9 SELECTED

DETECTIVE STORIES

Vitasta

Published by
Vitasta Publishing Pvt Ltd
2/15, Ansari Road, Daryaganj
New Delhi - 110 002
info@vitastapublishing.com

ISBN: 978-93-90961-78-8

First Edition 2023
MRP ₹ 350

We gratefully acknowledge Project Gutenberg, Digital Library University of Pennsylvania, Lit2Go, fadedpage.com, Westminster Detective Library, AmericanLiterature.com and The University of Virginia for making this book possible.

Compiled and Edited by Manukriti
Editorial Support by Abhishek Rana
Typeset & Cover Design by Somesh Kumar Mishra
Printed by Chaman Enterprises, Delhi

Contents

Publisher's Note

Dorothy L. Sayers once said, 'There certainly does seem a possibility that the detective story will come to an end, simply because the public will have learnt all the tricks.'

With this thought, let us understand detective fiction and in an attempt to understand the vitality and layers with which detective fiction came to be formed, it is integral to also understand the variety it brings out.

Detective fiction is an intelligent innovation to sprout from crime and mystery fiction. It challenges and influences a new style of writing and gives new ways of thinking about the society. In presenting a world around as defined by simple truths, masked under veils and layers of suspense, it is a genre that can always intrigue and instigate its readers into thinking and forming their own opinions about truth with clues and hints. Starting out in the form of modern short fiction in the early nineteenth century, it takes shape from increasing crime rate with the rampant modernisation of the world. However, when we look into the genre, it also has origins in ancient writings.

It can be concretely identified that certain ancient and religious texts bear similarities to what would later be called detective fiction. These stories have a specific premise and are intended to bring out the complexity that survives on the edge of social circumstances. Most people find that detective fiction as a concept takes shape with a play by Sophocles where his protagonist, Oedipus, goes on a hunt for the truth about the predecessor king. However, this archetypical undertone originates in the middle ages among the varied stories collected under *Arabian Nights*. Hence, the short story *The Three Apples* is added as the first story we'd like a detective fiction enthusiast to engage with.

Many times, the main characters in many detective stories are police officers. These stories can take many different forms, but many authors attempt to realistically depict the daily activities of a group of police officers who are frequently working on multiple cases at the same time. This trope is touched upon by William Evans Burton's *The Secret Cell* where one can drown in the suspense and rigour with which police officers investigate a case. This story is exemplary as it establishes not just what a brilliant story looks like but also provides base to the locked-room genre for the first time.

Logical reasoning is primary to detective fiction. It determines whether the truth of a conclusion for that rule can be defined solely on the truth of the premises. A very simple example would be that when it rains things outside get wet. The grass is outside, and therefore, when it rains, the grass gets wet. This theorisation and style is taken up by most detectives but in this collection, Edgar Allan Poe showcases the enigma with which Dupin would solve the case of *The Purloined Letter*. This story is unique and is an exemplary and iconic modern detective short fiction.

Deduction as a style is crafted by Arthur Conan Doyle intensely as he triggers the depth of Holmes' deductive skills in warding off new enemies in *The Final Problem* as he comes face-to-face with Professor Moriarty. Today, Holmes has a designated legacy to last eras and inspire others. This legendary detective deserved a well earned place in this collection beyond this specific root as they seemed to have influenced multiple directions for the genre.

While the above concepts underline detective fiction, it is the elements of crime and mystery that enables the survival of this ingenious fiction. In a detective story, murder and mystery narratives are central as they produce the conflict. Their investigative styles are what make them integral to detective fiction. While all of the stories contain either of the two,

Catherine Louisa Pirkis' *The Redhill Sisterhood* looks more into mystery. Pirkis' story induces the vitality of a strong intuitive sense. It intentionally fights for the brilliance with which a woman detective specifically thinks as Loveday Brooke challenges the simpletons in face of her intelligence.

Dr Richard Austin Freeman's *The Anthropologist at Large* rather projects on crime. Freeman poses his quality inverted fiction, which unravels itself from a structure in which the commission of the crime is shown or described at the beginning. With a medically charged legal professional, Dr Thorndyke, Freeman adds on a layer of a legality as well, which makes him and his work integral to detective fiction.

One of the most beloved sub genre of detective fiction is the locked room mystery, In which a crime—almost always murder—is committed under circumstances that make it appear impossible for the perpetrator to commit the crime and move out of the crime scene. Following other conventions of classic detective fiction, the reader is normally presented with the puzzle and all of the clues, and is encouraged to solve the mystery before the solution is revealed in a dramatic climax. Anna Katherine Green's *The Second Bullet* is exemplary to this type of a conflict as Violet Strange deals with one such murder.

Occult detective fiction is a sub genre of detective fiction that combines detective fiction tropes with supernatural horror fiction tropes. The occult detective, as opposed to the traditional detective, is used in cases involving ghosts, demons, curses, magic, monsters, and other supernatural elements. Some occult detectives are portrayed as knowing magic, being psychic, or possessing other paranormal abilities. In Sax Rohmer's *The Tragedies in the Greek Room*, this idea is perpetually focused as Moris Klaw attempts to solve the myth of a ghost.

Another widely appeasing sub genre is that of the whodunit, which is a colloquial elision of 'Who [has] done it?' It is an intricate plot-driven variety of detective fiction in which the main focus is the mystery of who committed the crime. The reader or viewer is given clues to the case from which the identity of the perpetrator can be deduced before the story itself provides the revelation at its climax. An eccentric, amateur, or semi-professional detective is usually in charge of the investigation.

Finally, this collection touches on mainstream hardboiled detective fiction and piques the reader's interest in the American criminal underworld. They were violent stories that focused on the mayhem and injustice surrounding the criminals rather than the circumstances surrounding the crime. Very often, there was no mystery at all: the books simply revolved around justice being served to those who deserved harsh treatment, which was described in explicit detail. To suffice this, *Pearls Are A Nuisance* by the legendary writer Raymond Chandler is added as it perfectly embodies the crisis in a hardboiled story.

In conclusion, detective fiction is multi-layered and overlays itself among each piece you look at. This quality makes these stories irresistible and provocative. We hope you enjoy this collection with the depth as we have tried to encapsulate all sub genres in our capacity.

9 SELECTED DETECTIVE STORIES

Arabian Nights

Anonymous

The Three Apples or *The Tale of the Murdered Woman* is a story which appears in the *One thousand and One Nights* collection, often known in English as the *Arabian Nights*. The story has been described as 'quintessential murder mystery' and its suspense arises from shocking revelation throughout its narrative.

The Three Apples

One night, after the adventure above described, the Khaleefeh Hároon Er-Rasheed said to Jaạfar, his Wezeer, We will go down to-night into the city, and inquire respecting the affairs of those who are at present in authority, and him against whom any one shall complain we will displace. Jaạfar replied, I hear and obey:—and when the Khaleefeh had gone forth with him and Mesroor, and they had passed through several of the market-streets, they proceeded along a lane, and saw there an old man, with a net and basket upon his head, and a staff in his hand, walking at his leisure, and reciting these verses:—

They say to me, Thou shinest among mankind, by thy knowledge, like the moonlight night: But I answer, Abstain from thus addressing me, since there is no knowledge without power: For if they would pawn me, and my knowledge with me, and all my papers and inkhorn too, For one day's food, they would never find the pledge accepted to the day of judgment. As for the poor, and his condition, and his whole life, how full of trouble! In the summer he fails to earn his food, and in winter he warms himself over the fire-pot. The dogs follow him wherever he goes, and any reviler, and he cannot repel him. If he states his case, and proves himself wronged, the judge will not admit his plea. Such, then, being the poor man's life, his fittest place is in the burial-ground.

The Khaleefeh, when he heard his recitation, said to Jaạfar, Observe this poor man, and consider these verses; for they indicate his necessity. Then approaching the man, he said to him, O sheykh, what is thine occupation?—O my master, answered the old man, I am a fisherman, and have a family to maintain, and I went forth from my house at noon, and have remained until now, but God hath allotted me nothing wherewith to obtain food for my household; therefore I have hated myself, and wished for death.—Wilt thou, said the Khaleefeh, return with us to the river, and station thyself on the bank of the Tigris, and cast thy net for my luck? If thou wilt do so I will purchase of thee whatever cometh up for a hundred pieces of gold.—The fisherman rejoiced when he heard these words, and said, On my head be your commands: I will return with you.—So he went again to the river, and cast his net, and, having waited till it sank, drew the cords, and dragged back the net, and there came up in it a chest, locked and heavy. When the Khaleefeh saw it, he felt its weight, and found it to be heavy; and he gave a hundred pieces of gold to the fisherman, who went away, while Mesroor, assisted by Jaạfar, took up the chest, and conveyed it, in company with the Khaleefeh, to the palace, where they lighted the candles, and placed the chest before the Khaleefeh. Jaạfar and Mesroor then broke it open, and they found in it a basket of palm-leaves sewed up with red worsted; and they cut the threads, and saw within it a piece of carpet, and, lifting up this, they found beneath it an izár, and when they had taken up the izár they discovered under it a damsel like molten silver, killed, and cut in pieces.

When the Khaleefeh beheld this, tears ran down his cheeks, and, looking towards Jaạfar, he exclaimed, O dog of Wezeers, shall people be murdered in my time, and be thrown into the river, and become burdens upon my responsibility? By Allah, I must retaliate for this damsel upon him who killed her, and put him to death!—Then said he to Jaạfar, By the truth of my descent from the Khaleefehs of the sons of El-'Abbás, if thou do not bring to me him who killed this woman, that I may avenge her upon him, I will crucify thee at the gate of my palace, together with forty of thy kinsmen! And the Khaleefeh was enraged.—Grant me, said Jaạfar, a delay of three days.—I grant thee the delay, replied the Khaleefeh. Jaạfar then went forth from his presence, and took his route through the city, sorrowful, and saying within himself, How shall I discover him who killed this damsel, that I may take him before the Khaleefeh? And if I take to him any other person, he will become a weight upon my conscience. I know not what to do.—For three days he remained in his house, and on the fourth day the Khaleefeh sent to summon him, and, when he had presented himself before him, said to him, Where is the murderer of the damsel?—O Prince of the Faithful, answered Jaạfar, am I acquainted with things hidden from the senses, that I should know who is her murderer? The Khaleefeh, incensed at this answer, gave orders to crucify him at the gate of his palace, and commanded a crier to proclaim through the streets of Baghdád, Whosoever desireth to amuse himself by seeing the crucifixion of Jaạfar El-Barmekee, the Wezeer of the Khaleefeh, and the crucifixion of his kinsmen, at the gate of the Khaleefeh's palace, let him come forth and amuse himself.—So the people came forth from every quarter to see the crucifixion of Jaạfar and his kinsmen; and they knew not the cause of this. The Khaleefeh then gave orders to set up the crosses; and they did so, and placed the Wezeer and his kinsmen beneath, to crucify them, and were awaiting the Khaleefeh's permission, while the people wept for Jaạfar and his relatives.

But while they were thus waiting, a handsome and neatly-dressed young man came forward quickly through the crowd, and, approaching the Wezeer, said to him, Safety to thee from this predicament, O chief of Emeers, and refuge of the poor! It was I who killed the woman whom ye found in the chest: kill me therefore for her, and retaliate her death upon me.—When Jaạfar heard these words, he rejoiced for his own deliverance, and grieved for the young man: but while he was speaking to him, lo, an old sheykh pressed hastily through the crowd to him and the young man, and, having saluted them, said, O Wezeer, believe not the words of this young man, for no one killed the damsel but myself; therefore retaliate her death upon me. The young man, however, said, O Wezeer, this is an old man, imbecile through age; he knoweth not what he saith: it was I who killed her; avenge her therefore upon me.—O my son, said the sheykh, thou art young, and wilt find pleasure in the world; and I am old, and satiated with the world: I will be a ransom for thee and for the Wezeer and his kinsmen; and no one killed the damsel but myself: by Allah, therefore, hasten to retaliate upon me.

On witnessing this scene, the Wezeer was astonished; and he took the young man and the sheykh to the Khaleefeh, and said, O Prince of the Faithful, the murderer of the damsel hath come.—Where is he? said the Khaleefeh. This young man, answered Jaạfar, saith, I am the murderer;—and this sheykh accuseth him of falsehood, and saith, Nay, but I am the murderer.—The Khaleefeh, looking towards the sheykh and the young man, said, Which of you killed this damsel? The young man answered, No one killed her but myself:—and the sheykh said also, No one killed her but myself. The Khaleefeh therefore said to Jaạfar, Take them both and crucify them.—If the murderer be one, replied Jaạfar, to kill the other would be unjust. The young man then said, By Him who raised the heavens and spread out the earth, it was I who killed the damsel:—and he gave an account of the manner of his killing her, and described what the Khaleefeh had found. The Khaleefeh therefore was convinced that the young man was he who had killed the damsel; and he was astonished, and said, What was the cause of thy killing this damsel unjustly, and of thy confessing the murder without being beaten, and thy saying, Retaliate her death upon me? The young man answered as follows:—

Know, O Prince of the Faithful, that this damsel was my wife, and the daughter of my uncle: this sheykh was her father, and is my uncle. I married her when she was a virgin, and God blessed me with three male children by her; and she loved me and served me, and I saw in her no evil. At the commencement of this month she was attacked by a severe illness, and I brought to her the physicians, who attended her until her health returned to her; and I desired them to send her to the bath; but she said to me, I want something before I enter the bath, for I have a longing for it.—What is it? said I. She answered, I have a longing for an apple, to smell it, and take a bite from it. So I went out immediately into the city, and searched for the apple, and would have bought it had its price been a piece of gold: but I could not find one. I passed the next night full of thought, and when the morning came I quitted my house again and went about to all the gardens, one after another; yet I found none in them. There met me, however, an old gardener, of whom I inquired for the apple, and he said to me, O my son, this is a rare thing, and not to be found here, nor anywhere except in the garden of the Prince of the Faithful at El-Baṣrah, and preserved there for the Khaleefeh. I returned therefore to my wife, and my love for her so constrained me that I prepared myself and journeyed fifteen days, by night and day, in going and returning, and brought her three apples which I purchased of the gardener at El-Baṣrah for three pieces of gold; and, going in, I handed them to her; but she was not pleased by them, and left them by her side. She was then suffering from a violent fever, and she continued ill during a period of ten days.

After this she recovered her health, and I went out and repaired to my shop, and sat there to sell and buy; and while I was thus occupied, at mid-day there passed by me a black slave, having in his hand an apple, with which he was playing: so I said to him, Whence didst thou get this apple, for I would procure one like it?—Upon which he laughed, and answered, I got it from my sweetheart: I had been absent, and came, and found her ill, and she had three apples; and she said to me, My unsuspecting husband journeyed to El-Baṣrah for them, and bought them for three pieces of gold:—and I took this apple from her.—When I heard the words of the slave, O Prince of the Faithful, the world became black before my face, and I shut up my shop, and returned to my house, deprived of my reason by excessive rage. I found not the third apple, and said to her, Where is the apple? She answered, I know not whither it is gone. I was convinced thus that the slave had spoken the truth, and I arose, and took a knife, and throwing myself upon her bosom, plunged the knife into her: I then cut off her head and limbs, and put them in the basket in haste, and covered them with the izár, over which I laid a piece of carpet: then I put the basket in the chest, and, having locked this, conveyed it on my mule, and threw it with my own hands into the Tigris.

And now, continued the young man, I conjure thee by Allah, O Prince of the Faithful, to hasten my death in retaliation for her murder, as I dread, otherwise, her appeal for vengeance upon me on the day of resurrection:9 for when I had thrown her into the Tigris without the knowledge of any one, I returned to my house, and found my eldest boy crying, though he knew not what I had done to his mother: so I said to him, What maketh thee cry?—and he answered, I took one of the apples that my mother had, and went down with it into the street to play with my brothers, and a tall black slave snatched it from me, and said to me, Whence came this to thee? I answered him, My father made a journey for it, and brought it from El-Baṣrah, for the sake of my mother; for she is sick: he bought three apples for three pieces of gold:—but he took it from me and beat me, and went away with it; and I am afraid that my mother may beat me on account of the apple.—When I heard my son's story, I discovered that the slave had forged a lie against the daughter of my uncle, and found that she had been killed unjustly; and as I was weeping bitterly for what I had done, this sheykh, my uncle and her father, came to me, and I informed him of the event; and he seated himself by me, and wept. We wept until midnight, and continued our mourning for her five days, ceasing not to the present day to bewail her death. By the honour of thine ancestors, therefore, hasten my death, to retaliate her murder upon me.

The Khaleefeh wondered at the young man's story, and said, By Allah, I will not put to death any but the wicked slave; for the young man is excusable. Then looking towards Jaạfar, he said to him, Bring before me this wicked slave who hath been the cause of the catastrophe; or, if thou bring him not, thou shalt be put to death in his stead. So the Wezeer departed weeping, and saying, Whence shall I bring him? Not every time that the jar is struck doth it escape being broken! I have no stratagem to employ in this affair: but He who delivered me in the first case may deliver me in the second. By Allah, I will not go out from my house for three days; and the Truth, whose perfection be extolled, will do what He willeth!—So he remained in his house three days, and on the fourth day he caused the Ḳáḍee to be brought, and made his testamentary arrangements; and as he was bidding farewell to his children, and weeping, lo, the messenger of the Khaleefeh came and said to him, The Prince of the Faithful is in a most violent rage, and hath sent me to thee; and he hath sworn that this day shall not pass until thou art put to death if thou do not bring to him the slave.

On hearing this, Jaạfar wept, and his children wept with him; and when he had bidden them all farewell except his youngest daughter, he approached her for the same purpose. He loved her more than all his other children; and he pressed her to his bosom, and wept at the thought of his separation from her; but, in doing this, he felt something round in her pocket, and said to her, What is in thy pocket? She answered, O my father, it is an apple; our slave Reyḥan brought it, and I have had it four days; he would not give it me until he had received from me two pieces of gold.—At this mention of the slave and the apple, Jaạfar rejoiced, and exclaimed, O ready Dispeller of trouble!—and immediately he ordered that the slave should be brought before him. He was therefore brought in, and he said to him, Whence came this apple?—O my master, he answered, I went out five days ago, and, entering one of the by-streets of the city, I saw some children playing, and one of them had this apple: and I snatched it from him, and beat him; and he cried, and said, That belongs to my mother, and she is sick: she wanted my father to bring her an apple, and he made a journey to El-Baṣrah, and brought back for her three apples which he bought for three pieces of gold; and I took this to play with it:—then he cried again; but, paying no regard to him, I took it away and brought it hither; and my little mistress bought it of me for two pieces of gold.—When he heard this story, Jaạfar was filled with wonder at discovering that this distressing event, and the murder of the damsel, had been occasioned by his slave; and he took the slave and went with him to the Khaleefeh, who ordered that the story should be committed to writing, and published.

William Evans Burton

(September 24, 1804 – February 10, 1860)

William Evans Burton was an English actor, playwright, theatre manager and publisher who worked closely with brilliant writers of his times. Having relocated to United States, his work was widely shared through magazines he himself curated. His short stories attracted a dedicated readership and it is believed that *The Secret Cell* went on to influence a major short story by Edgar Allan Poe.

The Secret Cell

I'll no more—the heart is torn
By views of woe we cannot heal;
Long shall I see these things forlorn,
And oft again their griefs shall feel,
As each upon the mind shall steal;
That wan projector's mystic style.
That lumpish idiot leering by,
That peevish idler's ceaseless wile,
And that poor maiden's half-form'd smile,
While struggling for the full-drawn sigh.
—Crabbe

About eight years ago, I was the humble means of unraveling a curious piece of villainy that occurred in one of the suburbs of London; it is well worth recording, in exemplification of that portion of 'Life' which is constantly passing in the holes and corners of the Great Metropolis. My tale, although romantic enough to be a fiction, is excessively commonplace in some of the details—it is a jumble of real life; a conspiracy, an abduction, a nunnery, and a lunatic asylum, are mixed up with constables, hackney-coaches, and an old washerwoman. I regret also that my heroine is not only without a lover, but is absolutely free from the influence of the passion, and is not persecuted on account of her transcendent beauty.

Mrs Lobenstein was the widow of a German coachman, who had accompanied a noble family from the continent of Europe; and, anticipating a lengthened stay, he had prevailed upon his wife to bring over their only child, a daughter, and settle down in the rooms apportioned to his use, over the stable, in one of the fashionable mews at the west end of London. But Mr Lobenstein had scarcely embraced his family, ere he was driven off, post haste, to the other world, leaving his destitute relict, with a very young daughter, to buffet her way along the rugged path of life.

With a little assistance from the nobleman in whose employ her husband had for some time been settled, Mrs Lobenstein was enabled to earn a respectable livelihood, and filled the honorable situation of laundress to many families of gentility, besides divers stray bachelors, dandies, and men about town. The little girl grew to be an assistance, instead of a drag, to her mother; and the widow found that her path was not entirely desolate, nor choked with the brambles of despair.

In the sixth year of her bereavement, Mrs Lobenstein, who presided over the destinies of my linen, called at my rooms, in company with a lady of equal width, breadth, and depth. Mrs L was of the genuine Hanseatic build—of the real Bremen beam—when in her presence, you felt the overwhelming nature of her pretensions to be considered a woman of some weight in the world, and standing in society. On the occasion of the visit in question, her friend was equally adipose, and it would have puzzled a conjurer to have turned the party into a tallowy trio. Mrs L begged leave to recommend her friend as her successor in the lavatorial line—for her own part, she was independent of work, thank heaven! and meant to retire from the worry of trade.

I congratulated her on the successful termination of her flourish with the washtubs.

"Oh, I have not made the money bless you! I might have scrubbed my fingers to the bones before I could have done more than earn my daily bread, and get, maybe, a black silk gown or so for Sundays. No, no! My Mary has done more with her quiet, meeting-day face in one year, than either the late Mr Lobenstein or myself could compass in our lives."

Mary Lobenstein, an artless, merry, blue-eyed girl of seventeen had attracted the attention of a bedridden lady whose linen she was in the habit of carrying home; and in compliance with the importunities of the old lady, she agreed to reside in her house as the invalid's sole and especial attendant. The old lady, luckily, was almost friendless; an hypocritical hyena of a niece, who expected, and had been promised, the reversion of her fortune, would occasionally give an inquiry relative to the state of her aunt's health; but so miserably did she conceal her joy at the approach of the old lady's dissolution, that the party in question perceived her selfish and mercenary nature, and disgusted at her evident security of purpose, called in an attorney, and executed an entirely new will. There was no other relative to select—Mary Lobenstein had been kind and attentive; and, more from revenge than good nature, the old lady bequeathed the whole of her property to the lucky little girl, accepting a trifling annuity to the old maid, her niece, who also held the chance of possession in case of Mary's death.

When this will was read by the man of law, who brought it forth in due season after the old lady's demise, Mary's wonder and delight almost equaled the rage and despair of the hyena of a niece, whom we shall beg leave to designate by the name of Elizabeth Bishop. She raved and swore the deadliest revenge against the innocent Mary, who one minute trembled at the denunciations of the thin and yellow spinster, and in the next chuckled and danced at the suddenness of her unexpected good fortune.

Mr Wilson, the lawyer, desired the disinherited to leave the premises to the legal owner, and staid by Miss Mary Lobenstein and her fat mama till they were in full and undisturbed possession. The 'good luck,' as Mrs L called it, had fallen so suddenly upon them, that a very heavy wash was left unfinished, to attend to the important business; and the complaints of the naked and destitute customers alone aroused the lucky laundress to a sense of her situation. The right and privilege of the routine of customers were sold to another fat lady, and Mrs Lobenstein called upon me, among the rest of her friends, to solicit the continuance of my washing for her stout successor.

A year passed away. I was lying in bed one wintry morning, and shivering with dread at the idea of poking my uncased legs into the cold air of the room, when my landlady disturbed my cogitations by knocking loudly at the room door, and requesting my instant appearance in the parlor, where 'a fat lady in tears' wished my presence. The existence of the obese Mrs Lobenstein had almost slipped my memory; and I was somewhat startled at seeing that lady, dressed in a gaudy colored silk gown, and velvet hat and feathers, in violent hysterics upon my crimson silk ottoman, that groaned beneath its burden. The attentions of my landlady and her domestic soon restored my ci-devant laundress to a state of comparative composure, when the distressed lady informed me that her daughter, her only child, had been missing for several days, and that, notwithstanding the utmost exertions of herself, her lawyer, and her friends, she had been unable to obtain the smallest intelligence respecting her beloved Mary. She had been to the police offices, had advertised in the newspapers, had personally inquired of all her friends or acquaintance, yet every exertion had resulted in disappointment.

"Everybody pities me, but no one suggests a means of finding my darling, and I am almost distracted. She left me one evening—it was quite early—to carry a small present to the chandlers' shop woman, who was so kind to us when I was left a destitute widow. My dear girl had but three streets to go, and ran out without a cloak or shawl; she made her gift to the poor woman, and instantly set out to return home. She never reached home—and, woe is me, I fear she never will. The magistrates at the police office said that she had eloped with some sweetheart; my Mary loved no one but her mother—and my heart tells me that my child could not willingly abandon her widowed parent for any new affection that might have entered her young breast. She had no followers—we were never for one hour apart, and I knew every thought of her innocent mind. One gentleman—he said he was a parson—called on me this morning, to administer consolation; yet he hinted that my poor girl had probably committed self-destruction—that the light of grace had suddenly burst upon her soul, and the sudden knowledge of her sinful state had been too much for her to bear, and, in desperation, she had hurried from the world. Alas! if my poor Mary is indeed no more, it was not by her own act that she appeared in haste before her Maker—God loved the little girl that he had made so good; the light of heavenly happiness glistened in her bright and pretty eyes; and she was too fond of this world's beauties, and the delights of life showered by the Almighty upon

His children, to think of repaying Him by gloom and suicide! No, no! Upon her bended knees, morning and night, she prayed to her Father in Heaven, that His will might be done; her religion, like her life, was simple, but pure. She was not of the creed professed by him who thought to cheer a parent's broken heart by speaking of a daughter's shameful death."

The plain, but earnest eloquence of the poor lady excited my warmest sympathy. She had called on me for advice; but I resolved to give her my personal assistance, and exert all my faculties in the clearance of this mystery. She denied the probability of any one being concerned in kidnapping, or conveying away her daughter—for, as she simply expressed herself, 'she was too insignificant to have created an enemy of such importance.'

I had a friend in the police department—a man who suffered not his intimacy with the villainy of the world to dull the humanities of nature. At the period of my tale, he was but little known, and the claims of a large family pressed hard upon him; yet his enemies have been unable to affix a stain upon his busy life. He has since attained a height of reputation that must ensure a sufficient income; he is established as the head of the private police of London—a body of men possessing rare and wonderful attainments. To this man I went; and, in a few words, excited his sympathy for the heart-stricken mother, and obtained a promise of his valuable assistance.

"The mother is rich," said I, "and if successful in your search, I can warrant you a larger reward than the sum total of your last year's earnings."

"A powerful inducement, I confess," replied L—, "but my professional pride is roused; it is a case deserving attention from its apparent inexplicability—to say nothing of the mother's misery, and that is something to a father and a son."

I mentioned every particular connected with the affair, and as he declined visiting Mrs Lobenstein's house, invited her to a conference with the officer at my lodgings, where he was made acquainted with many a curious item that seemed to have no connection with the subject we were in consultation upon. But this minute curiosity pleased the mother, and she went on her way rejoicing, for she was satisfied in her own mind that the officer would discover the fate of her child. Strange to say, although L— declared that he possessed not the slightest clue, this feeling on the part of the mother daily became stronger; a presentiment of the officer's success became the leading feature of her life; and she waited for many days with a placid face and a contented mind. The prophetic fancies of her maternal heart were confirmed; and L— eventually restored the pretty Mary to her mother's arms.

About ten days after the consultation, he called on me, and reported progress—requiring my presence at the police office for the purpose of making the affidavit necessary for the procuration of a search warrant.

"I have been hard at work," said he, "and if I have not found out where the young lady is concealed, I have at least made a singular discovery. My own inquiries in the mother's neighbourhood were not attended with any success; I therefore sent my wife, a shrewd woman, and well adapted for the business. She went without a shawl or bonnet, as if she had but stepped out from an adjacent house, into the baker's, the grocer's, the chandler's, and the beer shop; and while making her trifling purchases, she asked in a careless gossipping way, if any intelligence of Miss Lobenstein had been obtained? Everybody was willing to talk of such a remarkable circumstance; and my wife listened patiently to many different versions of the story but without obtaining any useful intelligence. One day, the last attempt that I had determined she should make, she observed that a huckster woman, who was standing in a baker's shop when the question was discussed, betrayed a violence of speech against the bereaved parent, and seemed to rejoice in her misfortunes. The womanly feeling of the rest of the gossips put down her inhuman chucklings, but my wife, with considerable tact, I must say, joined the huckster in her vituperation, rightly judging that there must be some peculiar reason for disliking a lady who seems generally esteemed, and who was then suffering under an affliction the most distressing to a female heart. The huckster invited my wife to walk down the street with her."

"I say—are you one of Joe's gang?" whispered the huckster.

'"Yes," said my wife.

'"I thought so, when I seed you grinning at the fat old Dutchey's trouble. Did Joe come down with the rhino pretty well to you about this business?"

'"Not to me," said my wife, at a venture.

'"Nor to me, neither, the shabby varmint. Where was your post?"

'This question rather bothered my wife, but she answered,

'"I swore not to tell."

'"Oh, stuff! They've got the girl, and it's all over now, in course; though Sal Brown who giv'd Joe the information about the girl, says that five pounds won't stop her mouth, when there's a hundred offered for the information—so we thought of splitting upon Joe, and touching the rhino. If you knows any more nor we do, and can make your share of the work, you may join our party, and come in for your whacks."

'"Well, I know a good deal, if I liked to tell it—what do you know?"

'"Why, I knows that four of us were employed to watch when Miss Lobenstein went out in the evening without her mother, and to let Joe know directly; and I know that we did watch for six months and more; and when Sal Brown *did* let him know, that the girl was missing that same night, and ha'n't been heard on since."

'"But do you know where she is?" said my wife in a whisper.

'"Well, I can't say that I do. My stall is at the corner near the mother's house; and Sal Brown was walking past, up and down the street, a following her profession. She's of opinion that the girl has been sent over the herring pond to some place abroad; but my idea is that she ha'n't far off, for Joe hasn't been away many hours together, I know."

'My wife declared that she was acquainted with every particular, and would join them in forcing Joe to be more liberal in his disbursements, or give him up to justice, and claim the reward. She regretted that she was compelled to go to Hornsey to her mother for the next few days, but agreed to call at the huckster's stall immediately on her return.

'There was one point more that my wife wished to obtain. "I saw the girl alone one night when it was quite dark, but Joe was not to be found when I went after him. Where did Sal Brown meet with him, when she told of the girl?"

'"Why, at the Blue Lion beer shop, to be sure," said the other.

'I was waiting in the neighborhood, well disguised. I received my wife's valuable information, and in a few minutes was sitting in the taproom of the Blue Lion, an humble public house of inferior pretensions. I was dressed in a shooting jacket, breeches, and gaiters, with a shot belt and powder horn slung round me. A huge pair of red whiskers circled my face, and a dark red shock of hair peeped from the sides of my broad-rimmed hat. I waited in the dull room, stinking of beer and tobacco, till the house closed for the night, but heard nothing of my Joe, although I listened attentively to the conversation of the incomers, a strange, uncouth set, entirely composed of the lower order of laborers, and seemingly unacquainted with each other.

'The whole of the next day, I lounged about the sanded tap room, and smoked my pipe, and drank my beer in silent gloominess. The landlord asked me a few questions, but when his curiosity was satisfied, he left me to myself. I pretended to be a runaway gamekeeper, hiding from my master's anger for selling his game without permission. The story satisfied the host, but I saw nothing of any stranger, nor did I hear any of the old faces called by the name I wished to hear. One of the visiters was an ill-looking thick-set fellow, and kept up a continual whispering with the landlord—I made sure that he was my man, when, to my great regret I heard him hailed by the name of George.

'I was standing inside the bar, chattering with the landlord, and settling for my pipes and my beer, when a good-looking, fresh-colored, smiling-faced young fellow, danced into the bar, and was immediately saluted by the host, "Hollo, Joe, where have you been these two days?"

'"Heavy business on hand, my buck—occupies all my time, but pays well. So give us a mug of your best, and d— the expense."

'I had no doubt but this was my man. I entered into

conversation with him, in my assumed manner, and my knowledge of the Somersetshire dialect materially assisted my disguise. Joe was evidently a sharp-witted fellow, who knew exactly what he was about. All my endeavors to draw him into talking of his own avocations completely failed; he would laugh, drink, and chatter, but not a word relative to the business that occupied his time could I induce him to utter.

'"Who's going to the hop in St. John street?" said the lively Joe. "I mean to have eighteen pennyworth of shake-a-leg there tonight, and have it directly too, for I must be back at my place at daybreak."

'This was enough for me. I walked with Joe to the vicinity of the dancing rooms, when, pleading a prior engagement, I quitted him, and returned home. My disguise was soon completely altered; my red wig and whiskers, drab hat and shooting dress were exchanged for a suit of black, with a small French cloak of dark cloth, and plain black hat. Thus attired, I watched the entrance of the humble ballroom, fearing that my man might leave it at an early period, for I knew not how far he had to journey to his place in the country, where he was compelled to be by the break of day. 'I walked the pavement of St. John street for six long hours, and was obliged to make myself known to the watchman to prevent his interference, for he doubted the honesty of my intentions. Just before the dawn of day, my friend Joe, who seemed determined to have enough dancing for his money, appeared in the street with a lady on each arm. I had to keep him in sight till he had escorted the damsels to their domiciles; when, buttoning up his coat, and pressing his hat down over his brows, he walked forward with a determined pace. I followed him at a convenient distance. I felt that he was in my power—that I was on the point of tracing the mystery of the girl's disappearance, and ascertaining the place of her detention.

'Joe walked rapidly towards Shoreditch Church. I was within a hundred feet of him, when the early Cambridge coach dashed down the Kingsland Road. Joe seized the guard's hold at the side of the back boot, placed his feet upon the hind spring, and in one moment was on the top of the coach, and trundling away from me at the rate of twelve miles an hour.

'I was beaten. It was impossible for me to overtake the coach. I thought of hiring a hack, but the rapid progress of the stage defied all idea of overtaking it. I returned dispirited to my home.

'My courage rose with the conception of fresh schemes. In the course of the day, I called on a friend, a stage coachman, and telling him some of the particulars of my object, asked him to introduce me to the driver of the Cambridge coach. I met him on his return to town the next day, and, by the help of my friend, overcame his repugnance to talk with strangers respecting the affairs of his passengers. I learnt, at last, that Joe never travelled more than half a dozen miles, but Elliott, the coachman, was unable to say who he was, or where he went to. My plan was soon arranged, and Elliott was bribed to assist me.

'The next morning by daybreak, I was sitting on the top of the Cambridge coach, well wrapped up in a large white top coat, with a shawl tied over my mouth. I got on the coach at the inn yard, and as we neared the church, looked out anxiously for my friend Joe; but he was not to be seen, nor could I discern any thing of him for six or seven miles along the road. The first stage was performed, and while the horses were being changed, Elliott, the coachman, pointed out a strange ill-looking man, in a close light waistcoat with white sleeves, white breeches, yarn stockings, and high-low shoes. "That fellow," said Elliott, "is always in company with the man you have been inquiring about. I have seen them frequently together come from over that style; he is now waiting for Joe, I'll bet a pound."

I alighted, and bargained with the landlord of the small roadside inn for the use of the front bedroom, upstairs. I took my post, and as the stage departed, began my watch. Joe did not appear till late in the afternoon—his friend eagerly seized him by the arm, and began to relate something with great anxiety of look and energy of action. They moved off over the style. I glided out of the house, and followed them. A footpath wound through an extensive meadow, and the men were rapidly nearing the farthest end. I hastened my pace, and gained the centre of the field, ere they were aware of my approach. I observed a telegraphic signal pass between them, and they instantly stopped their expedition, and turning back upon their path, sauntered slowly towards me. I kept on; we met—their eyes were searchingly bent upon me, but I maintained an easy gait and undisturbed countenance, and continued my walk for some minutes after they were past. As I climbed the farthest style, I observed them watching me from the other end of the field. I saw no more of Joe or his friend for the rest of that day and the whole of the next.

'I was much annoyed at my disappointment, and resolved not to be again outwitted. Every possible inquiry that could be made without exciting the curiosity of the neighbourhood, was instituted, but I was unable to obtain the smallest information, either of the abducted lady or of Joe's individuality. His friend was known as a vagabond of the first class—a discharged ostler, with a character that marked him ready for the perpetration of every crime.

'I was hunting in the dark. I had nothing but surmises to go upon, excepting the declaration of the huckster, that a man named Joe was the means of Miss [Lobenstein's] absence, but I was not sure that I was in pursuit of that identical Joe. The mystery attending the object of my suspicion gave an appearance of probability to my supposition, but it seemed as if I was not to proceed beyond the limits of uncertainty. I resolved, after waiting till the evening of the next day, to return to the taproom of the Blue Lion, and the impenetrability of my gamekeeper's disguise.

'Tying my rough coat up in my shawl, I clapped the bundle under my arm, and walked quietly along the road. As I passed through some posts on the sidewalk, a post-chaise was coming through the adjoining toll gate. A scuffle, accompanied with high oaths, in the interior of the chaise, attracted my attention; a hand was dashed through the carriage window, and cries for help were loudly vociferated. I ran towards the chaise; and ordered the postillion to stop; a coarse voice desired him to drive on; the command was repeated with violent imprecations, and the horses, severely lashed, bounded rapidly away. I was sufficiently near to catch hold of the back of the springs as the vehicle moved; the motion was violent, but I kept my grasp. The back board of the chaise, where the footman should stand, had been covered with a double row of iron spikes, to prevent the intrusion of idle boys; but, determined not to lose sight of the ruffians who were thus violating the peace of the realm, I pressed my bundle hard upon the spikes, and jumping nimbly up, found myself in a firm and pleasant seat.

'The carriage rolled speedily along. I determined, at the very first halting place, to summon assistance, and desire an explanation of the outcries and demands for help. If, as there seemed but little doubt, some act of lawless violence was being perpetrated. I resolved to arrest the principals upon the spot. While cogitating on the probabilities of the result, I received a tremendous cut across the face, from the thong of a heavy leather whip, jerked with considerable violence from the window of the post-chaise. A second well-directed blow drove me from my seat, and I fell into the road, severely lacerated, and almost blind.

'I rolled upon the dusty ground, and writhed in excessive agony. A thick wale crossed each cheek, and one of my eyes had been terrifically hit. It was yet early night, and the public nature of the road soon afforded me assistance. A young man passed me, driving a gig towards London; I hailed him, and requested his services. A slight detail of the cause in which I had received my injuries, induced him to turn round and receive me in the vacant seat. The promise of half a guinea tempted him to drive rapidly after the chaise, and in a few minutes we heard the sound of wheels. The young man cheered his horse to greater progress, but we were unable to pass the vehicle in advance, and it was not till we both drew up to the door of the roadside inn, where I had previously stopped, that we discovered that we had been in pursuit of a mail-coach instead of a post-chaise.

'The waiter declared that "nothin' of a four-veel natur, 'cept a vaggin and a *nearse*" had passed within the previous half hour. Placing my gig friend over some brandy and water, I sought the recesses of the kitchen, that I might procure some cooling liquid to bathe my face with. While busily employed at the yard pump, the sound of voices from an adjoining stable arrested my attention. The dim light of a lantern fell upon the figure of the ostler whom I had seen in company with mysterious Joe. I advanced lightly, in hopes of hearing the conversation. When I reached the door, I was startled by the sudden approach of someone from the other side of the yard, and compelled to hide behind the door. A stable helper popped his head into the building, and said—

'"See here, Billee, vot I found sticking on the spikes of the chay you've left in the lane."

'My luckless bundle was produced, and speedily untied. Directly Billy, for so was the suspicious ostler named, saw my rough, white, great coat, he exclaimed, with considerable energy—

'"I'm blessed if ve haint been looked arter. I seed this ere toggery a valking arter Joe and me in the meadow yonder. Ve thought it suspectable, so ve mizzled back. And I'm jiggered if the owner vornt sitting behind our conweyance, ven Joe hit him a vollop or two vith your vip to knock him off. Tommy, my tulip, I'll go back vi' you tonight, and vait a vhile till the vind changes."

'It was evident then, that Joe was connected with the abduction of the day—another convincing proof that he was the active agent in Miss Lobenstein's affair. With respect to my friend the ostler, I determined to try the effects of a little coercion, but concluded that it would be better to let him reach some distance from his usual haunts, to prevent alarming his comate Joe.

'In about an hour the post-chaise was driven to the

door; and the ostler, much the worse for his potations, was placed within the body of the vehicle. I was soon after them, in company with the young man in the gig, and we kept the chaise in sight till it had entered the still and deserted streets of the city. It was nearly midnight; the drunken ostler desired the scarcely sober postillion to put him out at the door of a tavern. I walked up to the astonished couple, and, arresting them on a charge of felony, slipped a pair of small but powerful spring handcuffs over the ostler's wrists. I conducted him, helpless and amazed, to an adjacent watch-house; and mentioning my name and office, desired his safe custody till I could demand his body.

The postillion, who was guarded by my gig friend, became much alarmed; and volunteered any information that I might desire. He confessed that he had been employed that afternoon, by one Joseph Mills, to carry a lunatic priest to the Franciscan Monastery, at Enfield Chase, from whence it was asserted that he had made his escape. The existence of a religious establishment in that neighborhood was entirely unknown to me, and I questioned the postillion respecting the number of its inmates, and the name of the superior, but he professed to know nothing beyond the locality of the building, and declared that he had never been inside the yard gate. He admitted that Joseph Mills had employed him several times upon the same business; and that, rather more than a fortnight ago, Billy, the ostler, had desired him to bring up a post-chaise from his master's yard at a minute's notice, and that a young lady was lifted, in a senseless state, into the chaise, and driven down to the building at Enfield as rapidly as the horses could be made to go.

'I took down his directions respecting the house, and at daybreak this morning I reconnoitered the front and back of the building. If I am any judge, that house is not devoted to monastic purposes alone; but you will see it tomorrow, I trust; for I wish you to accompany me as early in the morning as we can start, after procuring the warrants for a general search into the secrets of this most mysterious monastery.'

It was nearly noon the next day before we were enabled to complete our necessary arrangements. L—, Mr Wilson, the attorney, Mr R—, a police magistrate of some distinction, and the reader's humble servant, stepped into a private carriage, while a police officer, well armed, sat with the driver. The magistrate had been interested in the details necessary for the procuration of the warrant, and had invited himself to the development of the mystery. An hour's ride brought us to the entrance of a green lane that wound its mazy length between hedges of prickly holly and withered hawthorn trees. After traversing this lane for nearly two miles, we turned again to the left, by L—'s direction, and entered a narrow pass between a high brick wall and a huge bank, surmounted by a row of high and gloomy trees. The wall formed the boundary of the monastery grounds, and, at a certain place, where an ascent in the narrow road favored the purpose, we were desired by L—to mount the roof of the coach, and, by looking over the wall, to inspect the back front of the building. Massive bars of iron were fastened across every window of the house; in some places, the frames and glass were entirely removed, and the gratings were fixed in the naked brick work; or the apertures were fitted with thick boarding, excepting a small place at the top for the admission of the smallest possible quantity of light and air. The windows of a range of outhouses, which extended down one side of the extensive yard, were also securely barred; and a small square stone building stood in the middle of the garden, which immediately adjoined the yard. Two sides of this singular construction were visible from our coach top, yet neither door nor window were to be discerned.

One of our party pointed out a pale and wild-looking face glaring at us from one of the grated windows of the house. 'Let us away,' said L—, 'we are observed; and a farther gratification of our curiosity may prevent a successful issue to my scheme.'

'This looks more like a prison than a monastery or convent,' said the magistrate.

'I fear that we shall find it worse than either,' replied L—.

In a few minutes the carriage stopped at the gate of the building, the front of which exhibited but few points for the attachment of suspicion. The windows were shaded by blinds and curtains, but free from gratings or bars. The palings that enclosed a small fore court, were of massive oak, and being mounted on a dwarf wall, effectually prevented the intrusion of uninvited guests. The gates were securely closed, but the handle of a small bell invited attention, and a lusty pull by the driver gave notice of our presence.

L—, who had quitted the vehicle by the off door, requested the magistrate to keep out of sight, and with his brother officer, retired behind the coach. Our course of proceeding had been well arranged; when the door of the house was opened, I put my head from the carriage window, and requested to see the superior of the convent. The attendant, a short, ill-looking fellow in a fustian coat and gaiters, desired to know my business with him. 'It is of great secrecy and importance,' I replied; 'I cannot leave the carriage, because I have somebody here that requires my strictest attention. Give your master this card, and he will know exactly who I am, and what I require.'

Our scheme succeeded. The fellow left his post, and, unfastening the paling gate, advanced to the edge of the footpath, and put his hand in at the window of the carriage for my card. L— and the officer glided from their concealment, and secured possession of the outer gate and the door of the house, before the fellow had time to give the alarm. The driver, who had pretended to busy himself with the horses, immediately opened the carriage door; and in a few seconds, the whole of our party were mustered in the entrance hall. The man who had answered the bell, when he recovered his surprise, rushed to the door, and attempted to force his way to the interior of the house. The police officer stopped him, and an angry altercation ensued—he placed his finger in his mouth, and gave a loud and lengthy whistle. L—, who was busily engaged in searching for the fastenings of an iron screen, that crossed the width of the hall, observed the noise, and turning round to his mate, said quietly, 'If he's troublesome, Tommy, *give him a pair of gloves.'* In two minutes, the fellow was sitting helpless on the ground, securely handcuffed.

'Confound him,' said L—, 'he must have come out through this grating; there is no other entrance to the hall, and yet I cannot discover the doorway; and I am afraid that his signal has made it worse, for I heard the click of spring work directly after he gave his whistle.'

'This grating is a common appendage to a convent or religious house,' said Mr Wilson. 'Perhaps we are giving ourselves unnecessary trouble—let us ring the bell again, and we may obtain admission without the use of force.'

The officer and the magistrate exchanged a smile. The latter went to the man who had opened the door, and said, in a low tone of voice, 'We must get into the house, my man; show us how we can pass this grating, and I will give you five guineas. If you refuse, I shall commit you to jail, whether your connection with this establishment deserves it or no. I am a magistrate, and these, my officers, are acting under my direction.'

The man spoke not; but, raising his manacled hands to his mouth, gave another whistle of peculiar shrillness and modulation.

The hall in which we were detained, was of great height and extent. Beyond the iron screen, a heavy partition of wood work cut off the lower end, and a door of heavy oak opened from the room thus formed into the body of the hall. An open, but grated window, was immediately above the door, and extended almost from one end of the partition to the other. L—, observing this, climbed up the iron screen with the agility of the cat, and had scarcely attained the top, ere we observed him level a pistol towards some object in the enclosure, and exclaim, with a loud voice, 'Move one step, and I'll drive a couple of bullets through your skull.'

'What do you require?' exclaimed a tremulous voice from within.

'Send your friend there, Joe Mills, to open the door of the grating. If you move hand or foot, I'll pull trigger, and your blood be upon your own head.'

L—afterwards informed me, that upon climbing the screen, he discerned a gentleman in black in close consultation with a group of men. They were standing at the farther end of the enclosure against a window, the light of which enabled him to pick out the superior, and to discern the physiognomy of his old acquaintance Joe.

'Come, come, Joe, make haste,' said L—, 'my fingers are cramped, and I may fire in mistake.'

The threat was effectual in its operation. The man was afraid to move, and the door of the enclosure was opened by his direction. Joe walked trippingly across the hall, and, touching a spring in one of the iron rails, removed the fastenings from a portion of the screen, and admitted our party.

'How do you do, Mr Mills?' said L—'How are our friends at the Blue Lion? You must excuse me if I put you to a little inconvenience, but you are so volatile that we can't make sure of finding you when we want you, unless we take the requisite precaution. Tommy, tackle him to his friend, and by way of greater security, fasten them to the grating— but don't waste the gloves, for we have several more to fit.'

'Gentlemen,' said the man in black, advancing to the door of the enclosure, 'what is the reason of this violence? Why is the sanctity of this holy establishment thus defiled? Who are you, and what seek you here?'

'I am a magistrate, sir, and these men are officers of justice armed with proper authority to search this house for the person of Mary Lobenstein, and we charge you with her unlawful detention. Give her to our care, and you may save yourself much trouble.'

'I know nothing of the person you mean, nor are we subject to the supervision of your laws. This house is devoted to religious purposes—it is the abode of penitents who have abjured the world and all its vanities. We are under the protection of the Legate of His Holiness the Pope, and the laws of England do not forbid our existence. Foreigners only dwell within these walls, and I cannot allow the interference of any party unauthorised by the head of the church.'

'I shall not stop,' said the magistrate, 'to expose the errors of your statement; I am furnished with sufficient power to demand a right of search in any house in the kingdom. Independent of ascertaining the safety of the individual with whose abduction you are charged, it is my duty to inquire into the nature of an establishment assuming the right to capture the subjects of the king of this realm, and detain them in a place having all the appointments of a common prison, yet disowning the surveillance of the English laws. Mr L—, you will proceed in your search, and if any one attempts to oppose you, he must take the consequences.'

The countenance of the man in black betrayed the uneasiness he felt; the attendants, six in number, who, with our friend Mills, had formed the council whose deliberations were disturbed by the sight of L—'s pistol, were ranged beneath the window that looked into the yard, and waited the commands of the chief. This man, whose name we afterwards ascertained was Farrell, exchanged a look of cunning with his minions, and, with apparent resignation, replied,

'Well, sir, it is useless for me to contend with the authority you possess; Mr Nares, throw open the yard door, and, do you and your men attend the gentlemen round the circuit of the cells.'

The person addressed, unbolted the fastenings of

a huge door that opened into the yard, and bowed to our party as if waiting their precedence. Mr Wilson being nearest the door, went first, and Nares, with a bend of his head, motioned two of his party to follow. As they passed him, he gave them a knowing wink, and said, 'Take the gentlemen to the stone house first.' The magistrate was about to pass into the yard, when L— seized him by the collar of his coat, and violently pulling him back into the room, closed the door, and jerked the principal bolt into its socket.

'Excuse my rudeness, sir, but you will soon perceive that it was necessary. Your plan, Mr Nares, is a very good plan, but will scarcely answer your purpose. We do not intend placing ourselves at the mercy of your men in any of your stone houses, or cells with barred windows. You have the keys of the establishment at your girdle—go round with us yourself, and let those five or six fellows remain here instead of dancing at our heels. Come, come, sir, we are not to be trifled with; no hesitation, or I shall possess myself of your keys, and leave you securely affixed to your friend Mills.'

Nares grinned defiance, but made no reply; Farrell, whose pale face exhibited his dismay, took courage from the dogged bearing of his official, and stuttered out, 'Mr Nares, I desire that you will not give up your keys.' The hint was sufficient. Nares and his fellows, who were all furnished with bludgeons, raised their weapons in an attitude of attack, and a general fight was inevitable. The closing of the yard door had cut off one of our friends, but it also excluded two of the enemy. Still the odds were fearfully against us, not only in point of numbers, which rated five to four, but our antagonists were all of them armed, while the magistrate and I were totally unprovided with the means of defence.

Hostilities commenced by one of the men striking me a violent blow upon the fleshy part of the left shoulder, that sent me staggering to the other side of the room. Two of the ruffians simultaneously faced the police officer, as if to attack him; he received the blow of the nearest, upon his mace or staff of office, and before the fellow had time to lift his guard, returned him a smashing rap upon the fingers of his right hand, compelling him to drop his cudgel, and run howling into the corner of the room. The officer then turned his attention to the fellow who had assaulted me, and who was flourishing his stick with the intent of repeating the blow—but receiving a severe crack across his shins from the officer's mace, he was unable to keep his legs, and dropped upon the floor. I immediately wrested the bludgeon from his grasp, and left him *hors de combat.* The officer, while assisting me, received a knockdown blow from the fellow who had hesitated joining in the first attack, but, catlike, had been watching his opportunity for a pounce. I gave him in return a violent thump upon his head, and drove his hat over his eyes—then, rushing in upon him, I pinioned his arms, and held him till the officer rose and assisted me to secure him. While placing the handcuffs upon him, I was favored with a succession of kicks from the gentleman with the crippled hand.

L—, having drawn a pistol from his pocket, advanced to Nares and desired him to deliver up the keys; the ruffian answered him by striking a heavy blow on L—'s ear that immediately produced blood. The officer, exhibiting the utmost self-possession under these irritating circumstances, did not fire the pistol at his adversary, but dashed the weapon into his face, and inflicted a painful wound. Nares was a man of bulldog courage. He seized the pistol, and struggled fearfully for its possession. His gigantic frame and strength overpowered his antagonist; the pistol was discharged in the scuffle, luckily without wounding any one—and the ruffian, holding the conquered L— upon the ground, was twisting his cravat for the purpose of choking him, when, having satisfactorily arranged our men, we arrived to the rescue, and prevented the scoundrel from executing his villainous intention. But Nares, although defeated by numbers, evinced a determination to die game—it was with the utmost difficulty that we were enabled to secure his arms, and while slipping the handcuffs over his wrists, he continued to leave the marks of his teeth upon the fingers of the policeman.

While this furious *melée* was going on, the magistrate had been unceremoniously collared by the master of the house, and thrust forth into that part of the hall which adjoined the iron screen. But his worship did not reverence this ungentlemanly proceeding, and turned valiantly upon his assailer. Both of them were unprovided with weapons, and a furious bout of fisty-cuffs ensued, wherein his worship was considerably worsted. Mills and the porter, who had been fastened by the policeman to the railing of the screen, encouraged Farrell by their cheers. The magistrate was severely punished, and roared for help; Farrell, dreading collision with the conquerors of his party, left his man, and started off, through the open door of the grating; he ran down the lane with a speed that defied pursuit. The driver and the magistrate both endeavored to overtake him, but they soon lost sight of the nimble rogue, and returned discomforted to the house.

During the scuffle, the two men, who, with Mr Wilson, were shut out by the promptitude of L—, clamored loudly at the door for readmission. The attorney, as he afterwards confessed, was much alarmed at the position in which he found himself—cut off from all communication with his friends, and left at the mercy of two ill-looking scoundrels, in a strange place, and surrounded by a range of grated prisons, while a number of cadaverous, maniac looking faces glared at him from between the bars.

Upon mustering our party, we were all more or less wounded. The magistrate was outrageous in his denunciations of vengeance upon all the parties concerned ; his discolored eye and torn apparel, besides the bruises about his person, had inflamed his temper, and he declared that it was his firm determination to offer a large reward for the apprehension of the chief ruffian, Farrell. L— was much hurt, and for some time appeared unable to stand alone— his ear bled profusely, and relieved his head, which had been seriously affected by Nares's attempt at strangulation. The other officer had received a severe thumping, and his bitten hand gave him much pain. My left arm was almost useless, and many bloody marks exhibited the effects of the fellow's kicks upon my shins. Nevertheless, we had fought a good fight, and had achieved a perilous victory.

The magistrate threw up the window sash, and addressed the men in the yard from between the iron gratings. 'Harkee, you sirs, we have thrashed your fellows, and have them here in custody. If you attempt resistance, we shall serve you exactly in the same manner. But if either of you feel inclined to assist us in the discharge of our duty, and will freely answer every question, and render all the help in his power, you shall not only be forgiven for any part you may have taken in scenes of past violence, short of murder, but shall be well rewarded into the bargain.'

One of the men, and I must say that he was the most ill-looking of the whole lot, immediately stepped forward, and offered to turn 'king's evidence,' if the magistrate would swear to keep his promise. The other fellow growled his contempt of 'the sneak what would snitch,' and darted rapidly down the yard. As we never saw him again, it is supposed that he got into the garden, and found some means of escaping over the walls.

The yard door was opened, and the lawyer and the informer were admitted. The latter personage told us that his wife was the matron of the establishment, and, with her sister, would be found upstairs. The keys were taken from Nares, and we began our search. Mr Wilson desired the man to conduct us to Mary Lobenstein's room, but he positively denied the knowledge of any such person. His wife, a coarse, pock-marked, snub-nosed woman, with a loud, masculine voice, also declared that no female answering to that name, had ever been within the house. L— remarked that no credit was to be attached to their assertions, and ordered them to lead the way to the search.

It would occupy too much space to describe minutely the nature of the persons and events that we encountered in our rounds. Suffice it to say, we soon discovered that the suspicions of the police officer and the magistrate barely reached the truth. Farrell's establishment had no connection with any religious house, nor could we discover either monk, friar, nun, or novice in any of the cells. But the name was a good cloak for the villainous usages practised in the house, as it disarmed suspicion, and prevented the interference of the police. The house, in reality, was a private madhouse, but subject to the foulest abuses; wives who were tired of their husbands, and vice versa—reprobate sons, wishing to *dispose* of fathers— or villains who wanted to remove their rivals, either in love or wealth, could secure safe lodgings for the obnoxious personages in Farrell's Farm, as it was termed by the knowing few. Farrell could always obtain a certificate of the lunacy of the person to be removed; Nares had been bred to the pestle and the mortar; and as the act then stood, an apothecary's signature was sufficient authority for immuring a suspected person. Incurables, of the worst description, were received by Farrell, and boarded at the lowest rate. He generally contracted for a sum down, guaranteeing that their friends should never again be troubled by them—and, as the informer said, 'He gave them little enough to eat, and if they did not die, it wasn't his fault.'

The house was also appropriated to other purposes of secrecy and crime. Ladies in a delicate situation were accommodated with private rooms for their accouchement, and the children effectually provided for. Fugitives from justice were sure of concealment, if they could obtain admission to the farm. In short, Farrell's doors, although closed to the world and the eye of the law, were open to all who could afford to pay, or be paid for—from the titled seducer and his victim, whose ruin was effected in the elegant suite of rooms fronting the lane—to the outcast bedlamite, the refuse of the poorhouse, and the asylum, who was condemned to a slow, but certain death in the secret cells of this horrible abode.

It would fill a volume to recount the history of the sufferers whom we released from their almost hopeless imprisonment—a volume of crime, of suffering, and of sorrow.

After a painful and fruitless search through all the various rooms, cells, and hiding places of that singular house, we were compelled to acknowledge that the assertions of the under keeper and his wife were but too correct. Mary Lobenstein was not among the number of the *detenues* at the Farm, nor could we discover the slightest trace of her. Still L— clung to the hope that, in the confusion necessarily attending our first search, we had passed over some secret cell or dungeon in which the poor girl was immured. The square stone building in the centre of the garden afforded some ground for this surmise—we were unable to open the small iron-banded door that was fixed in the side of this apparently solid structure. The under keeper declared that the key was always in the possession of Farrell, his principal; and that no one ever entered the place but Nares and his master. He was not aware that any person was ever confined in it; a spring of water bubbled up within the building, and he believed that Farrell used it as a wine cellar only. He had seen wine carried in and out of the place. Indeed, the whole appearance of the building corroborated the man's statement—there was no window, air hole, or aperture of any description, excepting the small door before mentioned; and the contracted size of the place itself prevented the possibility of its containing a hiding hole for a human being, if a well or spring occupied the area, as the keeper affirmed.

Resigning this last hope of finding the poor girl, we gave our assistance to the magistrate in removing the prisoners, and placing the unfortunates whom we had released in temporary but appropriate abodes. In this service, the under keeper and his wife proved valuable auxiliaries, in pointing out the incurable mad folks, and those who, in his opinion, had been unjustly detained. The prisoners were placed in our carriage, and conveyed to London, under the superintendance of L— himself, who promised to return during the evening with additional assistance. The policeman was despatched to Enfield for several carriages and postchaises. Some of the most desperate and confirmed maniacs were sent to the lunatic asylum, with the magistrate's order for their admittance, and two or three of the sick and sorrowing were removed to the Middlesex hospital.

I assisted the lawyer and the magistrate in taking the depositions of several of the sufferers who appeared sane enough to warrant the truth of their stories. As night approached, I prepared for a departure, and Mr Wilson resolved to accompany me; we received the addresses of several persons from various inmates of the Farm, who requested us to let their families know of the place of their detention. As we drove down the lane, we met L—, and a posse of police officers, who were to accompany the magistrate in his night sojourn at the house, and assist him in the removal of the rest of the inmates in the morning.

During the evening, I called, with a heavy heart, upon Mrs Lobenstein, and communicated the melancholy result of our scheme. I related minutely the particulars of our transaction—she listened quietly to my story, and occasionally interrupted me, when describing the zeal of the officer L—, by invoking the blessings of heaven upon his head. When she learnt the unsuccessful issue of our search, she remained silent for a minute only—when, with a confident tone, and a cheerful voice, she said—'My daughter Mary is in that stone house. The workings of the fingers of Providence are too evident in the wonderful train of circumstances that led to the discovery of Farrell and his infamous mansion. My child is there, but you have not been able to penetrate the secret of her cell. I will go with you in the morning, if you can spare another day to assist a bereaved mother.'

I declared my readiness to accompany her, but endeavored to impress upon her mind the inutility of farther search. She relied securely upon the faith of her divine impression, as she termed it, and declared that God would never suffer so good a man as L—to be disappointed in his wonderful exertions; the keenness of a mother's eye, the instinct of a mother's love would help him in the completion of his sacred trust. It was impossible to argue with her; and I agreed to be with her at an early hour.

I slept but little during the night, for my bruised shins and battered shoulder pained me considerably, and the strange excitement of the day's events materially assisted to heighten both my corporeal and mental fever. When I arose in the morning, I felt so badly, that nothing but the earnest and confident tone of the poor childless widow induced me to undertake the annoyance of the trip—I could not bear to disappoint her. I found the carriage ready at the door—a couple of mechanics, with sledge hammers, crow bars, and huge bunches of skeleton keys, occupied the front seat, and having placed myself beside Mrs Lobenstein upon the other seat, the horses trotted briskly along the street. During our ride she informed me that a lawyer had called upon her from Elizabeth Bishop, the disappointed spinster, who, it will be recollected, had lost her expected fortune by the intervention of the gentle Mary Lobenstein. The man stated that Miss Bishop had heard of the disappearance of the inheritor of her aunt's estate, and had desired him to give notice that if proof was not forthcoming of Miss Lobenstein's existence, she should take possession of the property, agreeably to the provision existing in the will. 'I am sure,' said the mother, 'that woman is at the bottom of this affair—she has concerted the abduction of my daughter to obtain possession of the estate—but I trust in God that she will be disappointed in her foul design. A fearful whisper comes across my heart that those who would rob a mother of a child for gold, would not object to rob that child of her existence; but my trust is in the Most High, who tempers the wind to the shorn lamb, and will not consent to the spoliation of the widow and the fatherless.'

The probability of the poor girl's murder had been suggested by L— at the termination of our unsuccessful search, and had occupied a serious portion of my thoughts during the wakeful moments of the past night. Expecting nothing from the mother's repetition of the search, I determined to consult L— upon the feasibility of offering rewards to the villains Mills and Nares for a revelation of the truth, and if we failed in eliciting any intelligence, to institute a rigorous examination of the garden and the yard, and discover, if possible, the remains of the murdered girl.

The magistrate received Mrs Lobenstein with tenderness and respect, and sanctioned her desire to penetrate into the mystery of the square stone house. L—had nothing new to disclose, excepting that, in one of the rooms several articles of female apparel had been discovered, and he suggested that Mrs L should inspect them, as, perhaps, something that belonged to her daughter might be among them. The mother remarked that her daughter left home without a bonnet or a shawl, and it was scarcely likely that her body-clothes would be in the room: she, therefore, thought it useless to waste time in going upstairs, but requested the locksmith to accompany her to the stone house in the garden. It was impossible to help sympathising with Mrs Lobenstein in her anxiety; the magistrate deferred his return to London, where his presence was absolutely necessary to preside at the examination of Messrs. Nares, Mills, and Co., and the warm-hearted L—wiped the moisture from his eyes as he followed the mother across the yard, and heard her encourage the workmen to commence the necessary proceedings for the release of her darling child. The lock of the stone house was picked—the door was thrown wide open—and the maternal voice was heard in loud citation, but the dull echo of the stone room was the only reply—there was no living creature within the place.

We found the interior of the building to correspond with the description given by the underkeeper. The walls were hollowed into binns, which were filled with wine bottles, packed in sawdust; a circular well, bricked up a little above the level of the floor, filled the centre of the room; the water rose to within a foot of the ground—an old pulley and bucket, rotten from desuetude, clogged up one side of the doorway, and two or three wine barrels filled up the remaining vacancy of space. It was impossible that a human being could be concealed in any part of the building.

Mrs Lobenstein sighed, and her countenance told of her dismay; but the flame of hope had warmed her heart into a heat that was not to be immediately cooled. 'Gentlemen,' said she, 'accompany me once more round the cells and secret places—let me be satisfied with my own eyes that a thorough search has been made, and it will remove my doubts that you have overlooked some obscure nook wherein the wretches have concealed my little girl.' The range of chambers was again traversed, but without success, and the widow was compelled to admit that every possible place had been looked into, and that a farther sojourn in the house was entirely useless. The old lady sat down upon the last stair of the second flight, and with a grievous expression of countenance, looked into our several faces as we stood around her, as if she was searching for that consolation it was not in our power to bestow. Tears rolled down her cheeks, and mighty sobs told of the anguish of her heart. I was endeavoring to rouse her to exertion, as the only means of breaking the force of her grief, when my attention was drawn to the loud yelping of a dog, a small cocker spaniel, that had accompanied us in the carriage from Mrs Lobenstein's house, and in prowling round the building, had been accidentally shut up in one of the rooms. 'Poor Dash!' said the widow, 'I must not lose you; my dear Mary was fond of you, and I ought to be careful of her favorite.'

I took the hint, and walking down the gallery, opened the door of the room from whence the barking proceeded. It was the apartment that contained the articles of wearing apparel, which Mrs L had visited in her round, without discovering any token of her daughter. But the animal's superior instinct enabled him to detect the presence of a pair of shoes that had graced the feet of the little Mary when she quitted her mother's house, on the day of her abduction. Immediately the door was opened, the faithful creature gathered up the shoes in his mouth, and ran to his mistress, and dropped them at her feet, inviting her attention by a loud and sagacious bark. The old lady knew the shoes in a moment—'Yes, they are my girl's—I bought them myself for my darling—she has been here—has been murdered—and the body of my child is now mouldering in the grave.' A violent fit of hysterics ensued, and I consigned her to the care of the wife and sister of the underkeeper, who had not been allowed to leave the house.

I deemed the finding of the shoes to be of sufficient importance to recall the magistrate, who was in the carriage at the door, and about to start for London. He immediately alighted, and inquired into the particulars of the affair. Directly it was proved that Mary Lobenstein had been in the house, L— rushed upstairs, and dragged the keeper into the presence of the magistrate, who sternly asked the man why he had deceived him in declaring that the girl had never been there. The fellow was evidently alarmed, and protested vehemently that he knew no female of the name of Lobenstein—and the only clue he could give to the mystery of the shoes was, that a young girl answering our description of Mary, had been brought into the house at night time about a fortnight ago, but she was represented as an insane prostitute, of the name of Hill, who had been annoying some married gentlemen by riotous conduct at their houses—and it was said at first that she was to remain at the Farm for life—but that she had suddenly been removed by Nares, but where, he could not say. L— shook his head ominously when he heard this statement, and it was evident to us all that the mother's suspicions were right, and that a deed of blood had been recently perpetrated. The best means of ascertaining the place of burial was consulted on, and we adjourned to the garden to search for any appearance of freshly disturbed ground, or other evidence that might lead to a discovery of her remains. When we had crossed the yard, and were about entering the garden gate, L— suggested the propriety of fetching the little dog, whose excellent nose had afforded the only clue we had been able to obtain. I went back for the animal, but he refused to leave his mistress, and it was not without some danger of a bite, that I succeeded in catching him by the neck, and carrying him out of the room. I put him on his feet when we were past the garden gate, and endeavored to excite him to sprightliness by running along the walk, and whistling to him to follow, but he sneaked after me with a drooping tail and a bowed head, as if he felt his share of the general grief.

We walked round the garden without discovering any signs that warranted farther search. We had traversed every path in the garden, excepting a narrow, transverse one, that led from the gate to a range of green and hothouses that lined the farthest wall. We were on the point of leaving the place, satisfied that it was not in our power to remove the veil of mystery that shrouded the girl's disappearance, when the dog, who had strayed into the entrance of the narrow path, gave extraordinary signs of liveliness and emotion— his tail wagged furiously—his ears were thrown forward—and a short but earnest yaffle broke into a continuous bark as he turned rapidly from one side of the path to another, and finally ran down toward the green house with his nose bent to the ground.

'He scents her,' said L—; 'there is still a chance.'

Our party, consisting of the magistrate, L—, and two other officers, the underkeeper, the locksmiths, and myself, followed the dog down the narrow path into the centre of a piece of ground containing three or four cucumber beds, covered with sliding glass frames. The spaniel, after searching round the bed, jumped upon the centre frame, and howled piteously. It was evident that he had lost the scent. L— pointed out to our notice that the sliding lid was fastened to the frame by a large padlock—this extraordinary security increased our suspicions—he seized a crowbar from one of the smiths, and the lock was soon removed. The top of the frame was pulled up, and the dog jumped into the tan that filled the bed, and commenced scratching with all his might. L— thrust the bar into the yielding soil, and at the depth of a foot, the iron struck a solid substance. This intimation electrified us—we waited not for tools—our hands were dug into the bed, and the tan and black mould were dragged from the frame with an eagerness that soon emptied it, and exhibited the boarding of a large trap door, divided into two parts, but securely locked together. While the smiths essayed their skill upon the lock, the magistrate stood by with lifted hands and head uncovered—a tear was in the good man's eye—and he breathed short from the excess of his anxiety. Every one was visibly excited, and the loud and cheerful bark of the dog was hailed as an omen of success. L—'s impatience could not brook delay. He seized the sledge hammer of the smiths, and with a blow that might have knocked in the side of a house, demolished the lock and bolt, and the doors jumped apart in the recoil from the blow. They were raised—a black and yawning vault was below—and a small flight of wooden steps, green and mouldy, from the effects of the earth's dampness, led to the gloomy depths of the cavern.

The little dog dashed bravely down the stairway, and L—, requesting us to stand from between him and the light, picked his way down the narrow, slimy steps. One of the smiths followed, and the rest of us hung our heads anxiously over the edge of the vault's mouth, watching our friends as they receded in the distant gloom. A pause ensued; the dog was heard barking, and an indistinct muttering between L— and the smith ascended to the surface of the earth. I shouted to them, and was frightened at the reverberation of my voice. Our anxiety became painful in the extreme—the magistrate called to L—, but obtained no answer; and we were on the point of descending in a body, when the officer appeared at the foot of the stairs. 'We have found her,' said he—we gave a simultaneous shout. 'But she is dead,' was the appalling finish of his speech, as he emerged from the mouth of the vault.

The smith, with the lifeless body of Mary Lobenstein swung over his shoulder, was assisted up the stairs. The [corpse] of the little girl was placed on one of the garden settees, and, with heavy hearts and gloomy faces, we carried the melancholy burden into the house. The mother had not recovered from the shock which the anticipation of her daughter's death had given to her feelings; she was lying senseless upon the bed where she had been placed by the keeper's wife. We laid the body of her daughter in an adjoining room, and directed the woman to perform the last sad duties to the senseless clay while we awaited the parent's restoration. The magistrate returned to London; the smiths were packing up their tools preparatory to departure, and I was musing in melancholy mood over the events of the day, when the forbidding face of the keeper's wife peeped in at the half-opened door, and we were beckoned from the room.

'Please your honor, I never seed a dead body look like that there corpse of the little girl upstairs. I've seed a many corpses in my time, but there's something unnatural about that there one, not like a dead body ought to be.'

'What do you mean?'

'Why, though her feet and hands are cold, her jaw ain't dropped, and her eyes ain't open—and there's a limberness in her limbs that I don't like. I really believe she's only swounded.'

L— and I hurried upstairs, and the smiths, with their baskets of tools dangling at their backs, followed us into the room. I anxiously searched for any pulsation at the heart and the wrists of poor Mary, whose appearance certainly corroborated the woman's surmise, but the total absence of all visible signs of life denied us the encouragement of the flattering hope. One of the smiths took from his basket a tool of bright, fine-tempered steel; he held it for a few seconds against Mary's half-closed mouth, and upon withdrawing it, said, with a loud and energetic voice, 'She is alive! her breath has damped the surface of the steel!'

The man was right. Proper remedies were applied to the daughter and to her parent, and L— had the gratification of placing the lost Mary within her mother's arms.

Miss Lobenstein's explanation afforded but little additional information. When she was brought to the Farm by the villain Mills and his friend Billy the ostler, she was informed that it was to be the residence of her future life. She was subjected to the treatment of a maniac, her questions remained unanswered, and her supplications for permission to send to her mother were answered with a sneer. About three nights ago, she was ordered from her room, her shoes were taken off that she might noiselessly traverse the passages, and she was removed to the secret cell in the garden; some biscuits and a jug of water were placed beside her, and she had remained in undisturbed solitude till the instinct of her favorite dog led to her discovery, shortly after she had fainted from exhaustion and terror. There is little doubt but that the ruffians were alarmed at the watchings and appearances of the indefatigable L—, and withdrew their victim to the securest hiding place. I had the curiosity, in company with some of the officers, to descend into the Secret Cell; it had originally been dug out for the foundation of an intended house; the walls and partitions were solidly built, but the bankruptcy of the projector prevented any farther progress. When Farrell and his gang took possession of the place, it was deemed easier to cover the rafters of the cellar with boards and earth, than to fill it up—in time, the existence of the hole became forgotten, save by those most interested in its concealment. Farrell contrived the mode of entrance through the glass frame of the forcing bed, and when the adjacent greenhouses were constructed, an artificial flue or vent was introduced to the depths of the cell, and supplied it with a sufficiency of air.

Mrs Lobenstein refused to prosecute the spinster Bishop, the malignancy of whose temper preyed upon her own heart, and speedily consigned her unlamented to the grave. The true particulars of this strange affair were never given to the public, although I believe that its occurrence mainly contributed to effect an alteration in the English laws respecting private mad houses and other receptacles for lunatics. The magistracy of the county knew that they were to blame in permitting the existence of such a den as Farrell's Farm, and exerted themselves to quash proceedings against the fellows Mills and Nares, and their co-adjutors. A few months imprisonment was the only punishment awarded them, and that was in return for the assault upon the head of the police; but in Billy, the ostler, was recognized an old offender—various unpunished offences rose against him, and he was condemned to 'seven pennerth' aboard the hulks at Chatham. The greatest rogue escaped the arm of justice for a time; but L— has since assured me he has every reason to believe that Farrell was, under a feigned name, executed in Somersetshire for horse stealing. The Farm was converted into a Poor House for some of the adjacent parishes; L— received his reward, and when I left England, our heroine Mary was the blooming mother of a numerous family.

Edgar Allan Poe

(January 19, 1809 – October 7, 1849)

Edgar Allan Poe was a poet, editor, and literary critic from the United States. His poetry and, most notably, his short stories—tales of mystery and the macabre, are his most well-known works. He was one of the major figures responsible for the surge in popularity of the horror and detective genre. He is considered to have invented the modern short detective fiction through his works.

The Purloined Letter

Nil sapientiæ odiosius acumine nimio.

—*Seneca.*

At Paris, just after dark one gusty evening in the autumn of 18-, I was enjoying the twofold luxury of meditation and a meerschaum, in company with my friend C. Auguste Dupin, in his little back library, or book-closet, *au troisième*, No. 33, *Rue Dunôt, Faubourg St. Germain*. For one hour at least we had maintained a profound silence; while each, to any casual observer, might have seemed intently and exclusively occupied with the curling eddies of smoke that oppressed the atmosphere of the chamber. For myself, however, I was mentally discussing certain topics which had formed matter for conversation between us at an earlier period of the evening; I mean the affair of the Rue Morgue, and the mystery attending the murder of Marie Rogêt. I looked upon it, therefore, as something of a coincidence, when the door of our apartment was thrown open and admitted our old acquaintance, Monsieur G——, the Prefect of the Parisian police.

We gave him a hearty welcome; for there was nearly half as much of the entertaining as of the contemptible about the man, and we had not seen him for several years. We had been sitting in the dark, and Dupin now arose for the purpose of lighting a lamp, but sat down again, without doing so, upon G's saying that he had called to consult us, or rather to ask the opinion of my friend, about some official business which had occasioned a great deal of trouble.

'If it is any point requiring reflection,' observed Dupin, as he forebore to enkindle the wick, 'we shall examine it to better purpose in the dark.'

'That is another of your odd notions,' said the Prefect, who had a fashion of calling every thing 'odd' that was beyond his comprehension, and thus lived amid an absolute legion of 'oddities.'

'Very true,' said Dupin, as he supplied his visitor with a pipe, and rolled towards him a comfortable chair.

'And what is the difficulty now?' I asked. 'Nothing more in the assassination way, I hope?'

'Oh no; nothing of that nature. The fact is, the business is very simple indeed, and I make no doubt that we can manage it sufficiently well ourselves; but then I thought Dupin would like to hear the details of it, because it is so excessively odd.'

'Simple and odd,' said Dupin.

'Why, yes; and not exactly that, either. The fact is, we have all been a good deal puzzled because the affair is so simple, and yet baffles us altogether.'

'Perhaps it is the very simplicity of the thing which puts you at fault,' said my friend.

'What nonsense you do talk!' replied the Prefect, laughing heartily.

'Perhaps the mystery is a little too plain,' said Dupin.

'Oh, good heavens! who ever heard of such an idea?'

'A little too self-evident.'

'Ha! ha! ha—ha! ha! ha!—ho! ho! ho!' roared our visitor, profoundly amused, 'oh, Dupin, you will be the death of me yet!'

'And what, after all, is the matter on hand?' I asked.

'Why, I will tell you,' replied the Prefect, as he gave a long, steady and contemplative puff, and settled himself in his chair. 'I will tell you in a few words; but, before I begin, let me caution you that this is an affair demanding the greatest secrecy, and that I should most probably lose the position I now hold, were it known that I confided it to any one.'

'Proceed,' said I.

'Or not,' said Dupin.

'Well, then; I have received personal information, from a very high quarter, that a certain document of the last importance has been purloined from the royal apartments. The individual who purloined it is known;

this beyond a doubt; he was seen to take it. It is known, also, that it still remains in his possession.'

'How is this known?' asked Dupin.

'It is clearly inferred,' replied the Prefect, 'from the nature of the document, and from the non-appearance of certain results which would at once arise from its passing out of the robber's possession; that is to say, from his employing it as he must design in the end to employ it.'

'Be a little more explicit,' I said.

'Well, I may venture so far as to say that the paper gives its holder a certain power in a certain quarter where such power is immensely valuable.' The Prefect was fond of the cant of diplomacy.

'Still I do not quite understand,' said Dupin.

'No? Well; the disclosure of the document to a third person, who shall be nameless, would bring in question the honor of a personage of most exalted station; and this fact gives the holder of the document an ascendancy over the illustrious personage whose honor and peace are so jeopardized.'

'But this ascendancy,' I interposed, 'would depend upon the robber's knowledge of the loser's knowledge of the robber. Who would dare—'

'The thief,' said G., 'is the Minister D——, who dares all things, those unbecoming as well as those becoming a man. The method of the theft was not less ingenious than bold. The document in question—a letter, to be frank—had been received by the personage robbed while alone in the royal boudoir. During its perusal she was suddenly interrupted by the entrance of the other exalted personage from whom especially it was her wish to conceal it. After a hurried and vain endeavor to thrust it in a drawer, she was forced to place it, open as it was, upon a table. The address, however, was uppermost, and, the contents thus unexposed, the letter escaped notice. At this juncture enters the Minister D——. His lynx eye immediately perceives the paper, recognises the handwriting of the address, observes the confusion of the personage addressed, and fathoms her secret. After some business transactions, hurried through in his ordinary manner, he produces a letter somewhat similar to the one in question, opens it, pretends to read it, and then places it in close juxtaposition to the other. Again he converses, for some fifteen minutes, upon the public affairs. At length, in taking leave, he takes also from the table the letter to which he had no claim. Its rightful owner saw, but, of course, dared not call attention to the act, in the presence of the third personage who stood at her elbow. The minister decamped; leaving his own letter—one of no importance—upon the table.'

'Here, then,' said Dupin to me, 'you have precisely what you demand to make the ascendancy complete—the robber's knowledge of the loser's knowledge of the robber.'

'Yes,' replied the Prefect; 'and the power thus attained has, for some months past, been wielded, for political purposes, to a very dangerous extent. The personage robbed is more thoroughly convinced, every day, of the necessity of reclaiming her letter. But this, of course, cannot be done openly. In fine, driven to despair, she has committed the matter to me.'

'Than whom,' said Dupin, amid a perfect whirlwind of smoke, 'no more sagacious agent could, I suppose, be desired, or even imagined.'

'You flatter me,' replied the Prefect; 'but it is possible that some such opinion may have been entertained.'

'It is clear,' said I, 'as you observe, that the letter is still in possession of the minister; since it is this possession, and not any employment of the letter, which bestows the power. With the employment the power departs.'

'True,' said G.; 'and upon this conviction I proceeded. My first care was to make thorough search of the minister's hotel; and here my chief embarrassment lay in the necessity of searching without his knowledge. Beyond all things, I have been warned of the danger which would result from giving him reason to suspect our design.'

'But,' said I, 'you are quite au fait in these investigations. The Parisian police have done this thing often before.'

'Oh, yes; and for this reason I did not despair. The habits of the minister gave me, too, a great advantage. He is frequently absent from home all night. His servants are by no means numerous. They sleep at a distance from their master's apartment, and, being chiefly Neapolitans, are readily made drunk. I have keys, as you know, with which I can open any chamber or cabinet in Paris. For three months a night has not passed, during the greater part of which I have not been engaged, personally, in ransacking the D—— Hotel. My honor is interested, and, to mention a great secret, the reward is enormous. So I did not abandon the search until I had become fully satisfied that the thief is a more astute man than myself. I fancy that I have investigated every nook and corner of the premises in which it is possible that the paper can be concealed.'

'But is it not possible,' I suggested, 'that although the letter may be in possession of the minister, as it unquestionably is, he may have concealed it elsewhere than upon his own premises?'

'This is barely possible,' said Dupin. 'The present peculiar condition of affairs at court, and especially of those intrigues in which D—— is known to be involved, would render the instant availability of the document—its susceptibility of being produced at a moment's notice—a point of nearly equal importance with its possession.'

'Its susceptibility of being produced?' said I.

'That is to say, of being destroyed,' said Dupin.

'True,' I observed; 'the paper is clearly then upon the premises. As for its being upon the person of the minister, we may consider that as out of the question.'

'Entirely,' said the Prefect. 'He has been twice

waylaid, as if by footpads, and his person rigorously searched under my own inspection.'

'You might have spared yourself this trouble,' said Dupin. 'D——, I presume, is not altogether a fool, and, if not, must have anticipated these waylayings, as a matter of course.'

'Not altogether a fool,' said G., 'but then he's a poet, which I take to be only one remove from a fool.'

'True,' said Dupin, after a long and thoughtful whiff from his meerschaum, 'although I have been guilty of certain doggrel myself.'

'Suppose you detail,' said I, 'the particulars of your search.'

'Why the fact is, we took our time, and we searched everywhere. I have had long experience in these affairs. I took the entire building, room by room; devoting the nights of a whole week to each. We examined, first, the furniture of each apartment. We opened every possible drawer; and I presume you know that, to a properly trained police agent, such a thing as a secret drawer is impossible. Any man is a dolt who permits a "secret" drawer to escape him in a search of this kind. The thing is so plain. There is a certain amount of bulk—of space—to be accounted for in every cabinet. Then we have accurate rules. The fiftieth part of a line could not escape us. After the cabinets we took the chairs. The cushions we probed with the fine long needles you have seen me employ. From the tables we removed the tops.'

'Why so?'

'Sometimes the top of a table, or other similarly arranged piece of furniture, is removed by the person wishing to conceal an article; then the leg is excavated, the article deposited within the cavity, and the top replaced. The bottoms and tops of bedposts are employed in the same way.'

'But could not the cavity be detected by sounding?' I asked.

'By no means, if, when the article is deposited, a sufficient wadding of cotton be placed around it. Besides, in our case, we were obliged to proceed without noise.'

'But you could not have removed—you could not have taken to pieces all articles of furniture in which it would have been possible to make a deposit in the manner you mention. A letter may be compressed into a thin spiral roll, not differing much in shape or bulk from a large knitting-needle, and in this form it might be inserted into the rung of a chair, for example. You did not take to pieces all the chairs?'

'Certainly not; but we did better—we examined the rungs of every chair in the hotel, and, indeed the jointings of every description of furniture, by the aid of a most powerful microscope. Had there been any traces of recent disturbance we should not have failed to detect it instantly. A single grain of gimlet-dust, for example, would have been as obvious as an apple. Any disorder in the glueing—any unusual gaping in the joints—would have sufficed to insure detection.'

'I presume you looked to the mirrors, between the boards and the plates, and you probed the beds and the bed-clothes, as well as the curtains and carpets.'

'That of course; and when we had absolutely completed every particle of the furniture in this way, then we examined the house itself. We divided its entire surface into compartments, which we numbered, so that none might be missed; then we scrutinized each individual square inch throughout the premises, including the two houses immediately adjoining, with the microscope, as before.'

'The two houses adjoining!' I exclaimed; 'you must have had a great deal of trouble.'

'We had; but the reward offered is prodigious!'

'You include the grounds about the houses?'

'All the grounds are paved with brick. They gave us comparatively little trouble. We examined the moss between the bricks, and found it undisturbed.'

'You looked among D——'s papers, of course, and into the books of the library?'

'Certainly; we opened every package and parcel; we not only opened every book, but we turned over every leaf in each volume, not contenting ourselves with a mere shake, according to the fashion of some of our police officers. We also measured the thickness of every book-cover, with the most accurate admeasurement, and applied to each the most jealous scrutiny of the microscope. Had any of the bindings been recently meddled with, it would have been utterly impossible that the fact should have escaped observation. Some five or six volumes, just from the hands of the binder, we carefully probed, longitudinally, with the needles.'

'You explored the floors beneath the carpets?'

'Beyond doubt. We removed every carpet, and examined the boards with the microscope.'

'And the paper on the walls?'

'Yes.'

'You looked into the cellars?'

'We did.'

'Then,' I said, 'you have been making a miscalculation, and the letter is not upon the premises, as you suppose.'

'I fear you are right there,' said the Prefect. 'And now, Dupin, what would you advise me to do?'

'To make a thorough re-search of the premises.'

'That is absolutely needless,' replied G——. 'I am not more sure that I breathe than I am that the letter is not at the Hotel.'

'I have no better advice to give you,' said Dupin. 'You have, of course, an accurate description of the letter?'

'Oh yes!'—And here the Prefect, producing a memorandum-book, proceeded to read aloud a minute account of the internal, and especially of the external appearance of the missing document. Soon after finishing the perusal of this description, he took his departure, more entirely depressed in spirits than I had ever known the good gentleman before.

In about a month afterwards he paid us another visit, and found us occupied very nearly as before. He took a pipe and a chair and entered into some ordinary conversation. At length I said,—

'Well, but G——, what of the purloined letter? I presume you have at last made up your mind that there is no such thing as overreaching the Minister?'

'Confound him, say I—yes; I made the re-examination, however, as Dupin suggested—but it was all labor lost, as I knew it would be.'

'How much was the reward offered, did you say?' asked Dupin.

'Why, a very great deal—a very liberal reward—I don't like to say how much, precisely; but one thing I will say, that I wouldn't mind giving my individual check for fifty thousand francs to any one who could obtain me that letter. The fact is, it is becoming of more and more important every day; and the reward has been lately doubled. If it were trebled, however, I could do no more than I have done.'

'Why, yes,' said Dupin, drawlingly, between the whiffs of his meerschaum, 'I really—think, G——, you have not exerted yourself—to the utmost in this matter. You might—do a little more, I think, eh?'

'How?—in what way?'

'Why—puff, puff—you might—puff, puff—employ counsel in the matter, eh?—puff, puff, puff. Do you remember the story they tell of Abernethy?'

'No; hang Abernethy!'

'To be sure! hang him and welcome. But, once upon a time, a certain rich miser conceived the design of spunging upon this Abernethy for a medical opinion. Getting up, for this purpose, an ordinary conversation in a private company, he insinuated his case to the physician, as that of an imaginary individual.

'"We will suppose," said the miser, "that his symptoms are such and such; now, doctor, what would you have directed him to take?"

'"Take!" said Abernethy, "why, take advice, to be sure."'

'But,' said the Prefect, a little discomposed, 'I am perfectly willing to take advice, and to pay for it. I would really give fifty thousand francs to any one who would aid me in the matter.'

'In that case,' replied Dupin, opening a drawer, and producing a check-book, 'you may as well fill me up a check for the amount mentioned. When you have signed it, I will hand you the letter.'

I was astounded. The Prefect appeared absolutely thunder-stricken. For some minutes he remained speechless and motionless, looking incredulously at my friend with open mouth, and eyes that seemed starting from their sockets; then, apparently recovering himself in some measure, he seized a pen, and after several pauses and vacant stares, finally filled up and signed a check for fifty thousand francs, and handed it across the table to Dupin. The latter examined it carefully and deposited it in his pocket-book; then, unlocking an escritoire, took thence a letter and gave it to the Prefect. This functionary grasped it in a perfect agony of joy, opened it with a trembling hand, cast a rapid glance at its contents, and then, scrambling and struggling to the door, rushed at length unceremoniously from the room and from the house, without having uttered a syllable since Dupin had requested him to fill up the check.

When he had gone, my friend entered into some explanations.

'The Parisian police,' he said, 'are exceedingly able in their way. They are persevering, ingenious, cunning, and thoroughly versed in the knowledge which their duties seem chiefly to demand. Thus, when G—— detailed to us his mode of searching the premises at the Hotel D——, I felt entire confidence in his having made a satisfactory investigation—so far as his labors extended.'

'So far as his labors extended?' said I.

'Yes,' said Dupin. 'The measures adopted were not only the best of their kind, but carried out to absolute perfection. Had the letter been deposited within the range of their search, these fellows would, beyond a question, have found it.'

I merely laughed—but he seemed quite serious in all that he said.

'The measures, then,' he continued, 'were good in their kind, and well executed; their defect lay in their being inapplicable to the case, and to the man. A certain set of highly ingenious resources are, with the

Prefect, a sort of Procrustean bed, to which he forcibly adapts his designs. But he perpetually errs by being too deep or too shallow for the matter in hand; and many a schoolboy is a better reasoner than he. I knew one about eight years of age, whose success at guessing in the game of 'even and odd' attracted universal admiration. This game is simple, and is played with marbles. One player holds in his hand a number of these toys, and demands of another whether that number is even or odd. If the guess is right, the guesser wins one; if wrong, he loses one. The boy to whom I allude won all the marbles of the school. Of course he had some principle of guessing; and this lay in mere observation and admeasurement of the astuteness of his opponents. For example, an arrant simpleton is his opponent, and, holding up his closed hand, asks, 'are they even or odd?' Our schoolboy replies, 'odd,' and loses; but upon the second trial he wins, for he then says to himself, 'the simpleton had them even upon the first trial, and his amount of cunning is just sufficient to make him have them odd upon the second; I will therefore guess odd;'—he guesses odd, and wins. Now, with a simpleton a degree above the first, he would have reasoned thus: 'This fellow finds that in the first instance I guessed odd, and, in the second, he will propose to himself, upon the first impulse, a simple variation from even to odd, as did the first simpleton; but then a second thought will suggest that this is too simple a variation, and finally he will decide upon putting it even as before. I will therefore guess even;'—he guesses even, and wins. Now this mode of reasoning in the schoolboy, whom his fellows termed 'lucky,'—what, in its last analysis, is it?'

'It is merely,' I said, 'an identification of the reasoner's intellect with that of his opponent.'

'It is,' said Dupin; 'and, upon inquiring of the boy by what means he effected the thorough identification in which his success consisted, I received answer as follows: 'When I wish to find out how wise, or how stupid, or how good, or how wicked is any one, or what are his thoughts at the moment, I fashion the expression of my face, as accurately as possible, in accordance with the expression of his, and then wait to see what thoughts or sentiments arise in my mind or heart, as if to match or correspond with the expression.' This response of the schoolboy lies at the bottom of all the spurious profundity which has been attributed to Rochefoucault, to La Bougive, to Machiavelli, and to Campanella.'

'And the identification,' I said, 'of the reasoner's intellect with that of his opponent, depends, if I understand you aright, upon the accuracy with which the opponent's intellect is admeasured.'

'For its practical value it depends upon this,' replied Dupin; 'and the Prefect and his cohort fail so frequently, first, by default of this identification, and, secondly, by ill-admeasurement, or rather through non-admeasurement, of the intellect with which they are engaged. They consider only their own ideas of ingenuity; and, in searching for anything hidden, advert only to the modes in which they would have hidden it. They are right in this much—that their own ingenuity is a faithful representative of that of the mass; but when the cunning of the individual felon is diverse in character from their own, the felon foils them, of course. This always happens when it is above their own, and very usually when it is below. They have no variation of principle in their investigations; at best, when urged by some unusual emergency—by some extraordinary reward—they extend or exaggerate their old modes of practice, without touching their principles. What, for example, in this case of D——, has been done to vary the principle of action? What is all this boring, and probing, and sounding, and scrutinizing with the microscope and dividing the surface of the building into registered square inches—what is it all but an exaggeration of the application of the one principle or set of principles of search, which are based upon the one set of notions regarding human ingenuity, to which the Prefect, in the long routine of his duty, has been accustomed? Do you not see he has taken it for granted that all men proceed to conceal a letter,—not exactly in a gimlet hole bored in a chair-leg—but, at least, in some out-of-the-way hole or corner suggested by the same tenor of thought which would urge a man to secrete a letter in a gimlet-hole bored in a chair-leg? And do you not see also, that such recherchés nooks for concealment are adapted only for ordinary occasions, and would be adopted only by ordinary intellects; for, in all cases of concealment, a disposal of the article concealed—a disposal of it in this recherché manner,—is, in the very first instance, presumable and presumed; and thus its discovery depends, not at all upon the acumen, but altogether upon the mere care, patience, and determination of the seekers; and where the case is of importance—or, what amounts to the same thing in the political eyes, when the reward is of magnitude,—the qualities in question have never been known to fail. You will now understand what I meant in suggesting that, had the purloined letter been hidden any where within the limits of the Prefect's examination—in other words, had the principle of its concealment been comprehended within the principles of the Prefect—its discovery would have been a matter altogether beyond question. This functionary, however, has been thoroughly mystified; and the remote source of his defeat lies in the supposition that the Minister is a fool, because he has acquired renown as a poet. All fools are poets; this the Prefect feels; and he is merely guilty of a non distributio medii in thence inferring that all poets are fools.'

'But is this really the poet?' I asked. 'There are two brothers, I know; and both have attained reputation in letters. The Minister I believe has written learnedly on the Differential Calculus. He is a mathematician, and no poet.'

'You are mistaken; I know him well; he is both. As poet and mathematician, he would reason well; as mere mathematician, he could not have reasoned at all, and thus would have been at the mercy of the Prefect.'

'You surprise me,' I said, 'by these opinions, which have been contradicted by the voice of the world. You do not mean to set at naught the well-digested idea of centuries. The mathematical reason has long been regarded as the reason par excellence.'

'"Il y a à parièr,"' replied Dupin, quoting from Chamfort, '"que toute idée publique, toute convention reçue est une sottise, car elle a convenue au plus grand nombre." The mathematicians, I grant you, have done their best to promulgate the popular error to which you allude, and which is none the less an error for its promulgation as truth. With an art worthy a better cause, for example, they have insinuated the term "analysis" into application to algebra. The French are the originators of this particular deception; but if a term is of any importance—if words derive any value from applicability—then "analysis" conveys "algebra" about as much as, in Latin, "ambitus" implies "ambition," "*religio*" "religion," or "*homines honesti*" a set of *honorable* men.'

'You have a quarrel on hand, I see,' said I, 'with some of the algebraists of Paris; but proceed.'

'I dispute the availability, and thus the value, of that reason which is cultivated in any especial form other than the abstractly logical. I dispute, in particular, the reason educed by mathematical study. The mathematics are the science of form and quantity; mathematical reasoning is merely logic applied to observation upon form and quantity. The great error lies in supposing that even the truths of what is called pure algebra, are abstract or general truths. And this error is so egregious that I am confounded at the universality with which it has been received. Mathematical axioms are not axioms of general truth. What is true of relation—of form and quantity—is often grossly false in regard to morals, for example. In this latter science it is very usually untrue that the aggregated parts are equal to the whole. In chemistry also the axiom fails. In the consideration of motive it fails; for two motives, each of a given value, have not, necessarily, a value when united, equal to the sum of their values apart.

There are numerous other mathematical truths which are only truths within the limits of relation. But the mathematician argues, from his finite truths, through habit, as if they were of an absolutely general applicability—as the world indeed imagines them to be. Bryant, in his very learned "Mythology," mentions an analogous source of error, when he says that "although the Pagan fables are not believed, yet we forget ourselves continually, and make inferences from them as existing realities." With the algebraists, however, who are Pagans themselves, the "Pagan fables" are believed, and the inferences are made, not so much through lapse of memory, as through an unaccountable addling of the brains. In short, I never yet encountered the mere mathematician who could be trusted out of equal roots, or one who did not clandestinely hold it as a point of his faith that x^2+px was absolutely and unconditionally equal to q. Say to one of these gentlemen, by way of experiment, if you please, that you believe occasions may occur where x^2+px is not altogether equal to q, and, having made him understand what you mean, get out of his reach as speedily as convenient, for, beyond doubt, he will endeavor to knock you down.

'I mean to say,' continued Dupin, while I merely laughed at his last observations, 'that if the Minister had been no more than a mathematician, the Prefect would have been under no necessity of giving me this check. I know him, however, as both mathematician and poet, and my measures were adapted to his capacity, with reference to the circumstances by which he was surrounded. I knew him as a courtier, too, and as a bold intriguant. Such a man, I considered, could not fail to be aware of the ordinary policial modes of action. He could not have failed to anticipate—and events have proved that he did not fail to anticipate—the waylayings to which he was subjected. He must have foreseen, I reflected, the secret investigations of his premises. His frequent absences from home at night, which were hailed by the Prefect as certain aids to his success, I regarded only as ruses, to afford opportunity for thorough search to the police, and thus the sooner to impress them with the conviction to which G——, in fact, did finally arrive—the conviction that the letter was not upon the premises. I felt, also, that the whole train of thought, which I was at some pains in detailing to you just now, concerning the invariable principle of policial action in searches for articles concealed—I felt that this whole train of thought would necessarily pass through the mind of the Minister. It would imperatively lead him to despise all the ordinary nooks of concealment. He could not, I reflected, be so weak as not to see that the most intricate and remote recess of his hotel would be as open as his commonest closets to the eyes, to the probes, to the gimlets, and to the microscopes of the Prefect. I saw, in fine, that he would be driven, as a matter of course, to simplicity, if not deliberately induced to it as a matter of choice. You will remember, perhaps, how desperately the Prefect laughed when I suggested, upon our first interview, that it was just possible this mystery troubled him so much on account of its being so very self-evident.'

'Yes,' said I, 'I remember his merriment well. I really thought he would have fallen into convulsions.'

'The material world,' continued Dupin, 'abounds with very strict analogies to the immaterial; and thus some color of truth has been given to the rhetorical dogma, that metaphor, or simile, may be made to strengthen an argument, as well as to embellish a description. The principle of the vis inertiæ, for example, seems to be identical in physics and metaphysics. It is not more true in the former, that a large body is with more difficulty set in motion than a smaller one, and that its subsequent momentum is commensurate with this difficulty, than it is, in the latter, that intellects of the vaster capacity, while more forcible, more constant, and more eventful in their movements than those of inferior grade, are yet the less readily moved, and more embarrassed and full of hesitation in the first few steps of their progress. Again: have you ever noticed which of the street signs, over the shop-doors, are the most attractive of attention?'

'I have never given the matter a thought,' I said.

'There is a game of puzzles,' he resumed, 'which is played upon a map. One party playing requires another to find a given word—the name of town, river, state or empire—any word, in short, upon the motley and perplexed surface of the chart. A novice in the game generally seeks to embarrass his opponents by giving them the most minutely lettered names; but the adept selects such words as stretch, in large characters, from one end of the chart to the other. These, like the over-largely lettered signs and placards of the street, escape observation by dint of being excessively obvious; and here the physical oversight is precisely analogous with the moral inapprehension by which the intellect suffers to pass unnoticed those considerations which are too obtrusively and too palpably self-evident. But this is a point, it appears, somewhat above or beneath the understanding of the Prefect. He never once thought it probable, or possible, that the Minister had deposited the letter immediately beneath the nose of the whole world, by way of best preventing any portion of that world from perceiving it.

'But the more I reflected upon the daring, dashing, and discriminating ingenuity of D——; upon the fact that the document must always have been at hand, if he intended to use it to good purpose; and upon the decisive evidence, obtained by the Prefect, that it was not hidden within the limits of that dignitary's ordinary search—the more satisfied I became that, to conceal this letter, the Minister had resorted to the comprehensive and sagacious expedient of not attempting to conceal it at all.

'Full of these ideas, I prepared myself with a pair of green spectacles, and called one fine morning, quite by accident, at the Ministerial hotel. I found D—— at home, yawning, lounging, and dawdling, as usual, and pretending to be in the last extremity of ennui. He is, perhaps, the most really energetic human being now alive—but that is only when nobody sees him.

'To be even with him, I complained of my weak eyes, and lamented the necessity of the spectacles, under cover of which I cautiously and thoroughly surveyed the whole apartment, while seemingly intent only upon the conversation of my host.

'I paid especial attention to a large writing-table near which he sat, and upon which lay confusedly, some miscellaneous letters and other papers, with one or two musical instruments and a few books. Here, however, after a long and very deliberate scrutiny, I saw nothing to excite particular suspicion.

'At length my eyes, in going the circuit of the room, fell upon a trumpery fillagree card-rack of pasteboard, that hung dangling by a dirty blue ribbon, from a little brass knob just beneath the middle of the mantel-piece. In this rack, which had three or four compartments, were five or six visiting cards and a solitary letter. This last was much soiled and crumpled. It was torn nearly in two, across the middle—as if a design, in the first instance, to tear it entirely up as worthless, had been altered, or stayed, in the second. It had a large black seal, bearing the D—— cipher *very* conspicuously, and was addressed, in a diminutive female hand, to D——, the minister, himself. It was thrust carelessly, and even, as it seemed, contemptuously, into one of the uppermost divisions of the rack.

'No sooner had I glanced at this letter, than I concluded it to be that of which I was in search. To be sure, it was, to all appearance, radically different from the one of which the Prefect had read us so minute a description. Here the seal was large and black, with the D—— cipher; there it was small and red, with the ducal arms of the S—— family. Here, the address, to the Minister, diminutive and feminine; there the superscription, to a certain royal personage, was markedly bold and decided; the size alone formed a point of correspondence. But, then, the radicalness of these differences, which was excessive; the dirt; the soiled and torn condition of the paper, so inconsistent with the true methodical habits of D——, and so suggestive of a design to delude the beholder into an idea of the worthlessness of the document—these things, together with the hyper-obtrusive situation of this document, full in the view of every visitor, and thus exactly in accordance with the conclusions to which I had previously arrived; these things, I say, were strongly corroborative of suspicion, in one who came with the intention to suspect.

'I protracted my visit as long as possible, and, while I maintained a most animated discussion with the Minister upon a topic which I knew well had never failed to interest and excite him, I kept my attention really riveted upon the letter. In this examination, I committed to memory its external appearance and arrangement in the rack; and also fell, at length, upon a discovery which set at rest whatever trivial doubt I might have entertained. In scrutinizing the edges of the paper, I observed them to be more chafed than seemed necessary. They presented the broken appearance which is manifested when a stiff paper, having been once folded and pressed with a folder, is refolded in a reversed direction, in the same creases or edges which had formed the original fold. This discovery was sufficient. It was clear to me that the letter had been turned, as a glove, inside out, re-directed, and re-sealed. I bade the Minister good morning, and took my departure at once, leaving a gold snuff-box upon the table.

'The next morning I called for the snuff-box, when we resumed, quite eagerly, the conversation of the preceding day. While thus engaged, however, a loud report, as if of a pistol, was heard immediately beneath the windows of the hotel, and was succeeded by a series of fearful screams, and the shoutings of a terrified mob. D—— rushed to a casement, threw it open, and looked out. In the meantime, I stepped to the card-rack, took the letter, put it in my pocket, and replaced it by a fac-simile, (so far as regards externals,) which I had carefully prepared at my lodgings—imitating the D—— cipher, very readily, by means of a seal formed of bread.

'The disturbance in the street had been occasioned by the frantic behavior of a man with a musket. He had fired it among a crowd of women and children. It proved, however, to have been without ball, and the fellow was suffered to go his way as a lunatic or a drunkard. When he had gone, D—— came from the window, whither I had followed him immediately upon securing the object in view. Soon afterwards I bade him farewell. The pretended lunatic was a man in my own pay.'

'But what purpose had you,' I asked, 'in replacing the letter by a fac-simile? Would it not have been better, at the first visit, to have seized it openly, and departed?'

'D——,' replied Dupin, 'is a desperate man, and a man of nerve. His hotel, too, is not without attendants devoted to his interests. Had I made the wild attempt you suggest, I might never have left the Ministerial presence alive. The good people of Paris might have heard of me no more. But I had an object apart from these considerations. You know my political prepossessions. In this matter, I act as a partisan of the lady concerned. For eighteen months the Minister has had her in his power. She has now him in hers—since, being unaware that the letter is not in his possession, he will proceed with his exactions as if it was. Thus will he inevitably commit himself, at once, to his political destruction. His downfall, too, will not be more precipitate than awkward. It is all very well to talk about the facilis descensus Averni; but in all kinds of climbing, as Catalani said of singing, it is far more easy to get up than to come down. In the present instance I have no sympathy—at least no pity—for him who descends. He is that monstrum horrendum, an unprincipled man of genius. I confess, however, that I should like very well to know the precise character of his thoughts, when, being defied by her whom the Prefect terms 'a certain personage' he is reduced to opening the letter which I left for him in the card-rack.'

'How? did you put any thing particular in it?'

'Why—it did not seem altogether right to leave the interior blank—that would have been insulting. D——, at Vienna once, did me an evil turn, which I told him, quite good-humoredly, that I should remember. So, as I knew he would feel some curiosity in regard to the identity of the person who had outwitted him, I thought it a pity not to give him a clue. He is well acquainted with my MS., and I just copied into the middle of the blank sheet the words—

"'— — Un dessein si funeste,
S'il n'est digne d'Atrée, est digne de Thyeste.

They are to be found in Crébillon's 'Atrée.'"

Arthur Conan Doyle

(May 22, 1859 – July 7, 1930)

Arthur Conan Doyle was a Scottish physician and writer. He created Sherlock Holmes, one of the most famous fictional detectives in English literature and authored over fifty-six short tales and four novels about him and his companion, Dr Watson. In the subject of crime and detective fiction, the *Sherlock Holmes* stories are considered classics.

The Final Problem

It is with a heavy heart that I take up my pen to write these the last words in which I shall ever record the singular gifts by which my friend Mr Sherlock Holmes was distinguished. In an incoherent and, as I deeply feel, an entirely inadequate fashion, I have endeavoured to give some account of my strange experiences in his company from the chance which first brought us together at the period of the 'Study in Scarlet,' up to the time of his interference in the matter of the 'Naval Treaty'—an interference which had the unquestionable effect of preventing a serious international complication. It was my intention to have stopped there, and to have said nothing of that event which has created a void in my life which the lapse of two years has done little to fill. My hand has been forced, however, by the recent letters in which Colonel James Moriarty defends the memory of his brother, and I have no choice but to lay the facts before the public exactly as they occurred. I alone know the absolute truth of the matter, and I am satisfied that the time has come when no good purpose is to be served by its suppression. As far as I know, there have been only three accounts in the public press: that in the *Journal de Genève* on May 6th, 1891, the Reuter's despatch in the English papers on May 7th, and finally the recent letter to which I have alluded. Of these the first and second were extremely condensed, while the last is, as I shall now show, an absolute perversion of the facts. It lies with me to tell for the first time what really took place between Professor Moriarty and Mr Sherlock Holmes.

It may be remembered that after my marriage, and my subsequent start in private practice, the very intimate relations which had existed between Holmes and myself became to some extent modified. He still came to me from time to time when he desired a companion in his investigation, but these occasions grew more and more seldom, until I find that in the year 1890 there were only three cases of which I retain any record. During the winter of that year and the early spring of 1891, I saw in the papers that he had been engaged by the French government upon a matter of supreme importance, and I received two notes from Holmes, dated from Narbonne and from Nimes, from which I gathered that his stay in France was likely to be a long one. It was with some surprise, therefore, that I saw him walk into my consulting-room upon the evening of the 24th of April. It struck me that he was looking even paler and thinner than usual.

'Yes, I have been using myself up rather too freely,' he remarked, in answer to my look rather than to my words; 'I have been a little pressed of late. Have you any objection to my closing your shutters?'

The only light in the room came from the lamp upon the table at which I had been reading. Holmes edged his way round the wall and flinging the shutters together, he bolted them securely.

'You are afraid of something?' I asked.

'Well, I am.'

'Of what?'

'Of air-guns.'

'My dear Holmes, what do you mean?'

'I think that you know me well enough, Watson, to understand that I am by no means a nervous man. At the same time, it is stupidity rather than courage to refuse to recognise danger when it is close upon you. Might I trouble you for a match?' He drew in the smoke of his cigarette as if the soothing influence was grateful to him.

'I must apologise for calling so late,' said he, 'and I must further beg you to be so unconventional as to allow me to leave your house presently by scrambling over your back garden wall.'

'But what does it all mean?' I asked.

He held out his hand, and I saw in the light of the lamp that two of his knuckles were burst and bleeding.

'It is not an airy nothing, you see,' said he, smiling. 'On the contrary, it is solid enough for a man to break his hand over. Is Mrs Watson in?'

'She is away upon a visit.'

'Indeed! You are alone?'

'Quite.'

'Then it makes it the easier for me to propose that you should come away with me for a week to the Continent.'

'Where?'

'Oh, anywhere. It's all the same to me.'

There was something very strange in all this. It was not Holmes's nature to take an aimless holiday, and something about his pale, worn face told me that his nerves were at their highest tension. He saw the question in my eyes, and, putting his finger-tips together and his elbows upon his knees, he explained the situation.

'You have probably never heard of Professor Moriarty?' said he.

'Never.'

'Aye, there's the genius and the wonder of the thing!' he cried. 'The man pervades London, and no one has heard of him. That's what puts him on a pinnacle in the records of crime. I tell you, Watson, in all seriousness, that if I could beat that man, if I could free society of him, I should feel that my own career had reached its summit, and I should be prepared to turn to some more placid line in life. Between ourselves, the recent cases in which I have been of assistance to the royal family of Scandinavia, and to the French republic, have left me in such a position that I could continue to live in the quiet fashion which is most congenial to me, and to concentrate my attention upon my chemical researches. But I could not rest, Watson, I could not sit quiet in my chair, if I thought that such a man as Professor Moriarty were walking the streets of London unchallenged.'

'What has he done, then?'

'His career has been an extraordinary one. He is a man of good birth and excellent education, endowed by nature with a phenomenal mathematical faculty. At the age of twenty-one he wrote a treatise upon the Binomial Theorem, which has had a European vogue. On the strength of it he won the Mathematical Chair at one of our smaller universities, and had, to all appearances, a most brilliant career before him. But the man had hereditary tendencies of the most diabolical kind. A criminal strain ran in his blood, which, instead of being modified, was increased and rendered infinitely more dangerous by his extraordinary mental powers. Dark rumours gathered round him in the university town, and eventually he was compelled to resign his chair and to come down to London, where he set up as an Army coach. So much is known to the world, but what I am telling you now is what I have myself discovered.

'As you are aware, Watson, there is no one who knows the higher criminal world of London so well as I do. For years past I have continually been conscious of some power behind the malefactor, some deep organizing power which forever stands in the way of the law, and throws its shield over the wrong-doer. Again and again in cases of the most varying sorts—forgery cases, robberies, murders—I have felt the presence of this force, and I have deduced its action in many of those undiscovered crimes in which I have not been personally consulted. For years I have endeavoured to break through the veil which shrouded it, and at last the time came when I seized my thread and followed it, until it led me, after a thousand cunning windings, to ex-Professor Moriarty of mathematical celebrity.

'He is the Napoleon of crime, Watson. He is the organizer of half that is evil and of nearly all that is undetected in this great city. He is a genius, a philosopher, an abstract thinker. He has a brain of the first order. He sits motionless, like a spider in the centre of its web, but that web has a thousand radiations, and he knows well every quiver of each of them. He does little himself. He only plans. But his agents are numerous and splendidly organized. Is there a crime to be done, a paper to be abstracted, we will say, a house to be rifled, a man to be removed—the word is passed to the Professor, the matter is organized and carried out. The agent may be caught. In that case money is found for his bail or his defence. But the central power which uses the agent is never caught—never so much as suspected. This was the organization which I deduced, Watson, and which I devoted my whole energy to exposing and breaking up.

'But the Professor was fenced round with safeguards so cunningly devised that, do what I would, it seemed impossible to get evidence which would convict in a court of law. You know my powers, my dear Watson, and yet at the end of three months I was forced to confess that I had at last met an antagonist who was my intellectual equal. My horror at his crimes was lost in my admiration at his skill. But at last he made a trip—only a little, little trip—but it was more than he could afford when I was so close upon him. I had my chance, and, starting from that point, I have woven my net round him until now it is all ready to close. In three days—that is to say, on Monday next—matters will be ripe, and the Professor, with all the principal members of his gang, will be in the hands of the police. Then will come the greatest criminal trial of the century, the clearing up of over forty mysteries, and the rope for all of them; but if we move at all prematurely, you understand, they may slip out of our hands even at the last moment.

'Now, if I could have done this without the knowledge of Professor Moriarty, all would have been well. But he was too wily for that. He saw every step which I took to draw my toils round him. Again and again he strove to break away, but I as often headed him off. I tell you, my friend, that if a detailed account of that silent contest could be written, it would take its place as the most brilliant bit of thrust-and-parry work in the history of detection. Never have I risen to such a height, and never have I been so hard pressed by an opponent. He cut deep, and yet I just undercut him. This morning the last steps were taken, and three days only were wanted to complete the business. I was sitting in my room thinking the matter over, when the door opened and Professor Moriarty stood before me.

'My nerves are fairly proof, Watson, but I must confess to a start when I saw the very man who had been so much in my thoughts standing there on my threshhold. His appearance was quite familiar to me. He is extremely tall and thin, his forehead domes out in a white curve, and his two eyes are deeply sunken in his head. He is clean-shaven, pale, and ascetic-looking, retaining something of the professor in his features. His shoulders are rounded from much study, and his face protrudes forward, and is forever slowly oscillating from side to side in a curiously reptilian fashion. He peered at me with great curiosity in his puckered eyes.

'"You have less frontal development than I should have expected," said he, at last. "It is a dangerous habit to finger loaded firearms in the pocket of one's dressing-gown."

'The fact is that upon his entrance I had instantly recognised the extreme personal danger in which I lay. The only conceivable escape for him lay in silencing my tongue. In an instant I had slipped the revolver from the drawer into my pocket, and was covering him through the cloth. At his remark I drew the weapon out and laid it cocked upon the table. He still smiled and blinked, but there was something about his eyes which made me feel very glad that I had it there.

'"You evidently don't know me," said he.

'"On the contrary," I answered, "I think it is fairly evident that I do. Pray take a chair. I can spare you five minutes if you have anything to say."

'"All that I have to say has already crossed your mind," said he.

'"Then possibly my answer has crossed yours," I replied.

'"You stand fast?"

'"Absolutely."

'He clapped his hand into his pocket, and I raised the pistol from the table. But he merely drew out a memorandum-book in which he had scribbled some dates.

'"You crossed my path on the 4th of January," said he. "On the 23rd you incommoded me; by the middle of February I was seriously inconvenienced by you; at the end of March I was absolutely hampered in my plans; and now, at the close of April, I find myself placed in such a position through your continual persecution that I am in positive danger of losing my liberty. The situation is becoming an impossible one."

'"Have you any suggestion to make?" I asked.

'"You must drop it, Mr Holmes," said he, swaying his face about. "You really must, you know."

'"After Monday," said I.

'"Tut, tut," said he. "I am quite sure that a man of your intelligence will see that there can be but one outcome to this affair. It is necessary that you should withdraw. You have worked things in such a fashion that we have only one resource left. It has been an intellectual treat to me to see the way in which you have grappled with this affair, and I say, unaffectedly, that it would be a grief to me to be forced to take any extreme measure. You smile, sir, but I assure you that it really would."

'"Danger is part of my trade," I remarked.

'"That is not danger," said he. "It is inevitable destruction. You stand in the way not merely of an individual, but of a mighty organization, the full extent of which you, with all your cleverness, have been unable to realize. You must stand clear, Mr Holmes, or be trodden under foot."

'"I am afraid," said I, rising, "that in the pleasure of this conversation I am neglecting business of importance which awaits me elsewhere."

'He rose also and looked at me in silence, shaking his head sadly.

'"Well, well," said he, at last. "It seems a pity, but I have done what I could. I know every move of your game. You can do nothing before Monday. It has been a duel between you and me, Mr Holmes. You hope to place me in the dock. I tell you that I will never stand in the dock. You hope to beat me. I tell you that you will never beat me. If you are clever enough to bring destruction upon me, rest assured that I shall do as much to you."

'"You have paid me several compliments, Mr Moriarty," said I. "Let me pay you one in return when I say that if I were assured of the former eventuality I would, in the interests of the public, cheerfully accept the latter."

'"I can promise you the one, but not the other," he snarled, and so turned his rounded back upon me, and went peering and blinking out of the room.

'That was my singular interview with Professor Moriarty. I confess that it left an unpleasant effect upon my mind. His soft, precise fashion of speech leaves a conviction of sincerity which a mere bully could not produce. Of course, you will say: "Why not take police precautions against him?" the reason is that I am well convinced that it is from his agents the blow will fall. I have the best proofs that it would be so.'

'You have already been assaulted?'

'My dear Watson, Professor Moriarty is not a man who lets the grass grow under his feet. I went out about midday to transact some business in Oxford Street. As I passed the corner which leads from Bentinck Street on to the Welbeck Street crossing a two-horse van furiously driven whizzed round and was on me like a flash. I sprang for the foot-path and saved myself by the fraction of a second. The van dashed round by Marylebone Lane and was gone in an instant. I kept to the pavement after that, Watson, but as I walked down Vere Street a brick came down from the roof of one of the houses, and was shattered to fragments at my feet. I called the police and had the place examined. There were slates and bricks piled up on the roof preparatory to some repairs, and they would have me believe that the wind had toppled over one of these. Of course I knew better, but I could prove nothing. I took a cab after that and reached my brother's rooms in Pall Mall, where I spent the day. Now I have come round to you, and on my way I was attacked by a rough with a bludgeon. I knocked him down, and the police have him in custody; but I can tell you with the most absolute confidence that no possible connection will ever be traced between the gentleman upon whose front teeth I have barked my knuckles and the retiring mathematical coach, who is, I daresay, working out problems upon a blackboard ten miles away. You will not wonder, Watson, that my first act on entering your rooms was to close your shutters, and that I have been compelled to ask your permission to leave the house by some less conspicuous exit than the front door.'

I had often admired my friend's courage, but never more than now, as he sat quietly checking off a series of incidents which must have combined to make up a day of horror.

'You will spend the night here?' I said.

'No, my friend, you might find me a dangerous guest. I have my plans laid, and all will be well. Matters have gone so far now that they can move without my help as far as the arrest goes, though my presence is necessary for a conviction. It is obvious, therefore, that I cannot do better than get away for the few days which remain before the police are at liberty to act. It would be a great pleasure to me, therefore, if you could come on to the Continent with me.'

'The practice is quiet,' said I, 'and I have an accommodating neighbour. I should be glad to come.'

'And to start to-morrow morning?'

'If necessary.'

'Oh yes, it is most necessary. Then these are your instructions, and I beg, my dear Watson, that you will obey them to the letter, for you are now playing a double-handed game with me against the cleverest rogue and the most powerful syndicate of criminals in Europe. Now listen! You will dispatch whatever luggage you intend to take by a trusty messenger unaddressed to Victoria to-night. In the morning you will send for a hansom, desiring your man to take neither the first nor the second which may present itself. Into this hansom you will jump, and you will drive to the Strand end of the Lowther Arcade, handing the address to the cabman upon a slip of paper, with a request that he will not throw it away. Have your fare ready, and the instant that your cab stops, dash through the Arcade, timing yourself to reach the other side at a quarter-past nine.

You will find a small brougham waiting close to the curb, driven by a fellow with a heavy black cloak tipped at the collar with red. Into this you will step, and you will reach Victoria in time for the Continental express.'

'Where shall I meet you?'

'At the station. The second first-class carriage from the front will be reserved for us.'

'The carriage is our rendezvous, then?'

'Yes.'

It was in vain that I asked Holmes to remain for the evening. It was evident to me that he thought he might bring trouble to the roof he was under, and that that was the motive which impelled him to go. With a few hurried words as to our plans for the morrow he rose and came out with me into the garden, clambering over the wall which leads into Mortimer Street, and immediately whistling for a hansom, in which I heard him drive away.

In the morning I obeyed Holmes's injunctions to the letter. A hansom was procured with such precaution as would prevent its being one which was placed ready for us, and I drove immediately after breakfast to the Lowther Arcade, through which I hurried at the top of my speed. A brougham was waiting with a very massive driver wrapped in a dark cloak, who, the instant that I had stepped in, whipped up the horse and rattled off to Victoria Station. On my alighting there he turned the carriage, and dashed away again without so much as a look in my direction.

So far all had gone admirably. My luggage was waiting for me, and I had no difficulty in finding the carriage which Holmes had indicated, the less so as it was the only one in the train which was marked 'Engaged.' My only source of anxiety now was the non-appearance of Holmes. The station clock marked only seven minutes from the time when we were due to start. In vain I searched among the groups of travellers and leave-takers for the lithe figure of my friend. There was no sign of him. I spent a few minutes in assisting a venerable Italian priest, who was endeavouring to make a porter understand, in his broken English, that his luggage was to be booked through to Paris. Then, having taken another look round, I returned to my carriage, where I found that the porter, in spite of the ticket, had given me my decrepit Italian friend as a traveling companion. It was useless for me to explain to him that his presence was an intrusion, for my Italian was even more limited than his English, so I shrugged my shoulders resignedly, and continued to look out anxiously for my friend. A chill of fear had come over me, as I thought that his absence might mean that some blow had fallen during the night. Already the doors had all been shut and the whistle blown, when—

'My dear Watson,' said a voice, 'you have not even condescended to say good-morning.'

I turned in uncontrollable astonishment. The aged ecclesiastic had turned his face towards me. For an instant the wrinkles were smoothed away, the nose drew away from the chin, the lower lip ceased to protrude and the mouth to mumble, the dull eyes regained their fire, the drooping figure expanded. The next the whole frame collapsed again, and Holmes had gone as quickly as he had come.

'Good heavens!' I cried. 'How you startled me!'

'Every precaution is still necessary,' he whispered. 'I have reason to think that they are hot upon our trail. Ah, there is Moriarty himself.'

The train had already begun to move as Holmes spoke. Glancing back, I saw a tall man pushing his way furiously through the crowd, and waving his hand as if he desired to have the train stopped. It was too late, however, for we were rapidly gathering momentum, and an instant later had shot clear of the station.

'With all our precautions, you see that we have cut it rather fine,' said Holmes, laughing. He rose, and throwing off the black cassock and hat which had formed his disguise, he packed them away in a hand-bag.

'Have you seen the morning paper, Watson?'

'No.'

'You haven't seen about Baker Street, then?'

'Baker Street?'

'They set fire to our rooms last night. No great harm was done.'

'Good heavens, Holmes! This is intolerable.'

'They must have lost my track completely after their bludgeon-man was arrested. Otherwise they could not have imagined that I had returned to my rooms. They have evidently taken the precaution of watching you, however, and that is what has brought Moriarty to Victoria. You could not have made any slip in coming?'

'I did exactly what you advised.'

'Did you find your brougham?'

'Yes, it was waiting.'

'Did you recognise your coachman?'

'No.'

'It was my brother Mycroft. It is an advantage to get about in such a case without taking a mercenary into your confidence. But we must plan what we are to do about Moriarty now.'

'As this is an express, and as the boat runs in connection with it, I should think we have shaken him off very effectively.'

'My dear Watson, you evidently did not realize my meaning when I said that this man may be taken as being quite on the same intellectual plane as myself. You do not imagine that if I were the pursuer I should allow myself to be baffled by so slight an obstacle. Why, then, should you think so meanly of him?'

'What will he do?'

'What I should do?'

'What would you do, then?'

'Engage a special.'

'But it must be late.'

'By no means. This train stops at Canterbury; and there is always at least a quarter of an hour's delay at the boat. He will catch us there.'

'One would think that we were the criminals. Let us have him arrested on his arrival.'

'It would be to ruin the work of three months. We should get the big fish, but the smaller would dart right and left out of the net. On Monday we should have them all. No, an arrest is inadmissible.'

'What then?'

'We shall get out at Canterbury.'

'And then?'

'Well, then we must make a cross-country journey to Newhaven, and so over to Dieppe. Moriarty will again do what I should do. He will get on to Paris, mark down our luggage, and wait for two days at the depôt. In the meantime we shall treat ourselves to a couple of carpet-bags, encourage the manufactures of the countries through which we travel, and make our way at our leisure into Switzerland, via Luxembourg and Basle.'

At Canterbury, therefore, we alighted, only to find that we should have to wait an hour before we could get a train to Newhaven.

I was still looking rather ruefully after the rapidly disappearing luggage-van which contained my wardrobe, when Holmes pulled my sleeve and pointed up the line.

'Already, you see,' said he.

Far away, from among the Kentish woods there rose a thin spray of smoke. A minute later a carriage and engine could be seen flying along the open curve which leads to the station. We had hardly time to take our place behind a pile of luggage when it passed with a rattle and a roar, beating a blast of hot air into our faces.

'There he goes,' said Holmes, as we watched the carriage swing and rock over the points. 'There are limits, you see, to our friend's intelligence. It would have been a *coup-de-maître* had he deduced what I would deduce and acted accordingly.'

'And what would he have done had he overtaken us?'

'There cannot be the least doubt that he would have made a murderous attack upon me. It is, however, a game at which two may play. The question now is whether we should take a premature lunch here, or run our chance of starving before we reach the buffet at Newhaven.'

We made our way to Brussels that night and spent two days there, moving on upon the third day as far as Strasburg. On the Monday morning Holmes had telegraphed to the London police, and in the evening we found a reply waiting for us at our hotel. Holmes tore it open, and then with a bitter curse hurled it into the grate.

'I might have known it!' he groaned. 'He has escaped!'

'Moriarty?'

'They have secured the whole gang with the

exception of him. He has given them the slip. Of course, when I had left the country there was no one to cope with him. But I did think that I had put the game in their hands. I think that you had better return to England, Watson.'

'Why?'

'Because you will find me a dangerous companion now. This man's occupation is gone. He is lost if he returns to London. If I read his character right he will devote his whole energies to revenging himself upon me. He said as much in our short interview, and I fancy that he meant it. I should certainly recommend you to return to your practice.'

It was hardly an appeal to be successful with one who was an old campaigner as well as an old friend. We sat in the Strasburg *salle-à-manger* arguing the question for half an hour, but the same night we had resumed our journey and were well on our way to Geneva.

For a charming week we wandered up the Valley of the Rhone, and then, branching off at Leuk, we made our way over the Gemmi Pass, still deep in snow, and so, by way of Interlaken, to Meiringen. It was a lovely trip, the dainty green of the spring below, the virgin white of the winter above; but it was clear to me that never for one instant did Holmes forget the shadow which lay across him. In the homely Alpine villages or in the lonely mountain passes, I could tell by his quick glancing eyes and his sharp scrutiny of every face that passed us, that he was well convinced that, walk where we would, we could not walk ourselves clear of the danger which was dogging our footsteps.

Once, I remember, as we passed over the Gemmi, and walked along the border of the melancholy Daubensee, a large rock which had been dislodged from the ridge upon our right clattered down and roared into the lake behind us. In an instant Holmes had raced up on to the ridge, and, standing upon a lofty pinnacle, craned his neck in every direction. It was in vain that our guide assured him that a fall of stones was a common chance in the spring-time at that spot. He said nothing, but he smiled at me with the air of a man who sees the fulfillment of that which he had expected.

And yet for all his watchfulness he was never depressed. On the contrary, I can never recollect having seen him in such exuberant spirits. Again and again he recurred to the fact that if he could be assured that society was freed from Professor Moriarty he would cheerfully bring his own career to a conclusion.

'I think that I may go so far as to say, Watson, that I have not lived wholly in vain,' he remarked. 'If my record were closed to-night I could still survey it with equanimity. The air of London is the sweeter for my presence. In over a thousand cases I am not aware that I have ever used my powers upon the wrong side. Of late I have been tempted to look into the problems furnished by nature rather than those more superficial ones for which our artificial state of society is responsible. Your memoirs will draw to an end, Watson, upon the day that I crown my career by the capture or extinction of the most dangerous and capable criminal in Europe.'

I shall be brief, and yet exact, in the little which remains for me to tell. It is not a subject on which I would willingly dwell, and yet I am conscious that a duty devolves upon me to omit no detail.

It was on the 3rd of May that we reached the little village of Meiringen, where we put up at the Englischer Hof, then kept by Peter Steiler the elder. Our landlord was an intelligent man, and spoke excellent English, having served for three years as waiter at the Grosvenor Hotel in London. At his advice, on the afternoon of the 4th we set off together, with the intention of crossing the hills and spending the night at the hamlet of Rosenlaui. We had strict injunctions, however, on no account to pass the falls of Reichenbach, which are about half-way up the hill, without making a small détour to see them.

It is indeed, a fearful place. The torrent, swollen by the melting snow, plunges into a tremendous abyss, from which the spray rolls up like the smoke from a burning house. The shaft into which the river hurls itself is an immense chasm, lined by glistening coal-black rock, and narrowing into a creaming, boiling pit of incalculable depth, which brims over and shoots the stream onward over its jagged lip. The long sweep of green water roaring forever down, and the thick flickering curtain of spray hissing forever upward, turn a man giddy with their constant whirl and clamour. We stood near the edge peering down at the gleam of the breaking water far below us against the black rocks, and listening to the half-human shout which came booming up with the spray out of the abyss.

The path has been cut half-way round the fall to afford a complete view, but it ends abruptly, and the traveler has to return as he came. We had turned to do so, when we saw a Swiss lad come running along it with a letter in his hand. It bore the mark of the hotel which we had just left, and was addressed to me by the landlord. It appeared that within a very few minutes of our leaving, an English lady had arrived who was in the last stage of consumption.

She had wintered at Davos Platz, and was journeying now to join her friends at Lucerne, when a sudden hemorrhage had overtaken her. It was thought that she could hardly live a few hours, but it would be a great consolation to her to see an English doctor, and, if I would only return, etc. The good Steiler assured me in a postscript that he would himself look upon my compliance as a very great favour, since the lady absolutely refused to see a Swiss physician, and he could not but feel that he was incurring a great responsibility.

The appeal was one which could not be ignored. It was impossible to refuse the request of a fellow-countrywoman dying in a strange land. Yet I had my scruples about leaving Holmes. It was finally agreed, however, that he should retain the young Swiss messenger with him as guide and companion while I returned to Meiringen. My friend would stay some little time at the fall, he said, and would then walk slowly over the hill to Rosenlaui, where I was to rejoin him in the evening. As I turned away I saw Holmes, with his back against a rock and his arms folded, gazing down at the rush of the waters. It was the last that I was ever destined to see of him in this world.

When I was near the bottom of the descent I looked back. It was impossible, from that position, to see the fall, but I could see the curving path which winds over the shoulder of the hill and leads to it. Along this a man was, I remember, walking very rapidly.

I could see his black figure clearly outlined against the green behind him. I noted him, and the energy with which he walked but he passed from my mind again as I hurried on upon my errand.

It may have been a little over an hour before I reached Meiringen. Old Steiler was standing at the porch of his hotel.

'Well,' said I, as I came hurrying up, 'I trust that she is no worse?'

A look of surprise passed over his face, and at the first quiver of his eyebrows my heart turned to lead in my breast.

'You did not write this?' I said, pulling the letter from my pocket. 'There is no sick Englishwoman in the hotel?'

'Certainly not!' he cried. 'But it has the hotel

mark upon it! Ha, it must have been written by that tall Englishman who came in after you had gone. He said—'

But I waited for none of the landlord's explanations. In a tingle of fear I was already running down the village street, and making for the path which I had so lately descended. It had taken me an hour to come down. For all my efforts two more had passed before I found myself at the fall of Reichenbach once more. There was Holmes's Alpine-stock still leaning against the rock by which I had left him. But there was no sign of him, and it was in vain that I shouted. My only answer was my own voice reverberating in a rolling echo from the cliffs around me.

It was the sight of that Alpine-stock which turned me cold and sick. He had not gone to Rosenlaui, then. He had remained on that three-foot path, with sheer wall on one side and sheer drop on the other, until his enemy had overtaken him. The young Swiss had gone too. He had probably been in the pay of Moriarty, and had left the two men together. And then what had happened? Who was to tell us what had happened then?

I stood for a minute or two to collect myself, for I was dazed with the horror of the thing. Then I began to think of Holmes's own methods and to try to practise them in reading this tragedy. It was, alas, only too easy to do. During our conversation we had not gone to the end of the path, and the Alpine-stock marked the place where we had stood. The blackish soil is kept forever soft by the incessant drift of spray, and a bird would leave its tread upon it. Two lines of footmarks were clearly marked along the farther end of the path, both leading away from me.

There were none returning. A few yards from the end the soil was all ploughed up into a patch of mud, and the branches and ferns which fringed the chasm were torn and bedraggled. I lay upon my face and peered over with the spray spouting up all around me. It had darkened since I left, and now I could only see here and there the glistening of moisture upon the black walls, and far away down at the end of the shaft the gleam of the broken water. I shouted; but only the same half-human cry of the fall was borne back to my ears.

But it was destined that I should after all have a last word of greeting from my friend and comrade. I have said that his Alpine-stock had been left leaning against a rock which jutted on to the path. From the top of this boulder the gleam of something bright caught my eye, and, raising my hand, I found that it came from the silver cigarette-case which he used to carry. As I took it up a small square of paper upon which it had lain fluttered down on to the ground. Unfolding it, I found that it consisted of three pages torn from his note-book and addressed to me. It was characteristic of the man that the direction was a precise, and the writing as firm and clear, as though it had been written in his study.

'My dear Watson,' he said, 'I write these few lines through the courtesy of Mr Moriarty, who awaits my convenience for the final discussion of those questions which lie between us. He has been giving me a sketch of the methods by which he avoided the English police and kept himself informed of our movements. They certainly confirm the very high opinion which I had formed of his abilities. I am pleased to think that I shall be able to free society from any further effects of his presence, though I fear that it is at a cost which will give pain to my friends, and especially, my dear Watson, to you. I have already explained to you, however, that my career had in any case reached its crisis, and that no possible conclusion to it could be more congenial to me than this. Indeed, if I may make a full confession to you, I was quite convinced that the letter from Meiringen was a hoax, and I allowed you to depart on that errand under the persuasion that some development of this sort would follow. Tell Inspector Patterson that the papers which he needs to convict the gang are in pigeonhole M., done up in a blue envelope and inscribed 'Moriarty.' I made every disposition of my property before leaving England, and handed it to my brother Mycroft. Pray give my greetings to Mrs Watson, and believe me to be, my dear fellow,

'Very sincerely yours,
'Sherlock Holmes.'

A few words may suffice to tell the little that remains. An examination by experts leaves little doubt that a personal contest between the two men ended, as it could hardly fail to end in such a situation, in their reeling over, locked in each other's arms. Any attempt at recovering the bodies was absolutely hopeless, and there, deep down in that dreadful caldron of swirling water and seething foam, will lie for all time the most dangerous criminal and the foremost champion of the law of their generation. The Swiss youth was never found again, and there can be no doubt that he was one of the numerous agents whom Moriarty kept in his employ. As to the gang, it will be within the memory of the public how completely the evidence which Holmes had accumulated exposed their organization, and how heavily the hand of the dead man weighed upon them. Of their terrible chief few details came out during the proceedings, and if I have now been compelled to make a clear statement of his career it is due to those injudicious champions who have endeavoured to clear his memory by attacks upon him whom I shall ever regard as the best and the wisest man whom I have ever known.

Catherine Louisa Pirkis

Pseudonym C. L Pirkis
(6 October, 1839 – 4 October, 1910)

Catherine Louisa Pirkis was a British detective fiction author. Pirkis wrote behind the pen name 'C L Pirkis' throughout her career as a writer to avoid gender associations. *Disappeared from Her Home* was her first major novel and marked her entry into the mystery genre. It also served as a precursor to the invention of the female detective character Loveday Brooke, for which she is best known. She is often dubbed as 'the Female Sherlock Holmes.'

The Redhill Sisterhood

'They want you at Redhill, now,' said Mr Dyer, taking a packet of papers from one of his pigeon-holes. 'The idea seems gaining ground in manly quarters that in cases of mere suspicion, women detectives are more satisfactory than men, for they are less likely to attract attention. And this Redhill affair, so far as I can make out, is one of suspicion only.'

It was a dreary November morning; every gas jet in the Lynch Court office was alight, and a yellow curtain of outside fog draped its narrow windows.

'Nevertheless, I suppose one can't afford to leave it uninvestigated at this season of the year, with country-house robberies beginning in so many quarters,' said Miss Brooke.

'No; and the circumstances in this case certainly seem to point in the direction of the country-house burglar. Two days ago a somewhat curious application was made privately, by a man giving the name of John Murray, to Inspector Gunning, of the Reigate police–Redhill, I must tell you is in the Reigate police district. Murray stated that he had been a greengrocer somewhere in South London, had sold his business there, and had, with the proceeds of the sale, bought two small houses in Redhill, intending to let the one and live in the other. These houses are situated in a blind alley, known as Paved Court, a narrow turning leading off the London and Brighton coach road. Paved Court has been known to the sanitary authorities for the past ten years as a regular fever nest, and as the houses which Murray bought–numbers 7 and 8–stand at the very end of the blind alley, with no chance of thorough ventilation, I dare say the man got them for next to nothing. He told the Inspector that he had had great difficulty in procuring a tenant for the house he wished to let, number 8, and that consequently when, about three weeks back, a lady, dressed as a nun, made him an offer for it, he immediately closed with her. The lady gave her name simply as 'Sister Monica,' and stated that she was a member of an undenominational Sisterhood that had recently been founded by a wealthy lady, who wished her name kept a secret. Sister Monica gave no references, but, instead, paid a quarter's rent in advance, saying that she wished to take possession of the house immediately, and open it as a home for crippled orphans.'

'Gave no references–home for cripples,' murmured Loveday, scribbling hard and fast in her note-book.

'Murray made no objection to this,' continued Mr Dyer, 'and, accordingly, the next day, Sister Monica, accompanied by three other Sisters and some sickly children, took possession of the house, which they furnished with the barest possible necessaries from cheap shops in the neighbourhood. For a time, Murray said, he thought he had secured most desirable tenants, but during the last ten days suspicions as to their real character have entered his mind, and these suspicions he thought it his duty to communicate to the police. Among their possessions, it seems, these Sisters number an old donkey and a tiny cart, and this they start daily on a sort of begging tour through the adjoining villages, bringing back every evening a perfect hoard of broken victuals and bundles of old garments. Now comes the extraordinary fact on which Murray bases his suspicions. He says, and Gunning verifies his statement, that in whatever direction those Sisters turn the wheels of their donkey-cart, burglaries, or attempts at burglaries, are sure to follow. A week ago they went along towards Horley, where, at an outlying house, they received much kindness from a wealthy gentleman. That very night an attempt was made to break into that gentleman's house–an attempt, however, that was happily frustrated by the barking of the house-dog.

And so on in other instances that I need not go into. Murray suggests that it might be as well to have the daily movements of these sisters closely watched, and that extra vigilance should be exercised by the police in the districts that have had the honour of a morning call from them. Gunning coincides with this idea, and so has sent to me to secure your services.'

Loveday closed her note-book. 'I suppose Gunning will meet me somewhere and tell me where I'm to take up my quarters?' she said.

'Yes; he will get into your carriage at Merstham–the station before Redhill–if you will put your hand out of window, with the morning paper in it. By-the-way, he takes it for granted that you will save the 11.5 train from Victoria. Murray, it seems has been good enough to place his little house at the disposal of the police, but Gunning does not think espionage could be so well carried on there as from other quarters. The presence of a stranger in an alley of that sort is bound to attract attention. So he has hired a room for you in a draper's shop that immediately faces the head of the court. There is a private door to this shop of which you will have the key, and can let yourself in and out as you please. You are supposed to be a nursery governess on the lookout for a situation, and Gunning will keep you supplied with letters to give colour to the idea. He suggests that you need only occupy the room during the day, at night you will find far more comfortable quarters at Laker's Hotel, just outside the town.'

This was about the sum total of the instructions that Mr Dyer had to give.

The 11.5 train from Victoria, that carried Loveday to her work among the Surrey Hills, did not get clear of the London fog till well away on the other side of Purley. When the train halted at Merstham, in response to her signal a tall, soldier-like individual made for her carriage, and, jumping in, took the seat facing her. He introduced himself to her as Inspector Gunning, recalled to her memory a former occasion on which they had met, and then, naturally enough, turned the talk upon the present suspicious circumstances they were bent upon investigating.

'It won't do for you and me to be seen together,' he said; 'of course I am known for miles round, and anyone seen in my company will be at once set down as my coadjutor, and spied upon accordingly. I walked from Redhill to Merstham on purpose to avoid recognition on the platform at Redhill, and half-way here, to my great annoyance, found that I was being followed by a man in a workman's dress and carrying a basket of tools. I doubled, however, and gave him the slip, taking a short cut down a lane which, if he had been living in the place, he would have known as well as I did. By Jove!' this was added with a sudden start, 'there is the fellow, I declare; he has weathered me after all, and has no doubt taken good stock of us both, with the train going at this snail's pace. It was unfortunate that your face should have been turned towards that window, Miss Brooke.'

'My veil is something of a disguise, and I will put on another cloak before he has a chance of seeing me again,' said Loveday.

All she had seen in the brief glimpse that the train had allowed, was a tall, powerfully-built man walking along a siding of the line. His cap was drawn low over his eyes, and in his hand he carried a workman's basket.

Gunning seemed much annoyed at the circumstance. 'Instead of landing at Redhill,' he said, 'we'll go on to Three Bridges and wait there for a Brighton train to bring us back, that will enable you to get to your room somewhere between the lights; I don't want to have you spotted before you've so much as started your work.'

Then they went back to their discussion of the Redhill Sisterhood.

'They call themselves "undenominational," whatever that means,' said Gunning 'they say they are connected with no religious sect whatever, they attend sometimes one place of worship, sometimes another, sometimes none at all. They refuse to give up the name of the founder of their order, and really no one has any right to demand it of them, for, as no doubt you see, up to the present moment the case is one of mere suspicion, and it may be a pure coincidence that attempts at burglary have followed their footsteps in this neighbourhood. By-the-way, I have heard of a man's face being enough to hang him, but until I saw

Sister Monica's, I never saw a woman's face that could perform the same kind office for her. Of all the lowest criminal types of faces I have ever seen, I think hers is about the lowest and most repulsive.'

After the Sisters, they passed in review the chief families resident in the neighbourhood.

.'This,' said Gunning, unfolding a paper, 'is a map I have specially drawn up for you–it takes in the district for ten miles round Redhill, and every country house of any importance is marked with it in red ink. Here, in addition, is an index to those houses, with special notes of my own to every house.'

Loveday studied the map for a minute or so, then turned her attention to the index.

'Those four houses you've marked, I see, are those that have been already attempted. I don't think I'll run them through, but I'll mark them "doubtful," you see the gang–for, of course, it is a gang–might follow our reasoning on the matter, and look upon those houses as our weak point. Here's one I'll run through, "house empty during winter months," that means plate and jewellery sent to the bankers. Oh! and this one may as well be crossed off, "father and four sons all athletes and sportsmen," that means firearms always handy–I don't think burglars will be likely to trouble them. Ah! now we come to something! Here's a house to be marked "tempting" in a burglar's list. "Wootton Hall, lately changed hands and re-built, with complicated passages and corridors. Splendid family plate in daily use and left entirely to the care of the butler." I wonder, does the master of that house trust to his "complicated passages" to preserve his plate for him? A dismissed dishonest servant would supply a dozen maps of the place for half-a-sovereign. What do these initials, "E L," against the next house in the list, North Cape, stand for?'

'Electric lighted. I think you might almost cross that house off also. I consider electric lighting one of the greatest safeguards against burglars that a man can give his house.'

'Yes, if he doesn't rely exclusively upon it; it might be a nasty trap under certain circumstances. I see this gentleman also has magnificent presentation and other plate.'

'Yes. Mr Jameson is a wealthy man and very popular in the neighbourhood; his cups and epergnes are worth looking at.'

'Is it the only house in the district that is lighted with electricity?'

'Yes; and, begging your pardon, Miss Brooke, I only wish it were not so. If electric lighting were generally in vogue it would save the police a lot of trouble on these dark winter nights.'

'The burglars would find some way of meeting such a condition of things, depend upon it; they have reached a very high development in these days. They no longer stalk about as they did fifty years ago with blunderbuss and bludgeon; they plot, plan, contrive and bring imagination and artistic resource to their aid. By-the-way, it often occurs to me that the popular detective stories, for which there seems to large a demand at the present day, must be, at times, uncommonly useful to the criminal classes.'

At Three Bridges they had to wait so long for a return train that it was nearly dark when Loveday got back to Redhill. Mr Gunning did not accompany her thither, having alighted at a previous station. Loveday had directed her portmanteau to be sent direct to Laker's Hotel, where she had engaged a room by telegram from Victoria Station. So, unburthened by luggage, she slipped quietly out of the Redhill Station and made her way straight for the draper's shop in the London Road. She had no difficulty in finding it, thanks to the minute directions given her by the Inspector.

Street lamps were being lighted in the sleepy little town as she went along, and as she turned into the London Road, shopkeepers were lighting up their windows on both sides of the way. A few yards down this road, a dark patch between the lighted shops showed her where Paved Court led off from the thoroughfare. A side-door of one of the shops that stood at the corner of the court seemed to offer a post of observation whence she could see without being seen, and here Loveday, shrinking into the shadows, ensconced herself in order to take stock of the little alley and its inhabitants. She found it much as it had been described to her–a collection of four-roomed houses of which more than half were unlet. Numbers 7 and 8 at the head of the court presented a slightly less neglected appearance than the other tenements. Number 7 stood in total darkness, but in the upper window of number 8 there showed what seemed to be a night-light burning, so Loveday conjectured that this possibly was the room set apart as a dormitory for the little cripples.

While she stood thus surveying the home of the suspected Sisterhood, the Sisters themselves–two, at least, of them–came into view, with their donkey-cart and their cripples, in the main road. It was an odd little cortège. One Sister, habited in a nun's dress of dark blue serge, led the donkey by the bridle; another Sister, similarly attired, walked alongside the low cart, in which were seated two sickly-looking children. They were evidently returning from one of their long country circuits, and unless they had lost their way and been belated–it certainly seemed a late hour for the sickly little cripples to be abroad.

As they passed under the gas lamp at the corner of the court, Loveday caught a glimpse of the faces of the Sisters. It was easy, with Inspector Gunning's description before her mind, to identify the older and taller woman as Sister Monica, and a more coarse-featured and generally repellant face Loveday admitted to herself she had never before seen. In striking contrast to this forbidding countenance, was that of the younger Sister. Loveday could only catch a brief passing view of it, but that one brief view was enough to impress it on her memory as of unusual sadness and beauty. As the donkey stopped at the corner of the court, Loveday heard this sad-looking young woman addressed as 'Sister Anna' by one of the cripples, who asked plaintively when they were going to have something to eat.

'Now, at once,' said Sister Anna, lifting the little one, as it seemed to Loveday, tenderly out of the cart, and carrying him on her shoulder down the court to the door of number 8, which opened to them at their approach. The other Sister did the same with the other child; then both Sisters returned, unloaded the cart of sundry bundles and baskets, and, this done, led off the old donkey and trap down the road, possibly to a neighbouring costermonger's stables.

A man, coming along on a bicycle, exchanged a word of greeting with the Sisters as they passed, then swung himself off his machine at the corner of the court, and walked it along the paved way to the door of number 7. This he opened with a key, and then, pushing the machine before him, entered the house.

Loveday took it for granted that this man must be the John Murray of whom she had heard. She had closely scrutinized him as he had passed her, and had seen that he was a dark, well-featured man of about fifty years of age.

She congratulated herself on her good fortune in having seen so much in such a brief space of time, and coming forth from her sheltered corner turned her steps in the direction of the draper's shop on the other side of the road.

It was easy to find it. 'Golightly' was the singular name that figured above the shop-front, in which were displayed a variety of goods calculated to meet the wants of servants and the poorer classes generally. A tall, powerfully-built man appeared to be looking in at this window. Loveday's foot was on the doorstep of the draper's private entrance, her hand on the door-knocker, when this individual, suddenly turning, convinced her of his identity with the journeyman workman who had so disturbed Mr Gunning's equanimity. It was true he wore a bowler instead of a journeyman's cap, and he no longer carried a basket of tools, but there was no possibility for anyone, with so good an eye for an outline as Loveday possessed, not to recognize the carriage of the head and shoulders as that of the man she had seen walking along the railway siding. He gave her no time to make minute observation of his appearance, but turned quickly away, and disappeared down a by-street.

Loveday's work seemed to bristle with difficulties now. Here was she, as it were, unearthed in her own ambush; for there could be but little doubt that during the whole time she had stood watching those Sisters, that man, from a safe vantage point, had been watching her.

She found Mrs Golightly a civil and obliging person. She showed Loveday to her room above the shop, brought her the letters which Inspector Gunning had been careful to have posted to her during the day. Then she supplied her with pen and ink and, in response to Loveday's request, with some strong coffee that she said, with a little attempt at a joke, would 'keep a dormouse awake all through the winter without winking.'

While the obliging landlady busied herself about the room, Loveday had a few questions to ask about the Sisterhood who lived down the court opposite. On this head, however, Mrs Golightly could tell her no more than she already knew, beyond the fact that they started every morning on their rounds at eleven o'clock punctually, and that before that hour they were never to be seen outside their door.

Loveday's watch that night was to be a fruitless one. Although she sat, with her lamp turned out and safely screened from observation, until close upon midnight, with eyes fixed upon numbers 7 and 8 Paved Court, not so much as a door opening or shutting at either house rewarded her vigil. The lights flitted from the lower to the upper floors in both houses, and then disappeared somewhere between nine and ten in the evening; and after that, not a sign of life did either tenement show.

And all through the long hours of that watch, backwards and forwards there seemed to flit before her mind's eye, as if in some sort it were fixed upon its retina, the sweet, sad face of Sister Anna.

Why it was this face should so haunt her, she found it hard to say.

'It has a mournful past and a mournful future written upon it as a hopeless whole,' she said to herself. 'It is the face of an Andromeda! "here am I," it seems to say, "tied to my stake, helpless and hopeless."'

The church clocks were sounding the midnight hour as Loveday made her way through the dark streets to her hotel outside the town. As she passed under the railway arch that ended in the open country road, the echo of not very distant footsteps caught her ear. When she stopped they stopped, when she went on they went on, and she knew that once more she was being followed and watched, although the darkness of the arch prevented her seeing even the shadow of the man who was thus dogging her steps.

The next morning broke keen and frosty. Loveday studied her map and her country-house index over a seven o'clock breakfast, and then set off for a brisk walk along the country road. No doubt in London the streets were walled in and roofed with yellow fog; here, however, bright sunshine played in and out of the bare tree-boughs and leafless hedges on to a thousand frost spangles, turning the prosaic macadamized road into a gangway fit for Queen Titania herself and her fairy train.

Loveday turned her back on the town and set herself to follow the road as it wound away over the hill in the direction of a village called Northfield. Early as she was, she was not to have that road to herself. A team of strong horses trudged by on their way to their work in the fuller's-earth pits. A young fellow on a bicycle flashed past at a tremendous pace, considering the upward slant of the road. He looked hard at her as he passed, then slackened pace, dismounted, and awaited her coming on the brow of the hill.

'Good morning, Miss Brooke,' he said, lifting his cap as she came alongside of him. 'May I have five minutes' talk with you?'

The young man who thus accosted her had not the appearance of a gentleman. He was a handsome, bright-faced young fellow of about two-and-twenty, and was dressed in ordinary cyclists' dress; his cap was pushed back from his brow over thick, curly, fair hair, and Loveday, as she looked at him, could not repress the thought how well he would look at the head of a troop of cavalry, giving the order to charge the enemy.

He led his machine to the side of the footpath.

'You have the advantage of me,' said Loveday; 'I haven't the remotest notion who you are.'

'No,' he said; 'although I know you, you cannot possibly know me. I am a north country man, and I was present, about a month ago, at the trial of old Mr Craven, of Troyte's Hill–in fact, I acted as reporter for one of the local papers. I watched your face so closely as you gave your evidence that I should know it anywhere, among a thousand.'

'And your name is—?'

'George White, of Grenfell. My father is part proprietor of one of the Newcastle papers. I am a bit of a literary man myself, and sometimes figure as a reporter, sometimes as leader-writer, to that paper.' Here he gave a glance towards his side pocket, from which protruded a small volume of Tennyson's poems.

The facts he had stated did not seem to invite comment, and Loveday ejaculated merely:

'Indeed!'

The young man went back to the subject that was evidently filling his thoughts. 'I have special reasons for being glad to have met you this morning, Miss Brooke,' he want on, making his footsteps keep pace with hers. 'I am in great trouble, and I believe you are the only person in the whole world who can help me out of that trouble.'

'I am rather doubtful as to my power of helping anyone out of trouble,' said Loveday; 'so far as my experience goes, our troubles are as much a part of ourselves as our skins are of our bodies.'

'Ah, but not such trouble as mine,' said White eagerly. He broke off for a moment, then, with a sudden rush of words, told her what that trouble was. For the past year he had been engaged to be married to a young girl, who, until quite recently had been fulfilling the duties of a nursery governess in a large house in the neighbourhood of Redhill.

'Will you kindly give me the name of that house?' interrupted Loveday.

'Certainly; Wootton Hall, the place is called, and Annie Lee is my sweetheart's name. I don't care who knows it!' He threw his head back as he said this, as if he would be delighted to announce the fact to the whole world. 'Annie's mother,' he went on, 'died when she was a baby, and we both thought her father was dead also, when suddenly, about a fortnight ago, it came to her knowledge that instead of being dead, he was serving his time at Portland for some offence committed years ago.'

'Do you know how this came to Annie's knowledge?'

'Not the least in the world; I only know that I suddenly got a letter from her announcing the fact, and at the same time, breaking off her engagement with me. I tore the letter into a thousand pieces, and wrote back saying I would not allow the engagement to be broken off, but would marry her to-morrow if she would have me. To this letter she did not reply; there came instead a few lines from Mrs Copeland, the lady at Wootton Hall, saying that Annie had thrown up her engagement and joined some Sisterhood, and that she, Mrs Copeland, had pledged her word to Annie to reveal to no one the name and whereabouts of that Sisterhood.'

'And I suppose you imagine I am able to do what Mrs Copeland is pledged not to do?'

'That's just it, Miss Brooke,' cried the young man enthusiastically. 'You do such wonderful things; everyone knows you do. It seems as if, when anything is wanted to be found out, you just walk into a place, look round you and, in a moment, everything becomes clear as noonday.'

'I can't quite lay claim to such wonderful powers as that. As it happens, however, in the present instance, no particular skill is needed to find out what you wish to know, for I fancy I have already come upon the traces of Miss Annie Lee.'

'Miss Brooke!'

'Of course, I cannot say for certain, but is a matter you can easily settle for yourself–settle, too, in a way that will confer a great obligation on me.'

'I shall be only too delighted to be of any–the slightest service to you,' cried White, enthusiastically as before.

'Thank you. I will explain. I came down here specially to watch the movements of a certain Sisterhood who have somehow aroused the suspicions of the police. Well, I find that instead of being able to do this, I am myself so closely watched–possibly by confederates of these Sisters–that unless I can do my work by deputy I may as well go back to town at once.'

'Ah! I see–you want me to be that deputy.'

'Precisely. I want you to go to the room in Redhill that I have hired, take your place at the window–screened, of course, from observation–at which I ought to be seated–watch as closely as possible the movements of these Sisters and report them to me at the hotel, where I shall remain shut in from morning till night–it is the only way in which I can throw my persistent spies off the scent. Now, in doing this for me, you will be also doing yourself a good turn, for I have little doubt but what under the blue serge hood of one of the sisters you will discover the pretty face of Miss Annie Lee.'

As they had talked they had walked, and now stood on the top of the hill at the head of the one little street that constituted the whole of the village of Northfield.

On their left hand stood the village schools and the master's house; nearly facing these, on the opposite side of the road, beneath a clump of elms, stood the village pound. Beyond this pound, on either side of the way, were two rows of small cottages with tiny squares of garden in front, and in the midst of these small cottages a swinging sign beneath a lamp announced a 'Postal and Telegraph Office.'

'Now that we have come into the land of habitations again,' said Loveday, 'it will be best for us to part. It will not do for you and me to be seen together, or my spies will be transferring their attentions from me to you, and I shall have to find another deputy. You had better start on your bicycle for Redhill at once, and I will walk back at leisurely speed. Come to me at my hotel without fail at one o'clock and report proceedings. I do not say anything definite about remuneration, but I assure you, if you carry out my instructions to the letter, your services will be amply rewarded by me and by my employers.'

There were yet a few more details to arrange. White had been, he said, only a day and night in the neighbourhood, and special directions as to the locality had to be given to him. Loveday advised him not to attract attention by going to the draper's private door, but to enter the shop as if he were a customer, and then explain matters to Mrs Golightly, who, no doubt, would be in her place behind the counter; tell her he was the brother of the Miss Smith who had hired her room, and ask permission to go through the shop to that room, as he had been commissioned by his sister to read and answer any letters that might have arrived there for her.

'Show her the key of the side door–here it is,' said Loveday; 'it will be your credentials, and tell her you did not like to make use of it without acquainting her with the fact.'

The young man took the key, endeavoured to put it in his waistcoat pocket, found the space there occupied and so transferred it to the keeping of a side pocket in his tunic.

All this time Loveday stood watching him.

'You have a capital machine there,' she said, as the young man mounted his bicycle once more, 'and I hope you will turn it to account in following the movements of these Sisters about the neighbourood. I feel confident you will have something definite to tell me when you bring me your first report at one o'clock.'

White once more broke into a profusion of thanks, and then, lifting his cap to the lady, started his machine at a fairly good pace.

Loveday watched him out of sight down the slope of the hill, then, instead of following him as she had said she would 'at a leisurely pace,' she turned her steps in the opposite direction along the village street.

It was an altogether ideal country village. Neatly-dressed chubby-faced children, now on their way to the schools, dropped quaint little curtsies, or tugged at curly locks as Loveday passed; every cottage looked the picture of cleanliness and trimness, and although so late in the year, the gardens were full of late flowering chrysanthemums and early flowering Christmas roses.

At the end of the village, Loveday came suddenly into view of a large, handsome, red-brick mansion. It presented a wide frontage to the road, from which it lay back amid extensive pleasure grounds. On the right hand, and a little in the rear of the house, stood what seemed to be large and commodious stables, and immediately adjoining these stables was a low-built, red-brick shed, that had evidently been recently erected.

That low-build, red-brick shed excited Loveday's curiosity.

'Is this house called North Cape?' she asked of a man, who chanced at that moment to be passing with a pickaxe and shovel.

The man answered in the affirmative, and Loveday then asked another question: could he tell her what was that small shed so close to the house–it looked like a glorified cowhouse–now what could be its use?

The man's face lighted up as if it were a subject on which he liked to be questioned. He explained that that small shed was the engine-house where the electricity that lighted North Cape was made and stored. Then he dwelt with pride upon the fact, as if he held a personal interest in it, that North Cape was the only house, far or near, that was thus lighted.

'I suppose the wires are carried underground to the house,' said Loveday, looking in vain for signs of them anywhere.

The man was delighted to go into details on the matter. He had helped to lay those wires, he said: they were two in number, one for supply and one for return, and were laid three feet below ground, in boxes filled with pitch. These wires were switched on to jars in the engine-house, where the electricity was stored, and, after passing underground, entered the family mansion under its flooring at its western end.

Loveday listened attentively to these details, and then took a minute and leisurely survey of the house and its surroundings. This done, she retraced her steps through the village, pausing, however, at the 'Postal and Telegraph Office' to dispatch a telegram to Inspector Gunning.

It was one to send the Inspector to his cipher-book. It ran as follows:

> 'Rely solely on chemist and coal-merchant throughout the day.
>
> –L B'

After this, she quickened her pace, and in something over three-quarters of an hour was back again at her hotel.

There she found more of life stirring than when she had quitted it in the early morning. There was to be a meeting of the 'Surrey Stags,' about a couple of miles off, and a good many hunting men were hanging about the entrance to the house, discussing the chances of sport after last night's frost. Loveday made her way through the throng in leisurely fashion, and not a man but what had keen scrutiny from her sharp eyes. No, there was no cause for suspicion there: they were evidently one and all just what they seemed to be–loud-voiced, hard-riding men, bent on a day's sport; but–and here Loveday's eyes traveled beyond the hotel court-yard to the other side of the road–who was that man with a bill-hook hacking at the hedge there–a thin-featured, round-shouldered old fellow, with a bent-about hat? It might be as well not to take it too rashly for granted that her spies had withdrawn, and had left her free to do her work in her own fashion.

She went upstairs to her room. It was situated on the first floor in the front of the house, and consequently commanded a good view of the high road. She stood well back from the window, and at an angle whence she could see and not be seen, took a long, steady survey of the hedger. And the longer she looked the more convinced she was that the man's real work was something other than the bill-hook seemed to imply. He worked, so to speak, with his head over his shoulder, and when Loveday supplemented her eyesight with a strong field-glass, she could see more than one stealthy glance shot from beneath his bent-about hat in the direction of her window.

There could be little doubt about it: her movements were to be as closely watched to-day as they had been yesterday. Now it was of first importance that she should communicate with Inspector Gunning in the course of the afternoon: the question to solve was how it was to be done?

To all appearance Loveday answered the question in extraordinary fashion. She pulled up her blind, she drew back her curtain, and seated herself, in full view, at a small table in the window recess. Then she took a pocket inkstand from her pocket, a packet or correspondence cards from her letter-case, and with rapid pen, set to work on them.

About an hour and a half afterwards, White, coming in, according to his promise, to report proceedings, found her still seated at the window, not, however, with writing materials before her, but with needle and thread in her hand with which she was mending her gloves.

'I return to town by the first train to-morrow morning,' she said as he entered, 'and I find these wretched things want no end of stitches. Now for your report.'

White appeared to be in an elated frame of mind. 'I've seen her!' he cried, 'my Annie–they've got her, those confounded Sisters; but they sha'n't keep her–no, not if I have to pull the house down about their ears to get her out.'

'Well, now you know where she is, you can take your time about getting her out,' said Loveday. 'I hope, however, you haven't broken faith with me, and betrayed yourself by trying to speak with her, because, if so, I shall have to look out for another deputy.'

'Honour, Miss Brooke!' answered White indignantly. 'I stuck to my duty, though it cost me something to see her hanging over those kids and tucking them into the cart, and never say a word to her, never so much as wave my hand.'

'Did she go out with the donkey-cart to-day?'

'No, she only tucked the kids into the cart with a blanket, and then went back to the house. Two old Sisters, ugly as sin, went out with them. I watched them from the window, jolt, jolt, jolt, round the corner, out of sight, and then I whipped down the stairs, and on to my machine, and was after them in a trice and managed to keep them well in sight for over an hour and a half.'

'And their destination to-day was?'

'Wootton Hall.'

'Ah, just as I expected.'

'Just as you expected?' echoed White.

'I forgot. You do not know the nature of the suspicions that are attached to this Sisterhood, and the reasons I have for thinking that Wootton Hall, at this season of the year, might have an especial attraction for them.'

White continued staring at her. 'Miss Brooke,' he said presently, in an altered tone, 'whatever suspicions may attach to the Sisterhood, I'll stake my life on it, my Annie has had no share in any wickedness of any sort.'

'Oh, quite so; it is most likely that your Annie has, in some way, been inveigled into joining these Sisters–has been taken possession of by them, in fact, just as they have taken possession of the little cripples.'

'That's it!' he cried excitedly; 'that was the idea that occurred to me when you spoke to me on the hill about them, otherwise you may be sure—'

'Did they get relief of any sort at the Hall?' interrupted Loveday..

'Yes; one of the two ugly old women stopped outside the lodge gates with the donkey-cart, and the other beauty went up to the house alone. She stayed there, I should think, about a quarter of an hour, and when she came back, was followed by a servant, carrying a bundle and a basket.'

'Ah! I've no doubt they brought away with them something else beside old garments and broken victuals.'

White stood in front of her, fixing a hard, steady gaze upon her.

'Miss Brooke,' he said presently, in a voice that matched the look on his face, 'what do you suppose was the real object of these women in going to Wootton Hall this morning?'

'Mr White, if I wished to help a gang of thieves break into Wootton Hall tonight, don't you think I should be greatly interested in procuring from them the information that the master of the house was away from home; that two of the men servants, who slept in the house, had recently been dismissed and their places had not yet been filled; also that the dogs were never unchained at night, and that their kennels were at the side of the house at which the butler's pantry is not situated? These are particulars I have gathered in this house without stirring from my chair, and I am satisfied that they are likely to be true. A the same time, if I were a professed burglar, I should not be content with information that was likely to be true, but would be careful to procure such that was certain to be true, and so would set accomplices to work at the fountain head. Now do you understand?'

White folded his arms and looked down on her.

'What are you going to do?' he asked, in short, brusque tones.

Loveday looked him full in the face. 'Communicate with the police immediately,' she answered; 'and I should feel greatly obliged if you will at once take a note from me to Inspector Gunning at Reigate.'

'And what becomes of Annie?'

'I don't think you need have any anxiety on that head. I've no doubt that when the circumstances of her admission to the Sisterhood are investigated, it will be proved that she has been as much deceived and imposed upon as the man, John Murray, who so foolishly let his house to these women. Remember, Annie has Mrs Copeland's good word to support her integrity.'

White stood silent for awhile.

'What sort of a note do you wish me to take to the Inspector?' he presently asked.

'You shall read it as I write it, if you like,' answered Loveday. She took a correspondence card from her letter case, and, with an indelible pencil, wrote as follows–

> 'Wooton Hall is threatened to-night–concentrate attention there.
>
> —'L B'

White read the words as she wrote them with a curious expression passing over his handsome features.

'Yes,' he said, curtly as before. 'I'll deliver that, I give you my word, but I'll bring back no answer to you. I'll do no more spying for you–it's a trade that doesn't suit me. There's a straight-forward way of doing straight-forward work, and I'll take that way–no other–to get my Annie out of that den.'

He took the note, which she sealed and handed to him, and strode out of the room.

Loveday, from the window, watched him mount his bicycle. Was it her fancy, or did there pass a swift, furtive glance of recognition between him and the hedger on the other side of the way as he rode out of the court-yard?

Loveday seemed determined to make that hedger's work easy for him. The short winter's day was closing in now, and her room must consequently have been growing dim to outside observation. She lighted the gas chandelier which hung from the ceiling and, still with blinds and curtains undrawn, took her old place at the window, spread writing materials before her and commenced a long and elaborate report to her chief at Lynch Court.

About half-an-hour afterwards, as she threw a casual glance across the road, she saw that the hedger had disappeared, but that two ill-looking tramps sat munching bread and cheese under the hedge to which his bill-hook had done so little service. Evidently the intention was, one way or another, not to lose sight of her so long as she remained in Redhill.

Meantime, White had delivered Loveday's note to the Inspector at Reigate, and had disappeared on his bicycle once more.

Gunning read it without a change of expression. Then he crossed the room to the fire-place and held the card as close to the bars as he could without scorching it.

'I had a telegram from her this morning,' he explained to his confidential man, 'telling me to rely upon chemicals and coals throughout the day, and that, of course, meant that she would write to me in invisible ink. No doubt this message about Wootton Hall means nothing—'

He broke off abruptly, exclaiming: 'Eh! what's this!' as, having withdrawn the card from the fire, Loveday's real message stood out in bold, clear characters between the lines of the false one.

Thus it ran:

'North Cape will be attacked to-night–a desperate gang–be prepared for a struggle. Above all, guard the electrical engine-house. On no account attempt to communicate with me; I am so closely watched that any endeavour to do so may frustrate your chance of trapping the scoundrels. L B'

That night when the moon went down behind Reigate Hill an exciting scene was enacted at 'North Cape.' The *Surrey Gazette*, in its issue the following day, gave the subjoined account of it under the heading, 'Desperate encounter with burglars.'

'Last night, "North Cape," the residence of Mr Jameson, was the scene of an affray between the police and a desperate gang of burglars. "North Cape" is lighted throughout with electricity, and the burglars, four in number, divided in half–two being told off to enter and rob the house, and two to remain at the engine-shed, where the electricity is stored, so that, at a given signal, should need arise, the wires might be unswitched, the inmates of the house thrown into sudden darkness and confusion, and the escape of the marauders thereby facilitated. Mr Jameson, however, had received timely warning from the police of the intended attack, and he, with his two sons, all well armed, sat in darkness in the inner hall awaiting the coming of the thieves. The police were stationed, some in the stables, some in out-buildings nearer to the house, and others in more distant parts of the grounds. The burglars effected their entrance by means of a ladder placed to a window of the servants' stair case which leads straight down to the butler's pantry and to the safe where the silver is kept. The fellows, however, had no sooner got into the house than the police issuing from their hiding-place outside, mounted the ladder after them and thus cut off their retreat. Mr Jameson and his two sons, at the same moment, attacked them in front, and thus overwhelmed by numbers, the scoundrels were easily secured. It was at the engine-house outside that the sharpest struggle took place. The thieves had forced open the door of this engine-shed with their jimmies immediately on their arrival, under the very eyes of the police, who lay in ambush in the stables, and when one of the men, captured in the house, contrived to sound an alarm on his whistle, these outside watchers made a rush for the electrical jars, in order to unswitch the wires. Upon this the police closed upon them, and a hand-to-hand struggle followed, and if it had not been for the timely assistance of Mr Jameson and his sons, who had fortunately conjectured that their presence here might be useful, it is more than likely that one of the burglars, a powerfully-built man, would have escaped.

'The names of the captured men are John Murray, Arthur and George Lee (father and son), and a man with so many aliases that it is difficult to know which is his real name. The whole thing had been most cunningly and carefully planned. The elder Lee, lately released from penal servitude for a similar offence, appears to have been prime mover in the affair. This man had, it seems, a son and a daughter, who, through the kindness of friends, had been fairly well placed in life: the son at an electrical engineers' in London, the daughter as nursery governess at Wootton Hall. Directly this man was released from Portland, he seems to have found out his children and done his best to ruin them both. He was constantly at Wootton Hall endeavouring to induce his daughter to act as an accomplice to a robbery of the house. This so worried the girl that she threw up her situation and joined a Sisterhood that had recently been established in the neighbourhood. Upon this, Lee's thoughts turned in another direction. He induced his son, who had saved a little money, to throw up his work in London, and join him in his disreputable career. The boy is a handsome young fellow, but appears to have in him the makings of a first-class criminal. In his work as an electrical engineer he had made the acquaintance of the man John Murray, who, it is said, has been rapidly going downhill of late. Murray was the owner of the house rented by the Sisterhood that Miss Lee had joined, and the idea evidently struck the brains of these three scoundrels that this Sisterhood, whose antecedents were a little mysterious, might be utilized to draw off the attention of the police from themselves and from the especial house in the neighbourhood that they had planned to attack. With this end in view, Murray made an application to the police to have the Sisters watched, and still further to give colour to the suspicions he had endeavoured to set afloat concerning them, he and his confederates made feeble attempts at burglary upon the houses at which the Sisters had called, begging for scraps. It is a matter for congratulation that the plot, from beginning to end, has been thus successfully unearthed, and it is felt on all sides that great credit is due to Inspector Gunning and his skilled coadjutors for the vigilance and promptitude they have displayed throughout the affair.'

Loveday read aloud this report, with her feet on the fender of the Lynch Court office.

'Accurate, as far as it goes,' she said, as she laid down the paper.

'But we want to know a little more,' said Mr Dyer. 'In the first place, I would like to know what it was that diverted your suspicions from the unfortunate Sisters?'

'The way in which they handled the children,' answered Loveday promptly. 'I have seen female criminals of all kinds handling children, and I have noticed that although they may occasionally–even this is rare–treat them with a certain rough sort of kindness, of tenderness they are utterly incapable. Now Sister Monica, I must admit, is not pleasant to look at; at the same time, there was something absolutely beautiful in the way in which she lifted the little cripple out of the cart, put his tiny thin hand round her neck, and carried him into the house. By-the-way I would like to ask some rapid physiognolmist how he would account for Sister Monica's repulsiveness of feature as contrasted with young Lee's undoubted good looks–heredity, in this case, throws no light on the matter.'

'Another question,' said Mr Dyer, not paying much heed to Loveday's digression: 'how was it you transferred your suspicions to John Murray?'

'I did not do so immediately, although at the very first it had struck me as odd that he should be so anxious to do the work of the police for them. The chief thing I noticed concerning Murray, on the first and only occasion on which I saw him, was that he had had an accident with his bicycle, for in the right-hand corner of his lamp-glass there was a tiny star, and the lamp itself had a dent on the same side, had also lost its hook, and was fastened to the machine by a bit of electric fuse. The next morning as I was walking up the hill towards Northfield, I was accosted by a young man mounted on that self-same bicycle–not a doubt of it–star in glass, dent, fuse, all three.'

'Ah, that sounded an important keynote, and led you to connect Murray and the younger Lee immediately.'

'It did, and, of course, also at once gave the lie to his statement that he was a stranger in the place, and confirmed my opinion that there was nothing of the north-countryman in his accent. Other details in his manner and appearance gave rise to other suspicions. For instance, he called himself a press reporter by profession, and his hands were coarse and grimy as only a mechanic's could be. He said he was a bit of a literary man, but the Tennyson that showed so obtrusively from his pocket was new, and in parts uncut, and totally unlike the well-thumbed volume of the literary student. Finally, when he tried and failed to put my latch-key into his waistcoat pocket, I saw the reason lay in the fact that the pocket was already occupied by a soft coil of electric fuse, the end of which protruded. Now, an electric fuse is what an electrical engineer might almost unconsciously carry about with him, it is so essential a part of his working tools, but it is a thing that a literary man or a press reporter could have no possible use for.'

'Exactly, exactly. And it was no doubt, that bit of electric fuse that turned your thoughts to the one house in the neighbourhood lighted by electricity, and suggested to your mind the possibility of electrical engineers turning their talents to account in that direction. Now, will you tell me, what, at that stage of your day's work, induced you to wire to Gunning that you would bring your invisible-ink bottle into use?'

'That was simply a matter or precaution; it did not compel me to the use of invisible ink, if I saw other safe methods of communication. I felt myself being hemmed in on all sides with spies, and I could not tell what emergency might arise. I don't think I have ever had a more difficult game to play. As I walked and talked with the young fellow up the hill, it became clear to me that if I wished to do my work I must lull the suspicions of the gang, and seem to walk into their trap. I saw by the persistent way in which Wootton Hall was forced on my notice that it was wished to fix my suspicions there. I accordingly, to all appearance, did so, and allowed the fellows to think they were making a fool of me.'

'Ha! ha! Capital that–the biter bit, with a vengeance! Splendid idea to make that young rascal himself deliver the letter that was to land him and his pals in jail. And he all the time laughing in his sleeve and thinking what a fool he was making of you! Ha, ha, ha!' And Mr Dyer made the office ring again with his merriment.

'The only person one is at all sorry for in this affair is poor little Sister Anna,' said Loveday pityingly; 'and yet, perhaps, all things considered, after her sorry experience of life, she may not be so badly placed in a Sisterhood where practical Christianity–not religious hysterics–is the one and only rule of the order.'

Dr Richard Austin Freeman

(11 April, 1862 – 30 September, 1943)

Dr Richard Austin Freeman was a British author of detective fiction, most of which starred Dr Thorndyke, a medico-legal forensic investigator. He was the first to come up with the concept of an inverted detective story—Freeman's most notable contribution to the detective fiction genre. In his writings, Freeman drew on his early experiences as a colonial surgeon. Many of Dr Thorndyke's stories include true, though archaic, scientific knowledge from fields like tropical medicine, metallurgy, and toxicology.

The Anthropologist at Large

Thorndyke was not a newspaper reader. He viewed with extreme disfavour all scrappy and miscellaneous forms of literature, which, by presenting a disorderly series of unrelated items of information, tended, as he considered, to destroy the habit of consecutive mental effort.

'It is most important,' he once remarked to me, 'habitually to pursue a definite train of thought, and to pursue it to a finish, instead of flitting indolently from one uncompleted topic to another, as the newspaper reader is so apt to do. Still, there is no harm in a daily paper—so long as you don't read it.'

Accordingly, he patronized a morning paper, and his method of dealing with it was characteristic. The paper was laid on the table after breakfast, together with a blue pencil and a pair of office shears. A preliminary glance through the sheets enabled him to mark with the pencil those paragraphs that were to be read, and these were presently cut out and looked through, after which they were either thrown away or set aside to be pasted in an indexed book.

The whole proceeding occupied, on an average, a quarter of an hour.

On the morning of which I am now speaking he was thus engaged. The pencil had done its work, and the snick of the shears announced the final stage. Presently he paused with a newly-excised cutting between his fingers, and, after glancing at it for a moment, he handed it to me.

'Another art robbery,' he remarked. 'Mysterious affairs, these—as to motive, I mean. You can't melt down a picture or an ivory carving, and you can't put them on the market as they stand. The very qualities that give them their value make them totally unnegotiable.'

'Yet I suppose,' said I, 'the really inveterate collector—the pottery or stamp maniac, for instance—will buy these contraband goods even though he dare not show them.'

'Probably. No doubt the *cupiditas habendi*, the mere desire to possess, is the motive force rather than any intelligent purpose—'

The discussion was at this point interrupted by a knock at the door, and a moment later my colleague admitted two gentlemen. One of these I recognized as a Mr Marchmont, a solicitor, for whom we had occasionally acted; the other was a stranger—a typical Hebrew of the blonde type—good-looking, faultlessly dressed, carrying a bandbox, and obviously in a state of the most extreme agitation.

'Good-morning to you, gentlemen,' said Mr Marchmont, shaking hands cordially. 'I have brought a client of mine to see you, and when I tell you that his name is Solomon Löwe, it will be unnecessary for me to say what our business is.'

'Oddly enough,' replied Thorndyke, 'we were, at the very moment when you knocked, discussing the bearings of his case.'

'It is a horrible affair!' burst in Mr Löwe. 'I am distracted! I am ruined! I am in despair!'

He banged the bandbox down on the table, and flinging himself into a chair, buried his face in his hands.

'Come, come,' remonstrated Marchmont, 'we must be brave, we must be composed. Tell Dr Thorndyke your story, and let us hear what he thinks of it.'

He leaned back in his chair, and looked at his client with that air of patient fortitude that comes to us all so easily when we contemplate the misfortunes of other people.

'You must help us, sir,' exclaimed Löwe, starting up again—'you must, indeed, or I shall go mad. But I shall tell you what has happened, and then you must act at once. Spare no effort and no expense. Money is no object—at least, not in reason,' he added, with native caution. He sat down once more, and in perfect English, though with a slight German accent, proceeded volubly: 'My brother Isaac is probably known to you by name.'

Thorndyke nodded.

'He is a great collector, and to some extent a dealer—that is to say, he makes his hobby a profitable hobby.'

'What does he collect?' asked Thorndyke.

'Everything,' replied our visitor, flinging his hands apart with a comprehensive gesture—everything that is precious and beautiful—pictures, ivories, jewels, watches, objects of art and *vertu*—everything. He is a Jew, and he has that passion for things that are rich and costly that has distinguished our race from the time of my namesake Solomon onwards. His house in Howard Street, Piccadilly, is at once a museum and an art gallery. The rooms are filled with cases of gems, of antique jewellery, of coins and historic relics—some of priceless value—and the walls are covered with paintings, every one of which is a masterpiece. There is a fine collection of ancient weapons and armour, both European and Oriental; rare books, manuscripts, papyri, and valuable antiquities from Egypt, Assyria, Cyprus, and elsewhere. You see, his taste is quite catholic, and his knowledge of rare and curious things is probably greater than that of any other living man. He is never mistaken. No forgery deceives him, and hence the great prices that he obtains; for a work of art purchased from Isaac Löwe is a work certified as genuine beyond all cavil.'

He paused to mop his face with a silk handkerchief, and then, with the same plaintive volubility, continued:

'My brother is unmarried. He lives for his collection, and he lives with it. The house is not a very large one, and the collection takes up most of it; but he keeps a suite of rooms for his own occupation, and has two servants—a man and wife—to look after him. The man, who is a retired police sergeant, acts as caretaker and watchman; the woman as housekeeper and cook, if required, but my brother lives largely at his club. And now I come to this present catastrophe.'

He ran his fingers through his hair, took a deep breath, and continued:

'Yesterday morning Isaac started for Florence by way of Paris, but his route was not certain, and he intended to break his journey at various points as circumstances determined. Before leaving, he put his collection in my charge, and it was arranged that I should occupy his rooms in his absence. Accordingly, I sent my things round and took possession.

'Now, Dr Thorndyke, I am closely connected with the drama, and it is my custom to spend my evenings at my club, of which most of the members are actors. Consequently, I am rather late in my habits; but last night I was earlier than usual in leaving my club, for I started for my brother's house before half-past twelve. I felt, as you may suppose, the responsibility of the great charge I had undertaken; and you may, therefore, imagine my horror, my consternation, my despair, when, on letting myself in with my latchkey, I found a police-inspector, a sergeant, and a constable in the hall. There had been a robbery, sir, in my brief absence, and the account that the inspector gave of the affair was briefly this:

'While taking the round of his district, he had noticed an empty hansom proceeding in leisurely fashion along Howard Street. There was nothing remarkable in this, but when, about ten minutes later, he was returning, and met a hansom, which he believed to be the same, proceeding along the same street in the same direction, and at the same easy pace, the circumstance struck him as odd, and he made a note of the number of the cab in his pocket-book. It was 72,863, and the time was 11:35.

'At 11:45 a constable coming up Howard Street noticed a hansom standing opposite the door of my brother's house, and, while he was looking at it, a man came out of the house carrying something, which he put in the cab. On this the constable quickened his pace, and when the man returned to the house and reappeared carrying what looked like a portmanteau, and closing the door softly behind him, the policeman's suspicions were aroused, and he hurried forward, hailing the cabman to stop.

'The man put his burden into the cab, and sprang in himself. The cabman lashed his horse, which started off at a gallop, and the policeman broke into a run, blowing his whistle and flashing his lantern on to the cab. He followed it round the two turnings into Albemarle Street, and was just in time to see it turn into Piccadilly, where, of course, it was lost. However, he managed to note the number of the cab, which was 72,863, and he describes the man as short and thick-set, and thinks he was not wearing any hat.

'As he was returning, he met the inspector and the sergeant, who had heard the whistle, and on his report the three officers hurried to the house, where they knocked and rang for some minutes without any result. Being now more than suspicious, they went to the back of the house, through the mews, where, with great difficulty, they managed to force a window and effect an entrance into the house.

'Here their suspicions were soon changed to certainty, for, on reaching the first-floor, they heard strange muffled groans proceeding from one of the rooms, the door of which was locked, though the key had not been removed. They opened the door, and found the caretaker and his wife sitting on the floor, with their backs against the wall. Both were bound hand and foot, and the head of each was enveloped in a green-baize bag; and when the bags were taken off, each was found to be lightly but effectively gagged.

'Each told the same story. The caretaker, fancying he heard a noise, armed himself with a truncheon, and came downstairs to the first-floor, where he found the door of one of the rooms open, and a light burning inside. He stepped on tiptoe to the open door, and was peering in, when he was seized from behind, half suffocated by a pad held over his mouth, pinioned, gagged, and blindfolded with the bag.

'His assailant—whom he never saw—was amazingly strong and skilful, and handled him with perfect ease, although he—the caretaker—is a powerful man, and a good boxer and wrestler. The same thing happened to the wife, who had come down to look for her husband. She walked into the same trap, and was gagged, pinioned, and blindfolded without ever having seen the robber. So the only description that we have of this villain is that furnished by the constable.'

'And the caretaker had no chance of using his truncheon?' said Thorndyke.

'Well, he got in one backhanded blow over his right shoulder, which he thinks caught the burglar in the face; but the fellow caught him by the elbow, and gave his arm such a twist that he dropped the truncheon on the floor.'

'Is the robbery a very extensive one?'

'Ah!' exclaimed Mr Löwe, 'that is just what we cannot say. But I fear it is. It seems that my brother had quite recently drawn out of his bank four thousand pounds in notes and gold. These little transactions are often carried out in cash rather than by cheque'—here I caught a twinkle in Thorndyke's eye—'and the caretaker says that a few days ago Isaac brought home several parcels, which were put away temporarily in a strong cupboard. He seemed to be very pleased with his new acquisitions, and gave the caretaker to understand that they were of extraordinary rarity and value.

'Now, this cupboard has been cleared out. Not a vestige is left in it but the wrappings of the parcels, so, although nothing else has been touched, it is pretty clear that goods to the value of four thousand pounds have been taken; but when we consider what an excellent buyer my brother is, it becomes highly probable that the actual value of those things is two or three times that amount, or even more. It is a dreadful, dreadful business, and Isaac will hold me responsible for it all.'

'Is there no further clue?' asked Thorndyke. 'What about the cab, for instance?'

'Oh, the cab,' groaned Löwe—that clue failed. The police must have mistaken the number. They telephoned immediately to all the police stations, and a watch was set, with the result that number 72,863 was stopped as it was going home for the night. But it then turned out that the cab had not been off the rank since eleven o'clock, and the driver had been in the shelter all the time with several other men. But there is a clue; I have it here.'

Mr Löwe's face brightened for once as he reached out for the bandbox.

'The houses in Howard Street,' he explained, as he untied the fastening, 'have small balconies to the first-floor windows at the back. Now, the thief entered by one of these windows, having climbed up a rain-water pipe to the balcony. It was a gusty night, as you will remember, and this morning, as I was leaving the house, the butler next door called to me and gave me this; he had found it lying in the balcony of his house.'

He opened the bandbox with a flourish, and brought forth a rather shabby billycock hat.

'I understand,' said he, 'that by examining a hat it is possible to deduce from it, not only the bodily characteristics of the wearer, but also his mental and moral qualities, his state of health, his pecuniary position, his past history, and even his domestic relations and the peculiarities of his place of abode. Am I right in this supposition?'

The ghost of a smile flitted across Thorndyke's face as he laid the hat upon the remains of the newspaper. 'We must not expect too much,' he observed. 'Hats, as you know, have a way of changing owners. Your own hat, for instance' (a very spruce, hard felt), 'is a new one, I think.'

'Got it last week,' said Mr Löwe.

'Exactly. It is an expensive hat, by Lincoln and Bennett, and I see you have judiciously written your name in indelible marking-ink on the lining. Now, a new hat suggests a discarded predecessor. What do you do with your old hats?'

'My man has them, but they don't fit him. I suppose he sells them or gives them away.'

'Very well. Now, a good hat like yours has a long

life, and remains serviceable long after it has become shabby; and the probability is that many of your hats pass from owner to owner; from you to the shabby-genteel, and from them to the shabby ungenteel. And it is a fair assumption that there are, at this moment, an appreciable number of tramps and casuals wearing hats by Lincoln and Bennett, marked in indelible ink with the name S Löwe; and anyone who should examine those hats, as you suggest, might draw some very misleading deductions as to the personal habits of S Löwe.'

Mr Marchmont chuckled audibly, and then, remembering the gravity of the occasion, suddenly became portentously solemn.

'So you think that the hat is of no use, after all?' said Mr Löwe, in a tone of deep disappointment.

'I won't say that,' replied Thorndyke. 'We may learn something from it. Leave it with me, at any rate; but you must let the police know that I have it. They will want to see it, of course.'

'And you will try to get those things, won't you?' pleaded Löwe.

'I will think over the case. But you understand, or Mr Marchmont does, that this is hardly in my province. I am a medical jurist, and this is not a medico-legal case.'

'Just what I told him,' said Marchmont. 'But you will do me a great kindness if you will look into the matter. Make it a medico-legal case,' he added persuasively.

Thorndyke repeated his promise, and the two men took their departure.

For some time after they had left, my colleague remained silent, regarding the hat with a quizzical smile. 'It is like a game of forfeits,' he remarked at length, 'and we have to find the owner of "this very pretty thing."' He lifted it with a pair of forceps into a better light, and began to look at it more closely.

'Perhaps,' said he, 'we have done Mr Löwe an injustice, after all. This is certainly a very remarkable hat.'

'It is as round as a basin,' I exclaimed. 'Why, the fellow's head must have been turned in a lathe!'

Thorndyke laughed. 'The point,' said he, 'is this. This is a hard hat, and so must have fitted fairly, or it could not have been worn; and it was a cheap hat, and so was not made to measure. But a man with a head that shape has got to come to a clear understanding with his hat. No ordinary hat would go on at all.

'Now, you see what he has done—no doubt on the advice of some friendly hatter. He has bought a hat of a suitable size, and he has made it hot—probably steamed it. Then he has jammed it, while still hot and soft, on to his head, and allowed it to cool and set before removing it. That is evident from the distortion of the brim. The important corollary is, that this hat fits his head exactly—is, in fact, a perfect mould of it; and this fact, together with the cheap quality of the hat, furnishes the further corollary that it has probably only had a single owner.

'And now let us turn it over and look at the outside. You notice at once the absence of old dust. Allowing for the circumstance that it had been out all night, it is decidedly clean. Its owner has been in the habit of brushing it, and is therefore presumably a decent, orderly man. But if you look at it in a good light, you see a kind of bloom on the felt, and through this lens you can make out particles of a fine white powder which has worked into the surface.'

He handed me his lens, through which I could distinctly see the particles to which he referred.

'Then,' he continued, 'under the curl of the brim and in the folds of the hatband, where the brush has not been able to reach it, the powder has collected quite thickly, and we can see that it is a very fine powder, and very white, like flour. What do you make of that?'

'I should say that it is connected with some industry. He may be engaged in some factory or works, or, at any rate, may live near a factory, and have to pass it frequently.'

'Yes; and I think we can distinguish between the two possibilities. For, if he only passes the factory, the dust will be on the outside of the hat only; the inside will be protected by his head. But if he is engaged in the works, the dust will be inside, too, as the hat will hang on a peg in the dust-laden atmosphere, and his head will also be powdered, and so convey the dust to the inside.'

He turned the hat over once more, and as I brought

the powerful lens to bear upon the dark lining, I could clearly distinguish a number of white particles in the interstices of the fabric.

'The powder is on the inside, too,' I said.

He took the lens from me, and, having verified my statement, proceeded with the examination. 'You notice,' he said, 'that the leather head-lining is stained with grease, and this staining is more pronounced at the sides and back. His hair, therefore, is naturally greasy, or he greases it artificially; for if the staining were caused by perspiration, it would be most marked opposite the forehead.'

He peered anxiously into the interior of the hat, and eventually turned down the head-lining; and immediately there broke out upon his face a gleam of satisfaction.

'Ha!' he exclaimed. 'This is a stroke of luck. I was afraid our neat and orderly friend had defeated us with his brush. Pass me the small dissecting forceps, Jervis.'

I handed him the instrument, and he proceeded to pick out daintily from the space behind the head-lining some half a dozen short pieces of hair, which he laid, with infinite tenderness, on a sheet of white paper.

'There are several more on the other side,' I said, pointing them out to him.

'Yes, but we must leave some for the police,' he answered, with a smile. 'They must have the same chance as ourselves, you know.'

'But surely,' I said, as I bent down over the paper,

'these are pieces of horsehair!'

'I think not,' he replied; 'but the microscope will show. At any rate, this is the kind of hair I should expect to find with a head of that shape.'

'Well, it is extraordinarily coarse,' said I, 'and two of the hairs are nearly white.'

'Yes; black hairs beginning to turn grey. And now, as our preliminary survey has given such encouraging results, we will proceed to more exact methods; and we must waste no time, for we shall have the police here presently to rob us of our treasure.'

He folded up carefully the paper containing the hairs, and taking the hat in both hands, as though it were some sacred vessel, ascended with me to the laboratory on the next floor.

'Now, Polton,' he said to his laboratory assistant, 'we have here a specimen for examination, and time is precious. First of all, we want your patent dust-extractor.'

The little man bustled to a cupboard and brought forth a singular appliance, of his own manufacture, somewhat like a miniature vacuum cleaner. It had been made from a bicycle foot-pump, by reversing the piston-valve, and was fitted with a glass nozzle and a small detachable glass receiver for collecting the dust, at the end of a flexible metal tube.

'We will sample the dust from the outside first,' said Thorndyke, laying the hat upon the work-bench. 'Are you ready, Polton?'

The assistant slipped his foot into the stirrup of the pump and worked the handle vigorously, while Thorndyke drew the glass nozzle slowly along the hat-brim under the curled edge. And as the nozzle passed along, the white coating vanished as if by magic, leaving the felt absolutely clean and black, and simultaneously the glass receiver became clouded over with a white deposit.

'We will leave the other side for the police,' said Thorndyke, and as Polton ceased pumping he detached the receiver, and laid it on a sheet of paper, on which he wrote in pencil, 'Outside,' and covered it with a small bell-glass. A fresh receiver having been fitted on, the nozzle was now drawn over the silk lining of the hat, and then through the space behind the leather head-lining on one side; and now the dust that collected in the receiver was much of the usual grey colour and fluffy texture, and included two more hairs.

'And now,' said Thorndyke, when the second receiver had been detached and set aside, 'we want a mould of the inside of the hat, and we must make it by the quickest method; there is no time to make a paper mould. It is a most astonishing head,' he added, reaching down from a nail a pair of large callipers, which he applied to the inside of the hat; 'six inches and nine-tenths long by six and six-tenths broad, which gives us'—he made a rapid calculation on a scrap of paper—'the extraordinarily high cephalic index of 95·6.'

Polton now took possession of the hat, and, having

stuck a band of wet tissue-paper round the inside, mixed a small bowl of plaster-of-Paris, and very dexterously ran a stream of the thick liquid on to the tissue-paper, where it quickly solidified. A second and third application resulted in a broad ring of solid plaster an inch thick, forming a perfect mould of the inside of the hat, and in a few minutes the slight contraction of the plaster in setting rendered the mould sufficiently loose to allow of its being slipped out on to a board to dry.

We were none too soon, for even as Polton was removing the mould, the electric bell, which I had switched on to the laboratory, announced a visitor, and when I went down I found a police-sergeant waiting with a note from Superintendent Miller, requesting the immediate transfer of the hat.

'The next thing to be done,' said Thorndyke, when the sergeant had departed with the bandbox, 'is to measure the thickness of the hairs, and make a transverse section of one, and examine the dust. The section we will leave to Polton—as time is an object, Polton, you had better imbed the hair in thick gum and freeze it hard on the microtome, and be very careful to cut the section at right angles to the length of the hair—meanwhile, we will get to work with the microscope.'

The hairs proved on measurement to have the surprisingly large diameter of 1/135 of an inch—fully double that of ordinary hairs, although they were unquestionably human. As to the white dust, it presented a problem that even Thorndyke was unable to solve. The application of reagents showed it to be carbonate of lime, but its source for a time remained a mystery.

'The larger particles,' said Thorndyke, with his eye applied to the microscope, 'appear to be transparent, crystalline, and distinctly laminated in structure. It is not chalk, it is not whiting, it is not any kind of cement. What can it be?'

'Could it be any kind of shell?' I suggested. 'For instance—'

'Of course!' he exclaimed, starting up; 'you have hit it, Jervis, as you always do. It must be mother-of-pearl. Polton, give me a pearl shirt-button out of your oddments box.'

The button was duly produced by the thrifty Polton, dropped into an agate mortar, and speedily reduced to powder, a tiny pinch of which Thorndyke placed under the microscope.

'This powder,' said he, 'is, naturally, much coarser than our specimen, but the identity of character is unmistakable. Jervis, you are a treasure. Just look at it.'

I glanced down the microscope, and then pulled out my watch. 'Yes,' I said, 'there is no doubt about it, I think; but I must be off. Anstey urged me to be in court by 11:30 at the latest.'

With infinite reluctance I collected my notes and papers and departed, leaving Thorndyke diligently copying addresses out of the Post Office Directory.

My business at the court detained me the whole

of the day, and it was near upon dinner-time when I reached our chambers. Thorndyke had not yet come in, but he arrived half an hour later, tired and hungry, and not very communicative.

'What have I done?' he repeated, in answer to my inquiries. 'I have walked miles of dirty pavement, and I have visited every pearl-shell cutter's in London, with one exception, and I have not found what I was looking for. The one mother-of-pearl factory that remains, however, is the most likely, and I propose to look in there to-morrow morning. Meanwhile, we have completed our data, with Polton's assistance. Here is a tracing of our friend's skull taken from the mould; you see it is an extreme type of brachycephalic skull, and markedly unsymmetrical. Here is a transverse section of his hair, which is quite circular—unlike yours or mine, which would be oval. We have the mother-of-pearl dust from the outside of the hat, and from the inside similar dust mixed with various fibres and a few granules of rice starch. Those are our data.'

'Supposing the hat should not be that of the burglar after all?' I suggested.

'That would be annoying. But I think it is his, and I think I can guess at the nature of the art treasures that were stolen.'

'And you don't intend to enlighten me?'

'My dear fellow,' he replied, 'you have all the data. Enlighten yourself by the exercise of your own brilliant faculties. Don't give way to mental indolence.'

I endeavoured, from the facts in my possession, to construct the personality of the mysterious burglar, and failed utterly; nor was I more successful in my endeavour to guess at the nature of the stolen property; and it was not until the following morning, when we had set out on our quest and were approaching Limehouse, that Thorndyke would revert to the subject.

'We are now,' he said, 'going to the factory of Badcomb and Martin, shell importers and cutters, in the West India Dock Road. If I don't find my man there, I shall hand the facts over to the police, and waste no more time over the case.'

'What is your man like?' I asked.

'I am looking for an elderly Japanese, wearing a new hat or, more probably, a cap, and having a bruise on his right cheek or temple. I am also looking for a cab-yard; but here we are at the works, and as it is now close on the dinner-hour, we will wait and see the hands come out before making any inquiries.'

We walked slowly past the tall, blank-faced building, and were just turning to re-pass it when a steam whistle sounded, a wicket opened in the main gate, and a stream of workmen—each powdered with white, like a miller—emerged into the street. We halted to watch the men as they came out, one by one, through the wicket, and turned to the right or left towards their homes or some adjacent coffee-shop; but none of them answered to the description that my friend had given.

The outcoming stream grew thinner, and at length

ceased; the wicket was shut with a bang, and once more Thorndyke's quest appeared to have failed.

'Is that all of them, I wonder?' he said, with a shade of disappointment in his tone; but even as he spoke the wicket opened again, and a leg protruded. The leg was followed by a back and a curious globular head, covered with iron-grey hair, and surmounted by a cloth cap, the whole appertaining to a short, very thick-set man, who remained thus, evidently talking to someone inside.

Suddenly he turned his head to look across the street; and immediately I recognized, by the pallid yellow complexion and narrow eye-slits, the physiognomy of a typical Japanese. The man remained talking for nearly another minute; then, drawing out his other leg, he turned towards us; and now I perceived that the right side of his face, over the prominent cheekbone, was discoloured as though by a severe bruise.

'Ha!' said Thorndyke, turning round sharply as the man approached, 'either this is our man or it is an incredible coincidence.' He walked away at a moderate pace, allowing the Japanese to overtake us slowly, and when the man had at length passed us, he increased his speed somewhat, so as to maintain the distance.

Our friend stepped along briskly, and presently turned up a side street, whither we followed at a respectful distance, Thorndyke holding open his pocket-book, and appearing to engage me in an earnest discussion, but keeping a sharp eye on his quarry.

'There he goes!' said my colleague, as the man suddenly disappeared—'the house with the green window-sashes. That will be number thirteen.'

It was; and, having verified the fact, we passed on, and took the next turning that would lead us back to the main road.

Some twenty minutes later, as we were strolling past the door of a coffee-shop, a man came out, and began to fill his pipe with an air of leisurely satisfaction. His hat and clothes were powdered with white like those of the workmen whom we had seen come out of the factory. Thorndyke accosted him.

'Is that a flour-mill up the road there?'

'No, sir; pearl-shell. I work there myself.'

'Pearl-shell, eh?' said Thorndyke. 'I suppose that will be an industry that will tend to attract the aliens. Do you find it so?'

'No, sir; not at all. The work's too hard. We've only got one foreigner in the place, and he ain't an alien—he's a Jap.'

'A Jap!' exclaimed Thorndyke. 'Really. Now, I wonder if that would chance to be our old friend Kotei—you remember Kotei?' he added, turning to me.

'No, sir; this man's name is Futashima. There was another Jap in the works, a chap named Itu, a pal of Futashima's, but he's left.'

'Ah! I don't know either of them. By the way, usen't there to be a cab-yard just about here?'

'There's a yard up Rankin Street where they keep vans and one or two cabs. That chap Itu works there now. Taken to horseflesh. Drives a van sometimes. Queer start for a Jap.'

'Very.' Thorndyke thanked the man for his information, and we sauntered on towards Rankin Street. The yard was at this time nearly deserted, being occupied only by an ancient and crazy four-wheeler and a very shabby hansom.

'Curious old houses, these that back on to the yard,' said Thorndyke, strolling into the enclosure. 'That timber gable, now,' pointing to a house, from a window of which a man was watching us suspiciously, 'is quite an interesting survival.'

'What's your business, mister?' demanded the man in a gruff tone.

'We are just having a look at these quaint old houses,' replied Thorndyke, edging towards the back of the hansom, and opening his pocket-book, as though to make a sketch.

'Well, you can see 'em from outside,' said the man.

'So we can,' said Thorndyke suavely, 'but not so well, you know.'

At this moment the pocket-book slipped from his hand and fell, scattering a number of loose papers about the ground under the hansom, and our friend at the window laughed joyously.

'No hurry,' murmured Thorndyke, as I stooped to help him to gather up the papers—which he did in the most surprisingly slow and clumsy manner. 'It is fortunate that the ground is dry.' He stood up with the rescued papers in his hand, and, having scribbled down a brief note, slipped the book in his pocket.

'Now you'd better mizzle,' observed the man at the window.

'Thank you,' replied Thorndyke, 'I think we had;' and, with a pleasant nod at the custodian, he proceeded to adopt the hospitable suggestion.

'Mr Marchmont has been here, sir, with Inspector Badger and another gentleman,' said Polton, as we entered our chambers. 'They said they would call again about five.'

'Then,' replied Thorndyke, 'as it is now a quarter to five, there is just time for us to have a wash while you get the tea ready. The particles that float in the atmosphere of Limehouse are not all mother-of-pearl.'

Our visitors arrived punctually, the third gentleman being, as we had supposed, Mr Solomon Löwe. Inspector Badger I had not seen before, and he now impressed me as showing a tendency to invert the significance of his own name by endeavouring to 'draw' Thorndyke; in which, however, he was not brilliantly successful.

'I hope you are not going to disappoint Mr Löwe, sir,' he commenced facetiously. 'You have had a good look at that hat—we saw your marks on it—and he expects that you will be able to point us out the man, name and address all complete.' He grinned patronizingly at our unfortunate client, who was looking even more haggard and worn than he had been on the previous morning.

'Have you—have you made any—discovery?' Mr Löwe asked with pathetic eagerness.

'We examined the hat very carefully, and I think we have established a few facts of some interest.'

'Did your examination of the hat furnish any information as to the nature of the stolen property, sir?' inquired the humorous inspector.

Thorndyke turned to the officer with a face as expressionless as a wooden mask.

'We thought it possible,' said he, 'that it might consist of works of Japanese art, such as netsukes, paintings, and such like.'

Mr Löwe uttered an exclamation of delighted astonishment, and the facetiousness faded rather suddenly from the inspector's countenance.

'I don't know how you can have found out,' said he. 'We have only known it half an hour ourselves, and the wire came direct from Florence to Scotland Yard.'

'Perhaps you can describe the thief to us,' said Mr Löwe, in the same eager tone.

'I dare say the inspector can do that,' replied Thorndyke.

'Yes, I think so,' replied the officer. 'He is a short strong man, with a dark complexion and hair turning grey. He has a very round head, and he is probably a workman engaged at some whiting or cement works.

That is all we know; if you can tell us any more, sir, we shall be very glad to hear it.'

'I can only offer a few suggestions,' said Thorndyke, 'but perhaps you may find them useful. For instance, at 13, Birket Street, Limehouse, there is living a Japanese gentleman named Futashima, who works at Badcomb and Martin's mother-of-pearl factory. I think that if you were to call on him, and let him try on the hat that you have, it would probably fit him.'

The inspector scribbled ravenously in his notebook, and Mr Marchmont—an old admirer of Thorndyke's—leaned back in his chair, chuckling softly and rubbing his hands.

'Then,' continued my colleague, 'there is in Rankin Street, Limehouse, a cab-yard, where another Japanese gentleman named Itu is employed. You might find out where Itu was the night before last; and if you should chance to see a hansom cab there—number 22,481—have a good look at it. In the frame of the number-plate you will find six small holes. Those holes may have held brads, and the brads may have held a false number card. At any rate, you might ascertain where that cab was at 11:30 the night before last. That is all I have to suggest.'

Mr Löwe leaped from his chair. 'Let us go—now—at once—there is no time to be lost. A thousand thanks to you, doctor—a thousand million thanks. Come!'

He seized the inspector by the arm and forcibly dragged him towards the door, and a few moments later we heard the footsteps of our visitors clattering down the stairs.

'It was not worth while to enter into explanations with them,' said Thorndyke, as the footsteps died away—nor perhaps with you?'

'On the contrary,' I replied, 'I am waiting to be fully enlightened.'

'Well, then, my inferences in this case were perfectly simple ones, drawn from well-known anthropological facts. The human race, as you know, is roughly divided into three groups—the black, the white, and the yellow races. But apart from the variable quality of colour, these races have certain fixed characteristics associated especially with the shape of the skull, of the eye-sockets, and the hair.

'Thus in the black races the skull is long and narrow, the eye-sockets are long and narrow, and the hair is flat and ribbon-like, and usually coiled up like a watch-spring. In the white races the skull is oval, the eye-sockets are oval, and the hair is slightly flattened or oval in section, and tends to be wavy; while in the yellow or Mongol races, the skull is short and round, the eye-sockets are short and round, and the hair is straight and circular in section. So that we have, in the black races, long skull, long orbits, flat hair; in the white races, oval skull, oval orbits, oval hair; and in the yellow races, round skull, round orbits, round hair.

'Now, in this case we had to deal with a very short round skull. But you cannot argue from races to individuals; there are many short-skulled Englishmen. But when I found, associated with that skull, hairs which were circular in section, it became practically certain that the individual was a Mongol of some kind. The mother-of-pearl dust and the granules of rice starch from the inside of the hat favoured this view, for the pearl-shell industry is specially connected with China and Japan, while starch granules from the hat of an Englishman would probably be wheat starch.

'Then as to the hair: it was, as I mentioned to you, circular in section, and of very large diameter. Now, I have examined many thousands of hairs, and the thickest that I have ever seen came from the heads of Japanese; but the hairs from this hat were as thick as any of them. But the hypothesis that the burglar was a Japanese received confirmation in various ways. Thus, he was short, though strong and active, and the Japanese are the shortest of the Mongol races, and very strong and active.

'Then his remarkable skill in handling the powerful caretaker—a retired police-sergeant—suggested the Japanese art of ju-jitsu, while the nature of the robbery was consistent with the value set by the Japanese on works of art. Finally, the fact that only a particular collection was taken, suggested a special, and probably national, character in the things stolen, while their portability—you will remember that goods of the value of from eight to twelve thousand pounds were taken away in two hand-packages—was much more consistent with Japanese than Chinese works, of which the latter tend rather to be bulky and ponderous. Still, it was nothing but a bare hypothesis until we had seen Futashima—and, indeed, is no more now. I may, after all, be entirely mistaken.'

He was not, however; and at this moment there reposes in my drawing-room an ancient netsuke, which came as a thank-offering from Mr Isaac Löwe on the recovery of the booty from a back room in No. 13, Birket Street, Limehouse. The treasure, of course, was given in the first place to Thorndyke, but transferred by him to my wife on the pretence that but for my suggestion of shell-dust the robber would never have been traced. Which is, on the face of it, preposterous.

Anna Katharine Green

(November 11, 1846 – April 11, 1935)

Anna Katharine Green was a poet and novelist from the United States. She was one of America's first detective fiction writers, and was known for her well-crafted, legally precise works. Green has been dubbed 'the mother of the detective fiction,' and even today, is credited with creating detective series that moulded the detective fiction into its iconic form.

The Second Bullet

'You must see her.'

'No. No.'

'She's a most unhappy woman. Husband and child both taken from her in a moment; and now, all means of living as well, unless some happy thought of yours—some inspiration of your genius—shows us a way of re-establishing her claims to the policy voided by this cry of suicide.'

But the small wise head of Violet Strange continued its slow shake of decided refusal.

'I'm sorry,' she protested, 'but it's quite out of my province. I'm too young to meddle with so serious a matter.'

'Not when you can save a bereaved woman the only possible compensation left her by untoward fate?'

'Let the police try their hand at that.'

'They have had no success with the case.'

'Or you?'

'Nor I either.'

'And you expect—'

'Yes, Miss Strange. I expect you to find the missing bullet which will settle the fact that murder and not suicide ended George Hammond's life. If you cannot, then a long litigation awaits this poor widow, ending, as such litigation usually does, in favour of the stronger party. There's the alternative. If you once saw her—'

'But that's what I'm not willing to do. If I once saw her I should yield to her importunities and attempt the seemingly impossible. My instincts bid me say no. Give me something easier.'

'Easier things are not so remunerative. There's money in this affair, if the insurance company is forced to pay up. I can offer you—'

'What?'

There was eagerness in the tone despite her effort at nonchalance. The other smiled imperceptibly, and briefly named the sum.

It was larger than she had expected. This her visitor saw by the way her eyelids fell and the peculiar stillness which, for an instant, held her vivacity in check.

'And you think I can earn that?'

Her eyes were fixed on his in an eagerness as honest as it was unrestrained.

He could hardly conceal his amazement, her

desire was so evident and the cause of it so difficult to understand. He knew she wanted money—that was her avowed reason for entering into this uncongenial work. But to want it so much! He glanced at her person; it was simply clad but very expensively—how expensively it was his business to know. Then he took in the room in which they sat. Simplicity again, but the simplicity of high art—the drawing-room of one rich enough to indulge in the final luxury of a highly cultivated taste, viz.: unostentatious elegance and the subjection of each carefully chosen ornament to the general effect.

What did this favoured child of fortune lack that she could be reached by such a plea, when her whole being revolted from the nature of the task he offered her? It was a question not new to him; but one he had never heard answered and was not likely to hear answered now. But the fact remained that the consent he had thought dependent upon sympathetic interest could be reached much more readily by the promise of large emolument,—and he owned to a feeling of secret disappointment even while he recognized the value of the discovery.

But his satisfaction in the latter, if satisfaction it were, was of very short duration. Almost immediately he observed a change in her. The sparkle which had shone in the eye whose depths he had never been able to penetrate, had dissipated itself in something like a tear and she spoke up in that vigorous tone no one but himself had ever heard, as she said:

'No. The sum is a good one and I could use it; but I will not waste my energy on a case I do not believe in. The man shot himself. He was a speculator, and probably had good reason for his act. Even his wife acknowledges that he has lately had more losses than gains.'

'See her. She has something to tell you which never got into the papers.'

'You say that? You know that?'

'On my honour, Miss Strange.'

Violet pondered; then suddenly succumbed.

'Let her come, then. Prompt to the hour. I will receive her at three. Later I have a tea and two party calls to make.'

Her visitor rose to leave. He had been able to subdue all evidence of his extreme gratification, and now took on a formal air. In dismissing a guest, Miss Strange was invariably the society belle and that only. This he had come to recognize.

The case (well known at the time) was, in the fewest possible words, as follows:

On a sultry night in September, a young couple living in one of the large apartment houses in the extreme upper portion of Manhattan were so annoyed by the incessant crying of a child in the adjoining suite, that they got up, he to smoke, and she to sit in the window for a possible breath of cool air. They were congratulating themselves upon the wisdom they had shown in thus giving up all thought of sleep—for the child's crying had not ceased—when (it may have been two o'clock and it may have been a little later) there came from somewhere near, the sharp and somewhat peculiar detonation of a pistol-shot.

He thought it came from above; she, from the rear, and they were staring at each other in the helpless wonder of the moment, when they were struck by the silence. The baby had ceased to cry. All was as still in the adjoining apartment as in their own—too still—much too still. Their mutual stare turned to one of horror. 'It came from there!' whispered the wife. 'Some accident has occurred to Mr or Mrs Hammond—we ought to go—'

Her words—very tremulous ones—were broken by a shout from below. They were standing in their window and had evidently been seen by a passing policeman. 'Anything wrong up there?' they heard him cry. Mr Saunders immediately looked out. 'Nothing wrong here,' he called down. (They were but two stories from the pavement.) 'But I'm not so sure about the rear apartment. We thought we heard a shot. Hadn't you better come up, officer? My wife is nervous about it. I'll meet you at the stair-head and show you the way.'

The officer nodded and stepped in. The young couple hastily donned some wraps, and, by the time he appeared on their floor, they were ready to accompany him.

Meanwhile, no disturbance was apparent anywhere else in the house, until the policeman rang the bell of the Hammond apartment. Then, voices began to be heard, and doors to open above and below, but not the one before which the policeman stood.

Another ring, and this time an insistent one;—and still no response. The officer's hand was rising for the third time when there came a sound of fluttering from behind the panels against which he had laid his ear, and finally a choked voice uttering unintelligible words. Then a hand began to struggle with the lock, and the door, slowly opening, disclosed a woman clad in a hastily donned wrapper and giving every evidence of extreme fright.

'Oh!' she exclaimed, seeing only the compassionate faces of her neighbours. 'You heard it, too! a pistol-shot from there—there—my husband's room. I have not dared to go—I—I—O, have mercy and see if anything is wrong! It is so still—so still, and only a moment ago the baby was crying. Mrs Saunders, Mrs Saunders, why is it so still?'

She had fallen into her neighbour's arms. The hand with which she had pointed out a certain door had sunk to her side and she appeared to be on the verge of collapse.

The officer eyed her sternly, while noting her appearance, which was that of a woman hastily risen from bed.

'Where were you?' he asked. 'Not with your husband and child, or you would know what had happened there.'

'I was sleeping down the hall,' she managed to gasp out. 'I'm not well—I—Oh, why do you all stand still and do nothing? My baby's in there. Go! go!' and, with sudden energy, she sprang upright, her eyes wide open and burning, her small well featured face white as the linen she sought to hide.

The officer demurred no longer. In another instant he was trying the door at which she was again pointing.

It was locked.

Glancing back at the woman, now cowering almost to the floor, he pounded at the door and asked the man inside to open.

No answer came back.

With a sharp turn he glanced again at the wife.

'You say that your husband is in this room?'

She nodded, gasping faintly, 'And the child!'

He turned back, listened, then beckoned to Mr Saunders. 'We shall have to break our way in,' said he. 'Put your shoulder well to the door. Now!'

The hinges of the door creaked; the lock gave way (this special officer weighed two hundred and seventy-five, as he found out, next day), and a prolonged and sweeping crash told the rest.

Mrs Hammond gave a low cry; and, straining forward from where she crouched in terror on the floor, searched the faces of the two men for some hint of what they saw in the dimly-lighted space beyond. Something dreadful, something which made Mr Saunders come rushing back with a shout:

'Take her away! Take her to our apartment, Jennie. She must not see—'

Not see! He realized the futility of his words as his gaze fell on the young woman who had risen up at his approach and now stood gazing at him without speech, without movement, but with a glare of terror in her eyes, which gave him his first realization of human misery.

His own glance fell before it. If he had followed his instinct he would have fled the house rather than answer the question of her look and the attitude of her whole frozen body.

Perhaps in mercy to his speechless terror, perhaps in mercy to herself, she was the one who at last found the word which voiced their mutual anguish.

'Dead?'

No answer. None was needed.

'And my baby?'

O, that cry! It curdled the hearts of all who heard it. It shook the souls of men and women both inside and outside the apartment; then all was forgotten in the wild rush she made. The wife and mother had flung herself upon the scene, and, side by side with the not unmoved policeman, stood looking down upon the desolation made in one fatal instant in her home and heart.

They lay there together, both past help, both quite dead. The child had simply been strangled by the weight of his father's arm which lay directly across the upturned little throat. But the father was a victim of the shot they had heard. There was blood on his breast, and a pistol in his hand.

Suicide! The horrible truth was patent. No wonder they wanted to hold the young widow back. Her neighbour, Mrs Saunders, crept in on tiptoe and put her arms about the swaying, fainting woman; but there was nothing to say—absolutely nothing.

At least, they thought not. But when they saw her throw herself down, not by her husband, but by the child, and drag it out from under that strangling arm and hug and kiss it and call out wildly for a doctor, the officer endeavoured to interfere and yet could not find the heart to do so, though he knew the child was dead and should not, according to all the rules of the coroner's office, be moved before that official arrived. Yet because no mother could be convinced of a fact like this, he let her sit with it on the floor and try all her little arts to revive it, while he gave orders to the janitor and waited himself for the arrival of doctor and coroner.

She was still sitting there in wide-eyed misery, alternately fondling the little body and drawing back to consult its small set features for some sign of life, when the doctor came, and, after one look at the child, drew it softly from her arms and laid it quietly in the crib from which its father had evidently lifted it but a short time before. Then he turned back to her, and found her on her feet, upheld by her two friends. She had understood his action, and without a groan had accepted her fate. Indeed, she seemed incapable of any further speech or action. She was staring down at her husband's body, which she, for the first time, seemed fully to see. Was her look one of grief or of resentment for the part he had played so unintentionally in her child's death? It was hard to tell; and when, with slowly rising finger, she pointed to the pistol so tightly clutched in the other outstretched hand, no one there—and by this time the room was full—could foretell what her words would be when her tongue regained its usage and she could speak.

What she did say was this:

'Is there a bullet gone? Did he fire off that pistol?' A question so manifestly one of delirium that no one answered it, which seemed to surprise her, though she said nothing till her glance had passed all around the walls of the room to where a window stood open to the night,—its lower sash being entirely raised. 'There! look there!' she cried, with a commanding accent, and, throwing up her hands, sank a dead weight into the arms of those supporting her.

No one understood; but naturally more than one rushed to the window. An open space was before them. Here lay the fields not yet parcelled out into lots and built upon; but it was not upon these they looked, but upon the strong trellis which they found there, which, if it supported no vine, formed a veritable ladder between this window and the ground.

Could she have meant to call attention to this fact; and were her words expressive of another idea than the obvious one of suicide?

If so, to what lengths a woman's imagination can go! Or so their combined looks seemed to proclaim, when to their utter astonishment they saw the officer, who had presented a calm appearance up till now, shift his position and with a surprised grunt direct their eyes to a portion of the wall just visible beyond the half-drawn curtains of the bed. The mirror hanging there showed a star-shaped breakage, such as follows the sharp impact of a bullet or a fiercely projected stone.

'He fired two shots. One went wild; the other straight home.'

It was the officer delivering his opinion.

Mr Saunders, returning from the distant room where he had assisted in carrying Mrs Hammond, cast a look at the shattered glass, and remarked forcibly:

'I heard but one; and I was sitting up, disturbed by that poor infant. Jennie, did you hear more than one shot?' he asked, turning toward his wife.

'No,' she answered, but not with the readiness he had evidently expected. 'I heard only one, but that was not quite usual in its tone. I'm used to guns,' she explained, turning to the officer. 'My father was an army man, and he taught me very early to load and fire a pistol. There was a prolonged sound to this shot; something like an echo of itself, following close upon the first ping. Didn't you notice that, Warren?'

'I remember something of the kind,' her husband allowed.

'He shot twice and quickly,' interposed the policeman, sententiously. 'We shall find a spent bullet back of that mirror.'

But when, upon the arrival of the coroner, an investigation was made of the mirror and the wall behind, no bullet was found either there or any where else in the room, save in the dead man's breast. Nor had more than one been shot from his pistol, as five full chambers testified. The case which seemed so simple had its mysteries, but the assertion made by Mrs Saunders no longer carried weight, nor was the evidence offered by the broken mirror considered as indubitably establishing the fact that a second shot had been fired in the room.

Yet it was equally evident that the charge which had entered the dead speculator's breast had not been delivered at the close range of the pistol found clutched in his hand. There were no powder-marks to be discerned on his pajama-jacket, or on the flesh beneath. Thus anomaly confronted anomaly, leaving open but one other theory: that the bullet found in Mr Hammond's breast came from the window and the one he shot went out of it. But this would necessitate his having shot his pistol from a point far removed from where he was found; and his wound was such as made it difficult to believe that he would stagger far, if at all, after its infliction.

Yet, because the coroner was both conscientious and alert, he caused a most rigorous search to be made of the ground overlooked by the above mentioned window; a search in which the police joined, but which was without any result save that of rousing the attention of people in the neighbourhood and leading to a story being circulated of a man seen some time the night before crossing the fields in a great hurry. But as no further particulars were forthcoming, and not even a description of the man to be had, no emphasis would have been laid upon this story had it not transpired that the moment a report of it had come to Mrs Hammond's ears (why is there always some one to carry these reports?) she roused from the torpor into which she had fallen, and in wild fashion exclaimed:

'I knew it! I expected it! He was shot through the window and by that wretch. He never shot himself.' Violent declarations which trailed off into the one continuous wail, 'O, my baby! my poor baby!'

Such words, even though the fruit of delirium, merited some sort of attention, or so this good coroner thought, and as soon as opportunity offered and she was sufficiently sane and quiet to respond to his questions, he asked her whom she had meant by that wretch, and what reason she had, or thought she had, of attributing her husband's death to any other agency than his own disgust with life.

And then it was that his sympathies, although greatly roused in her favour began to wane. She met the question with a cold stare followed by a few ambiguous words out of which he could make nothing. Had she said wretch? She did not remember. They must not be influenced by anything she might have uttered in her first grief. She was well-nigh insane at the time. But of one thing they might be sure: her husband had not shot himself; he was too much afraid of death for such an act. Besides, he was too happy. Whatever folks might say he was too fond of his family to wish to leave it.

Nor did the coroner or any other official succeed in eliciting anything further from her. Even when she was asked, with cruel insistence, how she explained the fact that the baby was found lying on the floor instead of in its crib, her only answer was: 'His father was trying to soothe it. The child was crying dreadfully, as you have heard from those who were kept awake by him that night, and my husband was carrying him about when the shot came which caused George to fall and overlay the baby in his struggles.'

'Carrying a baby about with a loaded pistol in his hand?' came back in stern retort.

She had no answer for this. She admitted when informed that the bullet extracted from her husband's body had been found to correspond exactly with those remaining in the five chambers of the pistol taken from his hand, that he was not only the owner of this pistol but was in the habit of sleeping with it under his pillow; but, beyond that, nothing; and this reticence, as well as her manner which was cold and repellent, told against her.

A verdict of suicide was rendered by the coroner's

jury, and the life-insurance company, in which Mr Hammond had but lately insured himself for a large sum, taking advantage of the suicide clause embodied in the policy, announced its determination of not paying the same.

Such was the situation, as known to Violet Strange and the general public, on the day she was asked to see Mrs Hammond and learn what might alter her opinion as to the justice of this verdict and the stand taken by the Shuler Life Insurance Company.

The clock on the mantel in Miss Strange's rose-coloured boudoir had struck three, and Violet was gazing in some impatience at the door, when there came a gentle knock upon it, and the maid (one of the elderly, not youthful, kind) ushered in her expected visitor.

'You are Mrs Hammond?' she asked, in natural awe of the too black figure outlined so sharply against the deep pink of the sea-shell room.

The answer was a slow lifting of the veil which shadowed the features she knew only from the cuts she had seen in newspapers.

'You are—Miss Strange?' stammered her visitor; 'the young lady who—'

'I am,' chimed in a voice as ringing as it was sweet. 'I am the person you have come here to see. And this is my home. But that does not make me less interested in the unhappy, or less desirous of serving them. Certainly you have met with the two greatest losses which can come to a woman—I know your story well enough to say that—; but what have you to tell me in proof that you should not lose your anticipated income as well? Something vital, I hope, else I cannot help you; something which you should have told the coroner's jury—and did not.'

The flush which was the sole answer these words called forth did not take from the refinement of the young widow's expression, but rather added to it; Violet watched it in its ebb and flow and, seriously affected by it (why, she did not know, for Mrs Hammond had made no other appeal either by look or gesture), pushed forward a chair and begged her visitor to be seated.

'We can converse in perfect safety here,' she said. 'When you feel quite equal to it, let me hear what you have to communicate. It will never go any further. I could not do the work I do if I felt it necessary to have a confidant.'

'But you are so young and so—so—'

'So inexperienced you would say and so evidently a member of what New Yorkers call "society." Do not let that trouble you. My inexperience is not likely to last long and my social pleasures are more apt to add to my efficiency than to detract from it.'

With this Violet's face broke into a smile. It was not the brilliant one so often seen upon her lips, but there was something in its quality which carried encouragement to the widow and led her to say with obvious eagerness:

'You know the facts?'

'I have read all the papers.'

'I was not believed on the stand.'

'It was your manner—'

'I could not help my manner. I was keeping something back, and, being unused to deceit, I could not act quite naturally.'

'Why did you keep something back? When you saw the unfavourable impression made by your reticence, why did you not speak up and frankly tell your story?'

'Because I was ashamed. Because I thought it would hurt me more to speak than to keep silent. I do not think so now; but I did then—and so made my great mistake. You must remember not only the awful shock of my double loss, but the sense of guilt accompanying it; for my husband and I had quarreled that night, quarreled bitterly—that was why I had run away into another room and not because I was feeling ill and impatient of the baby's fretful cries.'

'So people have thought.' In saying this, Miss Strange was perhaps cruelly emphatic. 'You wish to explain that quarrel? You think it will be doing any good to your cause to go into that matter with me now?'

'I cannot say; but I must first clear my conscience and then try to convince you that quarrel or no quarrel, he never took his own life. He was not that kind. He had an abnormal fear of death. I do not like to say it but he was a physical coward. I have seen him turn pale at the least hint of danger. He could no more have turned that muzzle upon his own breast than he could have turned it upon his baby. Some other hand shot him, Miss Strange. Remember the open window, the shattered mirror; and I think I know that hand.'

Her head had fallen forward on her breast. The emotion she showed was not so eloquent of grief as of deep personal shame.

'You think you know the man?' In saying this, Violet's voice sunk to a whisper. It was an accusation of murder she had just heard.

'To my great distress, yes. When Mr Hammond and I were married,' the widow now proceeded in a more determined tone, 'there was another man—a very violent one—who vowed even at the church door that George and I should never live out two full years together. We have not. Our second anniversary would have been in November.'

'But—'

'Let me say this: the quarrel of which I speak was not serious enough to occasion any such act of despair on his part. A man would be mad to end his life on account of so slight a disagreement. It was not even on account of the person of whom I've just spoken, though that person had been mentioned between us earlier in the evening, Mr Hammond having come across him face to face that very afternoon in the subway. Up to this time neither of us had seen or heard of him since our wedding-day.'

'And you think this person whom you barely mentioned, so mindful of his old grudge that he sought out your domicile, and, with the intention of murder, climbed the trellis leading to your room and turned his pistol upon the shadowy figure which was all he could see in the semi-obscurity of a much lowered gas-jet?'

'A man in the dark does not need a bright light to see his enemy when he is intent upon revenge.'

Miss Strange altered her tone.

'And your husband? You must acknowledge that he shot off his pistol whether the other did or not.'

'It was in self-defence. He would shoot to save his own life—or the baby's.'

'Then he must have heard or seen—'

'A man at the window.'

'And would have shot there?'

'Or tried to.'

'Tried to?'

'Yes; the other shot first—oh, I've thought it all out—causing my husband's bullet to go wild. It was his which broke the mirror.'

Violet's eyes, bright as stars, suddenly narrowed.

'And what happened then?' she asked. 'Why cannot they find the bullet?'

'Because it went out of the window;—glanced off and went out of the window.'

Mrs Hammond's tone was triumphant; her look spirited and intense.

Violet eyed her compassionately.

'Would a bullet glancing off from a mirror, however hung, be apt to reach a window so far on the opposite side?'

'I don't know; I only know that it did,' was the contradictory, almost absurd, reply.

'What was the cause of the quarrel you speak of between your husband and yourself? You see, I must know the exact truth and all the truth to be of any assistance to you.'

'It was—it was about the care I gave, or didn't give, the baby. I feel awfully to have to say it, but George did not think I did my full duty by the child. He said there was no need of its crying so; that if I gave it the proper attention it would not keep the neighbours and himself awake half the night. And I—I got angry and insisted that I did the best I could; that the child was naturally fretful and that if he wasn't satisfied with my way of looking after it, he might try his. All of which was very wrong and unreasonable on my part, as witness the awful punishment which followed.'

'And what made you get up and leave him?'

'The growl he gave me in reply. When I heard that, I bounded out of bed and said I was going to the spare room to sleep; and if the baby cried he might just try what he could do himself to stop it.'

'And he answered?'

'This, just this—I shall never forget his words as long as I live—'If you go, you need not expect me to let you in again no matter what happens."

'He said that?'

'And locked the door after me. You see I could not tell all that.'

'It might have been better if you had. It was such a natural quarrel and so unprovocative of actual tragedy.'

Mrs Hammond was silent. It was not difficult to see that she had no very keen regrets for her husband personally. But then he was not a very estimable man nor in any respect her equal.

'You were not happy with him,' Violet ventured to remark.

'I was not a fully contented woman. But for all that he had no cause to complain of me except for the reason I have mentioned. I was not a very intelligent mother. But if the baby were living now—O, if he were living now—with what devotion I should care for him.'

She was on her feet, her arms were raised, her face impassioned with feeling. Violet, gazing at her, heaved a little sigh. It was perhaps in keeping with the situation, perhaps extraneous to it, but whatever its source, it marked a change in her manner. With no further check upon her sympathy, she said very softly:

'It is well with the child.'

The mother stiffened, swayed, and then burst into wild weeping.

'But not with me,' she cried, 'not with me. I am desolate and bereft. I have not even a home in which to hide my grief and no prospect of one.'

'But,' interposed Violet, 'surely your husband left

you something? You cannot be quite penniless?'

'My husband left nothing,' was the answer, uttered without bitterness, but with all the hardness of fact. 'He had debts. I shall pay those debts. When these and other necessary expenses are liquidated, there will be but little left. He made no secret of the fact that he lived close up to his means. That is why he was induced to take on a life insurance. Not a friend of his but knows his improvidence. I—I have not even jewels. I have only my determination and an absolute conviction as to the real nature of my husband's death.'

'What is the name of the man you secretly believe to have shot your husband from the trellis?'

Mrs Hammond told her.

It was a new one to Violet. She said so and then asked:

'What else can you tell me about him?'

'Nothing, but that he is a very dark man and has a club-foot.'

'Oh, what a mistake you've made.'

'Mistake? Yes, I acknowledge that.'

'I mean in not giving this last bit of information at once to the police. A man can be identified by such a defect. Even his footsteps can be traced. He might have been found that very day. Now, what have we to go upon?'

'You are right, but not expecting to have any difficulty about the insurance money I thought it would be generous in me to keep still. Besides, this is only surmise on my part. I feel certain that my husband was shot by another hand than his own, but I know of no way of proving it. Do you?'

Then Violet talked seriously with her, explaining how their only hope lay in the discovery of a second bullet in the room which had already been ransacked for this very purpose and without the shadow of a result.

A tea, a musicale, and an evening dance kept Violet Strange in a whirl for the remainder of the day. No brighter eye nor more contagious wit lent brilliance to these occasions, but with the passing of the midnight hour no one who had seen her in the blaze of electric lights would have recognized this favoured child of fortune in the earnest figure sitting in the obscurity of an up-town apartment, studying the walls, the ceilings, and the floors by the dim light of a lowered gas-jet. Violet Strange in society was a very different person from Violet Strange under the tension of her secret and peculiar work.

She had told them at home that she was going to spend the night with a friend; but only her old coachman knew who that friend was. Therefore a very natural sense of guilt mingled with her emotions at finding herself alone on a scene whose gruesome mystery she could solve only by identifying herself with the place and the man who had perished there.

Dismissing from her mind all thought of self, she strove to think as he thought, and act as he acted on the night when he found himself (a man of but little courage) left in this room with an ailing child.

At odds with himself, his wife, and possibly with the child screaming away in its crib, what would he be apt to do in his present emergency? Nothing at first, but as the screaming continued he would remember the old tales of fathers walking the floor at night with crying babies, and hasten to follow suit. Violet, in her anxiety to reach his inmost thought, crossed to where the crib had stood, and, taking that as a start, began pacing the room in search of the spot from which a bullet, if shot, would glance aside from the mirror in the direction of the window. (Not that she was ready to accept this theory of Mrs Hammond, but that she did not wish to entirely dismiss it without putting it to the test.)

She found it in an unexpected quarter of the room and much nearer the bed-head than where his body was found. This, which might seem to confuse matters, served, on the contrary to remove from the case one of its most serious difficulties. Standing here, he was within reach of the pillow under which his pistol lay hidden, and if startled, as his wife believed him to have been by a noise at the other end of the room, had but to crouch and reach behind him in order to find himself armed and ready for a possible intruder.

Imitating his action in this as in other things, she had herself crouched low at the bedside and was on the point of withdrawing her hand from under the pillow, when a new surprise checked her movement and held her fixed in her position, with eyes staring straight at the adjoining wall. She had seen there what he must have seen in making this same turn—the dark bars of the opposite window-frame outlined in the mirror—and understood at once what had happened. In the nervousness and terror of the moment, George Hammond had mistaken this reflection of the window for the window itself, and shot impulsively at the man he undoubtedly saw covering him from the trellis without. But while this explained the shattering of the mirror, how about the other and still more vital question, of where the bullet went afterward? Was the angle at which it had been fired acute enough to send it out of a window diagonally opposed? No; even if the pistol had been held closer to the man firing it than she had reason to believe, the angle still would be oblique enough to carry it on to the further wall.

But no sign of any such impact had been discovered on this wall. Consequently, the force of the bullet had been expended before reaching it, and when it fell—

Here, her glance, slowly traveling along the floor, impetuously paused. It had reached the spot where the two bodies had been found, and unconsciously her eyes rested there, conjuring up the picture of the bleeding father and the strangled child. How piteous and how dreadful it all was. If she could only understand—Suddenly she rose straight up, staring and immovable in the dim light. Had the idea—the explanation—

the only possible explanation covering the whole phenomena come to her at last?

It would seem so, for as she so stood, a look of conviction settled over her features, and with this look, evidences of a horror which for all her fast accumulating knowledge of life and its possibilities made her appear very small and very helpless.

A half-hour later, when Mrs Hammond, in her anxiety at hearing nothing more from Miss Strange, opened the door of her room, it was to find, lying on the edge of the sill, the little detective's card with these words hastily written across it:

I do not feel as well as I could wish, and so have telephoned to my own coachman to come and take me home. I will either see or write you within a few days. But do not allow yourself to hope. I pray you do not allow yourself the least hope; the outcome is still very problematical.

When Violet's employer entered his office the next morning it was to find a veiled figure awaiting him which he at once recognized as that of his little deputy. She was slow in lifting her veil and when it finally came free he felt a momentary doubt as to his wisdom in giving her just such a matter as this to investigate. He was quite sure of his mistake when he saw her face, it was so drawn and pitiful.

'You have failed,' said he.

'Of that you must judge,' she answered; and drawing near she whispered in his ear.

'No!' he cried in his amazement.

'Think,' she murmured, 'think. Only so can all the facts be accounted for.'

'I will look into it; I will certainly look into it,' was his earnest reply. 'If you are right—But never mind that. Go home and take a horseback ride in the Park. When I have news in regard to this I will let you know. Till then forget it all. Hear me, I charge you to forget everything but your balls and your parties.'

And Violet obeyed him.

Some few days after this, the following statement appeared in all the papers:

'Owing to some remarkable work done by the firm of —— & ——, the well-known private detective agency, the claim made by Mrs George Hammond against the Shuler Life Insurance Company is likely to be allowed without further litigation. As our readers will remember, the contestant has insisted from the first that the bullet causing her husband's death came from another pistol than the one found clutched in his own hand. But while reasons were not lacking to substantiate this assertion, the failure to discover more than the disputed track of a second bullet led to a verdict of suicide, and a refusal of the company to pay.

'But now that bullet has been found. And where? In the most startling place in the world, viz.: in the larynx of the child found lying dead upon the floor beside his father, strangled as was supposed by the weight of that father's arm. The theory is, and there seems to be none other, that the father, hearing a suspicious noise at the window, set down the child he was endeavouring to soothe and made for the bed and his own pistol, and, mistaking a reflection of the assassin for the assassin himself, sent his shot sidewise at a mirror just as the other let go the trigger which drove a similar bullet into his breast. The course of the one was straight and fatal and that of the other deflected. Striking the mirror at an oblique angle, the bullet fell to the floor where it was picked up by the crawling child, and, as was most natural, thrust at once into his mouth. Perhaps it felt hot to the little tongue; perhaps the child was simply frightened by some convulsive movement of the father who evidently spent his last moment in an endeavour to reach the child, but, whatever the cause, in the quick gasp it gave, the bullet was drawn into the larynx, strangling him.

'That the father's arm, in his last struggle, should have fallen directly across the little throat is one of those anomalies which confounds reason and misleads justice by stopping investigation at the very point where truth lies and mystery disappears.

'Mrs Hammond is to be congratulated that there are detectives who do not give too much credence to outward appearances.'

We expect soon to hear of the capture of the man who sped home the death-dealing bullet.

Sax Rohmer

(15 February, 1883 – 1 June, 1959)

Sax Rohmer was the pen name of Arthur Henry Ward, an English novelist. He is most known for the *Dr Fu Manchu* series of novels, in which he portrays the master criminal, Dr Fu Manchu. He went from writing for music hall artists to short stories and serials for publishing in magazines. The *Fu Manchu* stories, together with his more traditional detective series characters—Paul Harley, Gaston Max, Red Kerry, Morris Klaw (an occult investigator), and the Crime Magnet—made Rohmer one of the most popular and profitable authors of the 1920s and 1930s.

The Tragedies in the Greek Room

I

When did Moris Klaw first appear in London? It is a question which I am asked sometimes and to which I reply, 'To the best of my knowledge, shortly before the commencement of the strange happenings at the Menzies Museum.'

What I know of him I have gathered from various sources; and in these papers, which represent an attempt to justify the methods of one frequently accused of being an insane theorist, I propose to recount all the facts which have come to my knowledge. In some few of the cases I was personally though slightly concerned; but regard me merely as the historian and on no account as the principal or even minor character in the story. My friendship with Martin Coram led, then, to my first meeting with Moris Klaw—a meeting which resulted in my becoming his biographer, inadequate though my information unfortunately remains.

It was some three months after the appointment of Coram to the curatorship of the Menzies Museum that the first of a series of singular occurrences took place there.

This occurrence befell one night in August, and the matter was brought to my ears by Coram himself the following morning. I had, in fact, just taken my seat at the breakfast table, when he walked in unexpectedly and sank into an armchair. His dark, clean-shaven face looked more gaunt than usual and I saw, as he lighted the cigarette which I proffered, that his hand shook nervously.

'There's trouble at the Museum!' he said, abruptly. 'I want you to run around.'

I looked at him for a moment without replying, and, knowing the responsibility of his position, feared that he referred to a theft from the collection.

'Something gone?' I asked.

'No; worse!' was his reply.

'What do you mean, Coram?'

He threw the cigarette, unsmoked, into the hearth.

'You know Conway?' he said; 'Conway, the night attendant? Well—he's dead!' I stood up from the table, my breakfast forgotten, and stared incredulously. 'Do you mean that he died in the night?' I inquired.

'Yes. Done for, poor devil!'

'What! murdered?'

'Without a doubt, Searles! He's had his neck broken!'

I waited for no further explanatians, but, hastily dressing, accompanied Coram to the Museum. It consists, I should mention, of four long, rectangular rooms, the windows of two overlooking South Grafton Square, those of the third giving upon the court that leads to the curator's private entrance, and the fourth adjoining an enclosed garden attached to the building. This fourth room is on the ground floor and is entered through the hall from the Square, the other three, containing the principle and more valuable exhibits, are upon the first floor and are reached by a flight of stairs from the hall. The remainder of the building is occupied by an office and the curator's private apartments, and is completely shut off from that portion open to the public, the only communicating door—an iron one—being kept locked.

The room described in the catalogue as the 'Greek Room' proved to be the scene of the tragedy. This room is one of the two overlooking the Square and contains some of the finest items of the collection. The Museum is not open to the public until ten o'clock, and I found, upon arriving there, that the only occupants of the Greek Room were the commissionaire on duty, two constables, a plain-clothes officer and an inspector—that is, if I except the body of poor Conway.

He had not been touched, but lay as he was found

by Beale, the commissionaire who took charge of the upper rooms during the day, and, indeed, it was patent that he was beyond medical aid. In fact, the position of his body was so extraordinary as almost to defy description.

There are three windows in the Greek Room, with wall cases between, and, in the gap corresponding to the east window and just by the door opening into the next room, is a chair for the attendant. Conway lay downward on the polished floor with his limbs partly under this chair and his clenched fists thrust straight out before him. His head, turned partially to one side, was doubled underneath his breast in a most dreadful manner, indisputably pointing to a broken neck, and his commissionaire's cap lay some distance away, under a table supporting a heavy case of vases.

So much was revealed at a glance, and I immediately turned blankly to Coram.

'What do you make of it?' he said.

I shook my head in silence. I could scarce grasp the reality of the thing; indeed, I was still staring at the huddled figure when the doctor arrived. At his request we laid the dead man flat upon the floor to facilitate an examination, and we then saw that he was greatly cut and bruised about the head and face, and that his features were distorted in a most extraordinary manner, almost as though he had been suffocated.

The doctor did not fail to notice this expression.

'Made a hard fight of it!' he said. 'He must have

been in the last stages of exhaustion when his neck was broken!'

'My dear fellow!' cried Coram, somewhat irritably, 'what do you mean when you say that he made a hard fight? There could not possibly have been any one else in these rooms last night!'

'Excuse me, sir!' said the inspector, 'but there certainly was something going on here. Have you seen the glass case in the next room?'

'Glass case?' muttered Coram, running his hand distractedly through his thick black hair. 'No; what of a glass case?'

'In here, sir,' explained the inspector, leading the way into the adjoining apartment.

At his words, we all followed, and found that he referred to the glass front of a wall case containing statuettes and images of Egyptian deities. The centre pane of this was smashed into fragments, the broken glass strewing the floor and the shelves inside the case.

'That looks like a struggle, sir, doesn't it?' said the inspector.

'Heaven help us! What does it mean?' groaned poor Coram. 'Who could possibly have gained access to the building in the night, or, having done so, have quitted it again, when all the doors remained locked?'

'That we must try and find out!' replied the inspector. 'Meanwhile, here are his keys. They lay on the floor in a corner of the Greek Room.' Coram took them, mechanically. 'Beale,' he said to the commissionaire, 'see if any of the cases are unlocked.'

The man proceeded to go around the rooms. He had progressed no farther than the Greek Room when he made a discovery. 'Here's the top of this unfastened, sir!' he suddenly cried, excitedly. We hurriedly joined him, to find that he stood before a marble pedestal surmounted by a thick glass case containing what Coram had frequently assured me was the gem of the collection—the Athenean Harp.

It was alleged to be of very ancient Greek workmanship, and was constructed of fine gold inlaid with jewels. It represented two reclining female figures, their arms thrown above their heads, their hands meeting; and the strings, several of which were still intact, were of incredibly fine gold wire. The instrument was said to have belonged to a Temple of Pallas in an extremely remote age, and at the time it was brought to light much controversy had waged concerning its claims to authenticity, several connoisseurs proclaiming it the work of a famous goldsmith of medieval Florence, and nothing but a clever forgery. However, Greek or Florentine, amazingly ancient or comparatively modern, it was a beautiful piece of workmanship and of very great intrinsic value, apart from its artistic worth and unique character.

'I thought so!' said the plain-clothes man. 'A clever museum thief!'

Coram sighed wearily. 'My good fellow,' he replied, 'can you explain, by any earthly hypothesis, how a man could get into these apartments and leave them again during the night?'

'Regarding that, sir,' remarked the detective, 'there are a few questions I should like to ask you. In the first place, at what time does the Museum close?'

'At six o'clock in the summer.'

'What do you do when the last visitor has gone?'

'Having locked the outside door, Beale, here, thoroughly examines every room to make certain that no one remains concealed. He next locks the communicating doors and comes down into the hall. It was then his custom to hand me the keys. I gave them into poor Conway's keeping when he came on duty at half-past six, and every hour he went through the Museum, relocking all the doors behind him.'

'I understand that there is a tell-tale watch in each room?'

'Yes. That in the Greek Room registers 4 A. M., so that it was about then that he met his death. He had evidently opened the door communicating with the next room—that containing the broken glass case; but he did not touch the detector and the door was found open this morning.'

'Someone must have lain concealed there and sprung upon him as he entered.'

'Impossible! There is no other means of entrance or exit. The three windows are iron-barred and they have not been tampered with. Moreover, the watch shows that he was there at three o'clock, and nothing larger than a mouse could find shelter in the place; there is nowhere a man could hide.'

'Then the murderer followed him into the Greek Room.'

'Might I venture to point out that, had he done so, he would have been there this morning when Beale arrived? The door of the Greek Room was locked and the keys were found inside upon the floor!'

'The thief might have had a duplicate set.'

'Quite impossible; but, granting the impossible, how did he get in, since the hall door was bolted and barred barred?'

'We must assume that he succeeded in concealing himself before the Museum was closed.'

'The assumption is not permissible, in view of the fact that Beale and I both examined the rooms last night prior to handing the keys to Conway. However, again granting the impossible, how did he get out?'

The Scotland Yard man removed his hat and mopped his forehead with his handkerchief. 'I must say, sir, it is a very strange thing,' he said; 'but how about the iron door here?'

'It leads to my own apartments. I, alone, hold a key. It was locked.' A brief examination served to show that exit from any of the barred windows was impossible.

'Well, sir,' said the detective, 'if the man had keys he could have come down into the hall and the lower room.'

'Step down and look,' was Coram's invitation. The windows of the room on the ground floor were also heavily protected, and it was easy to see that none of them had been opened.

'Upon my word,' exclaimed the inspector, 'it's uncanny! He couldn't have gone out by the hall door, because you say it was bolted and barred on the inside.'

'It was,' replied Coram.

'One moment, sir,' interrupted the plain-clothes. man. 'If that was so, how did you get in this morning?'

'It was Beale's custom,' said Coram, 'to come around by the private entrance to my apartments. We then entered the Museum together by the iron door into the Greek Room and relieved Conway of the keys. There are several little matters to be attended to in the morning before admitting the public, and the other door is never unlocked before ten o'clock.'

'Did you lock the door behind you when you came through this morning?'

'Immediately on finding poor Conway.'

'Could any one have come through this door in the night, provided he had a duplicate key?'

'No. There is a bolt on the private side.'

'And you were in your rooms all last night?'

'From twelve o'clock, yes.'

The police looked at one another silently; then the inspector gave an embarrassed laugh. 'Frankly, sir,' he said, 'I'm completely puzzled!'

We passed upstairs again and Coram turned to the doctor. 'Anything else to report about poor Conway?' he asked.

'His face is all cut by the broken glass and he seems to have had a desperate struggle, although, curiously enough, his body bears no other marks of violence. The direct cause of death was, of course, a broken neck.'

'And how should you think he came by it?'

'I should say that he was hurled upon the floor by an opponent possessing more than ordinary strength!'

Thus the physician was about to depart when there came a knocking upon the iron door. 'It is Hilda,' said Coram, slipping the key in the lock—my daughter,' he added, turning to the detective.

II

The heavy door swinging open, there entered Hilda Coram, a slim, classical figure, with the regular features of her father and the pale gold hair of her dead mother. She looked unwell, and stared about her apprehensively.

'Good morning, Mr Searles,' she greeted me. 'Is it not dreadful about poor Conway!'—and then glanced at Coram that she held a card in her hand. 'Father, there is such a singular old man asking to see you.'

She handed the card to Coram, who in turn passed it to me. It was that of Douglas Glade of the Daily Cable, and had written upon it in Glade's hand the words, 'To introduce Mr Moris Klaw.' 'I suppose it is all right if Mr Glade vouches for him,' said Coram. 'But does anybody here know Moris Klas Klaw?'

'I do,' replied the Scotland Yard man, smiling

shortly. 'He's an antique dealer or something of the kind; got a ramshackle old place by Wapping Old Stairs—sort of a cross between Jamrach's and a rag shop. He's lately been hanging about the Central Criminal Court a lot. Seems to fancy his luck as an amateur investigator. He's certainly smart,' he added, grudgingly, 'but cranky.'

'Ask Mr Klaw to come through, Hilda,' said Coram.

Shortly afterward entered a strange figure. It was that of a tall man who stooped, so that his apparent height was diminished—a very old man who carried his many years lightly, or younger man prematurely aged; none could say which. His skin had the hue of dirty vellum, and his hair, his shaggy brows, his scanty beard were so toneless as to defy classification in terms of colour. He wore an archaic brown bowler, smart, gold-rimmed pince-nez, and a black silk muffler. A long, caped black cloak completely enveloped the stooping figure; from beneath its mud-spattered edge peeped long-toed continental boots.

He removed his hat. 'Good morning, Mr Coram,' he said. His voice reminded me of the distant rumbling of empty casks; his accent was wholly indescribable. 'Good morning' (to the detective), 'Mr Grimsby. Good morning, Mr Searles. Your friend, Mr Glade, tells me I shall find you here. Good morning, Inspector. To Miss Coram I already have said good morning.' From the lining of the flat-topped hat he took out one of those small cylindrical scent sprays and played its contents upon his high, bald brow. An odour of verbena filled the air. He replaced the spray in the hat, the hat upon his scantily thatched crown.

'There is here a smell of dead men!' he explained. I turned aside to hide my smiles, so grotesque was my first impression of the amazing individual known as Moris Klaw.

'Mr Coram,' he continued, 'I am an old fool who sometimes has wise dreams. Crime has been the hobby of a busy life. I have seen crime upon the Gold Coast, where the black fever it danced in the air above the murdered one like a lingering soul, and I have seen blood flow in Arctic Lapland, where it was frozen up into red ice almost before it left the veins. Have I your permit to see if I can help?'

All of us, the police included, were strangely impressed now.

'Certainly,' said Coram; 'will you step this way?' Moris Klaw bent over the dead man.

'You have moved him!' he said, sharply. It was explained that this had been for the purpose of a medical examination. He nodded absently. With the aid of a large magnifying glass he was scrutinizing poor Conway. He examined his hair, his eyes, his hands, his fingernails. He rubbed long, flexible fingers upon the floor beside the body—and sniffed at the dust.

'Someone so kindly will tell me all about it,' he said, turning out the dead man's pockets.

Coram briefly recounted much of the foregoing,

and replied to the oddly chosen questions which from time to time Moris Klaw put to him. Throughout the duologue, the singular old man conducted a detailed search of every square inch, I think, of the Greek Room. Before the case containing the harp he stood, peering.

'It is here that the trouble centres,' he muttered.

'What do I know of such a Grecian instrument? Let me think.' He threw back his head, closing his eyes.

'Such valuable curios,' he rumbled, 'have his tories and the crimes they occasion operate in cycles.' He waved his hand in a slow circle. 'If I but knew the history of this harp! Mr Coram!'

He glanced toward my friend.

'Thoughts are things, Mr Coram. If I might spend a night hereupon the very spot of floor where the poor Conway fell—I could from the surrounding atmosphere (it is a sensitive plate) recover a picture of the thing in his mind—indicating Conway at the last!'

The Scotland Yard man blew down his nose.

'You snort, my friend,' said Moris Klaw, turning upon him. 'You would snort less if you had waked screaming, out in the desert; screaming out with fear of the dripping beaks of the vultures—the last dreadful fear which the mind had known of him who had died of thirst upon that haunted spot!'

The words and the manner of their delivery thrilled us all.

'What is it,' continued the weird old man, 'but the odic force, the ether—say it how you please—which carries the wireless message, the lightning? It is a huge, subtile, sensitive plate. Inspiration, what you call bad luck and good luck—all are but reflections from it. The supreme thought preceding cons it. Death is imprinted on the surrounding atmosphere like a photograph. I have trained this'—he tapped his brow—'to reproduce those photographs! May I sleep here to-night, Mr Coram?'

Somewhere beneath the ramshackle exterior we had caught a glimpse of a man of power. From behind the thick pebbles momentarily had shone out the light of a tremendous and original mind. 'I should be most glad of your assistance,' answered my friend. 'No police must be here to-night,' rumbled Moris Klaw. 'No heavy-footed constables, filling the room with thoughts of large cooks and small Basses, must fog my negative!'

'Can that be arranged?' asked Coram of the inspector. 'The men on duty can remain in the hall, if you wish it, sit.'

'Good!' rumbled Moris Klaw.

He moistened his brow with verbena, bowed uncouthly, and shuffled from the Greek Room.

III

Moris Klaw reappeared in the evening, accompanied by a strikingly beautiful brunette. The change of face upon the part of Mr Grimsby of New Scotland Yard was singular. 'My daughter—Isis,' explained Moris

Klaw. 'She assists to develop my negatives.' Grimsby became all attention. Leaving two men on duty in the hall, Moris Klaw, his daughter, Grimsby, Coram, and I went up to the Greek Room.

Its darkness was relieved by a single lamp. 'I've had the stones in the Athenean Harp examined by a lapidary,' said Coram. 'It occurred to me that they might have been removed and paste substituted. It was not so, however. 'No,' rumbled Klaw. 'I thought of that, too. No visitors have been admitted here during the day?'

'The Greek Room has been closed.'

'It is well, Mr Coram. Let no one disturb me until my daughter comes in the morning.'

Isis Klaw placed a red silk cushion upon the spot where the dead man had lain.

'Some pillows and a blanket, Mr Klaw?' suggested the suddenly attentive Mr Grimsby.

'I thank you, no,' was the reply. 'They would be saturated with alien impressions. My cushion it is odically sterilized! The "etheric storm" created by Conway's last mental emotion reaches my brain unpolluted. Good-night, gentlemen. Good-night, Isis!'

We withdrew, leaving Moris Klaw to his ghostly vigil.

'I suppose Mr Klaw is quite trustworthy?' whispered Coram to the detective. 'Oh, undoubtedly!' was the reply. 'In any case, he can do no harm. My men will be on duty downstairs here all night.'

'Do you speak of my father, Mr Grimsby?' came a

soft, thrilling voice.

Grimsby turned, and met the flashing black eyes of Isis Klaw.

'I was assuring Mr Coram,' he answered, readily, 'that Mr Klaw's methods have several times proved successful!'

'Several times!' she cried, scornfully. 'What! has he ever failed?'

Her accent was certainly French, I determined; her voice, her entire person, as certainly charming—to which the detective's manner bore witness. 'I'm afraid I'm not familiar with all his cases, miss,' he said. 'Can I call you a cab?'

'I thank you, no.' She rewarded him with a dazzling smile. 'Good-night.' Coram opened the doors of the Museum, and she passed out. Leaving the men on duty in the hall, Coram and I shortly afterward also quitted the Museum by the main entrance, in order to avoid disturbing Moris Klaw by using the curator's private door.

To my friend's study Hilda Coram brought us coffee. She was unnaturally pale, and her eyes were feverishly bright. I concluded that the tragedy was responsible.

'Perhaps, to an extent,' said Coram; 'but she is studying music and, I fear, overworking in order to pass a stiff exam.'

Coram and I surveyed the Greek Room problem from every conceivable standpoint, but were unable to surmise how the thief had entered, how left, and why he had fled without his booty.

'I don't mind confessing,' said Coram, 'that I am very ill at ease. We haven't the remotest idea how the murderer got into the Greek Room or how he got out again. Bolts and bars, it is evident, do not prevail against him, so that we may expect a repetition of the dreadful business at any time!'

'What precautions do you propose to take?'

'Well, there will be a couple of police on duty in the Museum for the next week or so, but, after that, we shall have to rely upon a night watchman. The funds only allow of the appointment of four attendants: three for day and one for night duty.'

'Do you think you'll find any difficulty in getting a man?'

'No,' replied Coram. 'I know of a steady man who will come as soon as we are ready for him.' I slept but little that night, and was early afoot and around to the Museum. Isis Klaw was there before me, carrying the red cushion, and her father was deep in conversation with Coram.

Detective-Inspector Grimsby approached me.

'I see you're looking at the cushion, sir!' he said, smilingly. 'But it's not a "plant." He's not an up-to-date cracksman. Nothing's missing!'

'You need not assure me of that,' I replied. 'I do not doubt Mr Klaw's honesty of purpose.'

'Wait till you hear his mad theory, though!' he said, with a glance aside at the girl.

'Mr Coram,' Moris Klaw was saying, in his odd, rumbling tones, 'my psychic photograph is of a woman! A woman dressed all in white!'

Grimsby coughed—then flushed as he caught the eye of Isis.

'Poor Conway's mind,' continued Klaw, 'is filled with such a picture when he breathes his last—great wonder he has for the white woman and great fear for the Athenean Harp, which she carries!'

'Which she carries!' cried Coram. 'Some woman took the harp from its case a few minutes before Conway died!' affirmed Moris Klaw. 'I have much research to make now, and with aid from Isis shall develop my negative! Yesterday I learnt from the constable who was on night duty at the corner of the Square that a heavy pantechnicon van went driving round at four o'clock. It was shortly after four o'clock that the tragedy occurred. The driver was unaware that there was no way out, you understand. Is it important? I cannot say. It often is such points that matter. We must, however, waste no time. Until you hear from me again you will lay dry plaster of Paris all around the stand of the Athenean Harp each night. Good morning, gentlemen!' His arm linked in his daughter's, he left the Museum.

IV

For some weeks after this mysterious affair, all went well at the Menzies Museum. The new night watchman, a big Scot, by name John Macalister, seemed to have fallen thoroughly into his duties, and everything was proceeding smoothly. No clue concerning the previous outrage had come to light, the police being clearly at a loss. From Moris Klaw we heard not a word. But Macalister did not appear to suffer from nervousness, saying that he was quite big enough to look after himself.

Poor Macalister! His bulk did not save him from a dreadful fate. He was found, one fine morning, lying flat on his back in the Greek Room—dead. As in the case of Conway, the place showed unmistakable signs of a furious struggle. The attendant's chair had been dashed upon the floor with such violence as to break three of the legs; a bust of Pallas, that had occupied a corner position upon a marble pedestal, was found to be hurled down; and the top of the case which usually contained the Athenean Harp had been unlocked, and the priceless antique lay close by, upon the floor!

The cause of death, in Macalister's case, was heart failure, an unsuspected weakness of that organ being brought to light at the inquest; but, according to the medical testimony, deceased must have undergone unnaturally violent exertions to bring about death. In other respects, the circumstances of the two cases were almost identical. The door of the Greek Room was locked upon the inside and the keys were found on the floor. From the detector watches in the other rooms it was evident that his death must have taken place about three o'clock. Nothing was missing, and the jewels in the harp had not been. tampered with.

But, most amazing circumstance of all, imprinted upon the dry plaster of Paris which, in accordance. with the instructions of the mysteriously absent Moris Klaw, had nightly been placed around the case containing the harp, were the marks of little bare feet!

A message sent, through the willing agency of Inspector Grimsby, to the Wapping abode of the old curio dealer, resulted in the discovery that Moris Klaw was abroad. His daughter, however, reported having received a letter from her father which contained the words—

'Let Mr Coram keep the key of the case containing the Athenean Harp under his pillow at night.'

'What does she mean?' asked Coram. 'That I am to detach that particular key from the bunch or place them all beneath my pillow?' Grimsby shrugged his shoulders.

'I'm simply telling you what she told me, sir.'

'I should suspect the man to be an impostor,' said Coram, 'if it were not for the extraordinary. confirmation of his theory furnished by the footprints. They certainly looked like those of a woman!'

Remembering how Moris Klaw had acted, I sought out the constable who had been on duty at the corner of South Grafton Square on the night of the second tragedy. From him I elicited a fact which, though insignificant in itself, was, when associated with another circumstance, certainly singular.

A Pickford traction engine, drawing two heavy wagons, had been driven round the Square at 3 A. M., the driver thinking that he could get out on the other side.

That was practically all I learned from the constable, but it served to set me thinking. Was it merely a coincidence that, at almost the exact hour of the previous tragedy, a heavy pantechnicon had passed the Museum?

'It's not once in six months,' the man assured me, 'that any vehicle but a tradesman's cart goes round the Square. You see, it doesn't lead any where, but this Pickford chap he was rattling by before I could stop him, and though I shouted he couldn't hear me, the engine making such a noise, so I just let him drive round and find out for himself.'

I now come to the event which concluded this extraordinary case, and, that it may be clearly understood, I must explain the positions which we took up during the nights of the following week; for Coram had asked me to take a night watch, with himself, Grimsby, and Beale, in the Museum.

Beale, the commissionaire, remained in the hall and lower room—it was catalogued as the 'Bronze Room'—Coram patrolled the room at the top of the stairs, Grimsby the next, or Greek Room, and I the Egyptian Room. None of the doors was locked, and Grimsby, by his own special request, held the keys of the cases in the Greek Room.

We commenced our vigil on the Saturday, and I, for one, found it a lugubrious business. One electric lamp was usually left burning in each apartment throughout the night, and I sat as near to that in the Egyptian Room as possible and endeavoured to distract my thoughts with a bundle of papers with which I had provided myself.

In the next room I could hear Grimsby walking about incessantly, and, at regular intervals, the scratching of a match as he lighted a cigar. He was an inveterate cheroot smoker.

Our first night's watching, then, was productive of no result, and the five that followed were equally monotonous.

Upon Grimsby's suggestion we observed great secrecy in the matter of these dispositions. Even Coram's small household was kept in ignorance of this midnight watching. Grimsby, following out some theory of his own, now determined to dispense altogether with light in the Greek Room. Friday was intensely hot, and occasional fitful breezes brought with them banks of black thundercloud, which, however, did not break; and, up to the time that we assumed our posts at the Museum, no rain had fallen. At about twelve o'clock I looked out into South Grafton Square and saw that the sky was entirely obscured by a heavy mass of inky cloud, ominous of a gathering storm.

Returning to my chair beneath the electric lamp, I took up a work of Mark Twain's, which I had brought as a likely antidote to melancholy or nervousness. As I commenced to read, for the twentieth time, 'The Jumping Frog,' I heard the scratch of Grimsby's match in the next room and knew that he had lighted his fifth cigar.

It must have been about one o'clock when the rain came. I heard the big drops on the glass roof, followed by the steady pouring of the deluge. For perhaps five minutes it rained steadily, and then it ceased as abruptly as it had begun. Above the noise of the water rushing down the metal gutters, I distinctly detected the sound of Grimsby striking another match. Then, with a mighty crash, came the thunder.

Directly above the Museum it seemed as though the very heavens had burst, and the glass roof rattled as if a shower of stones had fallen, the thunderous report echoing and reverberating hollowly through the building.

As the lightning flashed with dazzling brilliance, I started from my chair and stood, breathless, with every sense on the alert; for, strangely intermingling with the patter of the rain that now commenced to fall again, came a low wailing, like nothing so much as the voice of a patient succumbing to an anæsthetic. There was something indefinably sweet, but indescribably weird, in the low and mysterious music.

Not knowing from whence it proceeded, I stood undetermined what to do; but, just as the thunder boomed again, I heard a wild cry—undoubtedly proceeding from the Greek Room! Springing to the door, I threw it open.

All was in darkness, but, as I entered, a vivid flash of lightning illuminated the place.

I saw a sight which I can never forget. Grimsby lay flat upon the floor by the farther door. But, dreadful as that spectacle was, it scarce engaged my attention; nor did I waste a second glance upon the Athencan Harp, which lay close beside its empty case.

For the figure of a woman, draped in flimsy white, was passing across the Greek Room!

Grim fear took me by the throat, since I could not doubt that what I saw was a supernatural manifestation. Darkness followed. I heard a loud wailing cry and a sound as of a fall.

Then Coram came running through the Greek Room.

Trembling violently, I joined him; and together we stood looking down at Grimsby. 'Good God!' whispered Coram; 'this is awful. It cannot be the work of mortal hands! Poor Grimsby is dead!' 'Did you see the woman?' I muttered. I will confess it: my courage had completely deserted me. He shook his head; but, as Beale came running to join us, glanced fearfully into the shadows of the Greek Room. The storm seemed to have passed, and, as we three frightened men stood around Grimsby's recumbent body, we could almost hear the beating of each other's hearts.

Suddenly, giving a great start, Coram clutched my

arm. 'Listen!' he said. 'What's that?'

I held my breath and listened. 'It's the thunder in the distance,' said Beale. 'You are wrong,' I answered. 'It is someone knocking at the hall entrance! There goes the bell, now!'

Coram gave a sigh of relief. 'Heavens!' he said; 'I've no nerves left! Come on and see who it

The three of us, keeping very close together, passed quickly through the Greek Room and down into the hall.

As the ringing continued, Coram unbolted the door—and there, on the steps, stood Moris Klaw. Some vague idea of his mission flashed through my mind. 'You are too late!' I cried. 'Grimsby has gone!'

I saw a look of something like anger pass over his large pale features, and then he had darted past us and vanished up the stairs.

V

Having rebolted the door, we rejoined Moris Klaw in the Greek Room. He was kneeling beside Grimsby in the dim light—and Grimsby, his face ghastly pale, was sitting up and drinking from a flask!

'I am in time!' said Moris Klaw. 'He has only fainted!'

'It was the ghost!' whispered the Scotland Yard man. 'My God! I'm prepared for anything human—but when the lightning came and I saw that white thing—playing the harp—'

Coram turned aside and was about to pick up the harp, which lay upon the floor near, when—

'Ah!' cried Moris Klaw, 'do not touch it! It is death!'

Coram started back as though he had been stung as Grimsby very unsteadily got upon his feet. 'Turn up lights,' directed Moris Klaw, 'and I will show you!'

The curator went out to the switchboard and the Greek Room became brightly illuminated. The ramshackle figure of Moris Klaw seemed to be invested with triumphant majesty. Behind the pebbles his eyes gleamed.

'Observe,' he said, 'I raise the harp from the floor.' He did so. 'And I live. For why? Because I do not take hold upon it in a natural manner—by the top! I take it by the side! Conway and Macalister took hold upon it at the top; and where are they—Conway and Macalister?'

'Mr Klaw,' said Coram, 'I cannot doubt that this black business is all clear to your very unusual intelligence; but to me it is a profound mystery. I have, myself, in the past, taken up the harp in the way you describe as fatal, and without injury—'

'But not immediately after it had been played upon!' interrupted Moris Klaw. 'Played upon! I have never attempted to play upon it!'

'Even had you done so you might yet have escaped, provided you set it down before touching the top part! Note, please!'

He ran his long white fingers over the golden strings. Instantly there stole upon my ears that weird, wailing music which had heralded the strange happenings of the night!

'And now,' continued our mentor, 'whilst I who am cunning hold it where the ladies' gold feet join, observe the top where the hand would in ordinary rest in holding it.'

We gathered around him.

'A needle-point,' he rumbled, impressively, 'protruding! The player touches it not! But who takes it from the hand of the player dies! By placing the harp again upon its base the point again retires! Shall I say what is upon that point, to drive a man mad like a dog with rabies, to stay potent for generations? I cannot. It is a secret buried with the ugly body of Cæsar Borgia!'

'Cesar Borgia!' we cried in chorus.

'Ah!' rumbled Moris Klaw, 'your Athenean Harp was indeed made by Paduano Zelloni, the Florentine! It is a clever forge! I have been in Rome until yesterday. You are surprised? I am sorry, for the poor Macalister died. Having perfected, with the aid of Isis, my mind photograph of the lady who plays the harp, I go to Rome to perfect the story of the harp. For why? At my house I have records, but incomplete, useless. In Rome I have a friend, of so old a family, and once so wicked, I shall not name it!

'He has recourse to the great Vatican Library—to the annals of his race. There he finds me an account of such a harp. In those priceless parchments it is called "a Greek lyre of gold." It is described. I am convinced. I am sure!

'Once the beautiful Lucrece Borgia play upon this harp. To one who is distasteful to her she says: 'Replace for me my harp.' He does so. He is a dead man! God! what cleverness!

'Where has it lain for generations before your Sir Menzies find it? No man knows. But it has still its virtues! How did the poor Menzies die? Throw himself from his room window, I recently learn. This harp certainly was in his room. Conway, after dashing, mad, about the place, springs head downward from the attendant's chair. Macalister dies in exhaustion and convulsions!'

A silence; when—

'What caused the harp to play?' asked Coram. Moris Klaw looked hard at him. Then a thrill of new horror ran through my veins. A low moan came from somewhere hard by! Coram turned in a flash!

'Why, my private door is open!' he whispered.

'Where do you keep your private keys?' rumbled Klaw.

'In my study.' Coram was staring at the open door, but seemed afraid to approach it. 'We have been using the attendant's keys at night. My own are on my study mantelpiece now.'

'I think not,' continued the thick voice. 'Your daughter has them!'

'My daughter!' cried Coram, and sprang to the open door. 'Heavens! Hilda! Hilda!'

'She is somnambulistic!' whispered Moris Klaw in my ear. 'When certain unusual sounds—such as heavy vehicles at night—reach her in her sleep (ah! how little we know of the phenomenon of sleep!), she arises, and, in common with many sleepwalkers, always acts the same. Something, in the case of Miss Hilda, attracts her to the golden harp—'

'She is studying music!'

'She must rest from it. Her brain is overwrought! She unlocks the case and strikes the cords of the harp, relocking the door, replacing the keys—I before have known such cases—then retires as she came. Who takes the harp from her hands, or raises it, if she has laid it down upon its side, dies! These dead attendants were brave fellows both, for, hearing the music, they came running, saw how the matter was, and did not waken the sleeping player. Conway was poisoned as he returned the harp to its case; Macalister, as he took it up from where it lay. Something to-night awoke her ere she could relock the door. The fright of so awaking made her to swoon.'

Coram's kindly voice and the sound of a girl sobbing affrightedly reached us.

'It was my yell of fear, Mr Klaw!' said Grimsby, shamefacedly. 'She looked like a ghost!'

'I understand,' rumbled Moris Klaw, soothingly. 'As I see her in my sleep she is very awesome! I will show you the picture Isis has made from my etheric photograph. I saw it, finished, earlier to night. It confirmed me that the Miss Hilda with the harp in her hand was poor Conway's last thought in life!'

'Mr Klaw,' said Grimsby, earnestly, 'you are a very remarkable man!'

'Yes?' he rumbled, and gingerly placed in its case the 'Greek lyre of gold' which Paduano Zelloni had wrought for Cæsar Borgia.

From the brown hat he took out his scent spray and squirted verbena upon his heated forehead.

'That harp,' he explained, 'it smells of dead men!'

Raymond Chandler

(July 23, 1888 – March 26, 1959)

Raymond Chandler was a novelist and screenwriter of American-British origin. Chandler became a detective fiction writer in 1932, at the age of forty-four, after losing his job as an oil company executive during the Great Depression. His first short story, *Blackmailers Don't Shoot,* was published in the popular pulp magazine *Black Mask* in 1933. In addition to his short stories, Chandler published seven novels during his lifetime. He was also elected president of the Mystery Writers of America a year before his death. Chandler's hardboiled fiction has a huge stylistic influence on detective literature even today.

Pearls are a Nuisance

1

It is quite true that I wasn't doing anything that morning except looking at a blank sheet of paper in my typewriter and thinking about writing a letter. It is also quite true that I don't have a great deal to do any morning. But that is no reason why I should have to go out hunting for old Mrs Penruddock's pearl necklace. I don't happen to be a policeman.

It was Ellen Macintosh who called me up, which made a difference, of course. 'How are you, darling?' she asked. 'Busy?'

'Yes and no,' I said. 'Mostly no. I am very well. What is it now?'

'I don't think you love me, Walter. And anyway you ought to get some work to do. You have too much money. Somebody has stolen Mrs Penruddock's pearls and I want you to find them.'

'Possibly you think you have the police department on the line,' I said coldly. 'This is the residence of Walter Gage. Mr Gage talking.'

'Well, you can tell Mr Gage from Miss Ellen Macintosh,' she said, 'that if he is not out here in half an hour, he will receive a small parcel by registered mail containing one diamond engagement ring.'

'And a lot of good it did me,' I said. 'That old crow will live for another fifty years.'

But she had already hung up so I put my hat on and went down and drove off in the Packard. It was a nice late April morning, if you care for that sort of thing. Mrs Penruddock lived on a wide quiet street in Carondelet Park.

The house had probably looked exactly the same for the last fifty years, but that didn't make me any better pleased that Ellen Macintosh might live in it another fifty years, unless old Mrs Penruddock died and didn't need a nurse any more. Mr Penruddock had died a few years before, leaving no will, a thoroughly tangled-up estate, and a list of pensioners as long as a star boarder's arm. I rang the front doorbell and the door was opened, not very soon, by a little old woman with a maid's apron and a strangled knot of gray hair on the top of her head. She looked at me as if she had never seen me before and didn't want to see me now.

'Miss Ellen Macintosh, please,' I said. 'Mr Walter

Gage calling.'

She sniffed, turned without a word and we went back into the musty recesses of the house and came to a glassed-in porch full of wicker furniture and the smell of Egyptian tombs. She went away, with another sniff.

In a moment the door opened again and Ellen Macintosh came in. Maybe you don't like tall girls with honey-colored hair and skin like the first strawberry peach the grocer sneaks out of the box for himself. If you don't, I'm sorry for you.

'Darling, so you did come,' she cried. 'That was nice of you, Walter. Now sit down and I'll tell you all about it.'

We sat down.

'Mrs Penruddock's pearl necklace has been stolen, Walter.'

'You told me that over the telephone. My temperature is still normal.'

'If you will excuse a professional guess,' she said, 'it is probably subnormal—permanently. The pearls are a string of forty-nine matched pink ones which Mr Penruddock gave to Mrs Penruddock for her golden wedding present. She hardly ever wore them lately, except perhaps on Christmas or when she had a couple of very old friends in to dinner and was well enough to sit up. And every Thanksgiving she gives a dinner to all the pensioners and friends and old employees Mr Penruddock left on her hands, and she wore them then.'

'You are getting your verb tenses a little mixed,' I said, 'but the general idea is clear. Go on.'

'Well, Walter,' Ellen said, with what some people call an arch look, 'the pearls have been stolen. Yes, I know that is the third time I told you that, but there's a strange mystery about it. They were kept in a leather case in an old safe which was open half the time and which I should judge a strong man could open with his fingers even when it was locked. I had to go there for a paper this morning and I looked in at the pearls just to say hello—'

'I hope your idea in hanging on to Mrs Penruddock has not been that she might leave you that necklace,' I said stiffly. 'Pearls are all very well for old people and fat blondes, but for tall willowy—'

'Oh shut up, darling,' Ellen broke in. 'I should certainly not have been waiting for these pearls—because they were false.'

I swallowed hard and stared at her. 'Well,' I said, with a leer, 'I have heard that old Penruddock pulled some cross-eyed rabbits out of the hat occasionally, but giving his own wife a string of phony pearls on her golden wedding gets my money.'

'Oh, don't be such a fool, Walter! They were real enough then. The fact is Mrs Penruddock sold them and had imitations made. One of her old friends, Mr Lansing Gallemore of the Gallemore Jewelry Company, handled it all for her very quietly, because of course she didn't want anyone to know. And that is why the police have not been called in. You *will* find them for her, won't you, Walter?'

'How? And what did she sell them for?'

'Because Mr Penruddock died suddenly without making any provision for all these people he had been supporting. Then the depression came, and there was hardly any money at all. Only just enough to carry on the household and pay the servants, all of whom have been with Mrs Penruddock so long that she would rather starve than let any of them go.'

'That's different,' I said. 'I take my hat off to her. But how the dickens am I going to find them, and what does it matter anyway—if they were false?'

'Well, the pearls—imitations, I mean—cost two hundred dollars and were specially made in Bohemia and it took several months and the way things are over there now she might never be able to get another set of really good imitations. And she is terrified somebody will find out they were false, or that the thief will blackmail her, when he finds out they were false. You see, darling, I know who stole them.'

I said, 'Huh?' a word I very seldom use as I do not think it part of the vocabulary of a gentleman.

'The chauffeur we had here a few months, Walter—a horrid big brute named Henry Eichelberger. He left suddenly the day before yesterday, for no reason at all. Nobody ever leaves Mrs Penruddock. Her last chauffeur was a very old man and he died. But Henry Eichelberger left without a word and I'm sure he had stolen the pearls. He tried to kiss me once, Walter.'

'Oh, he did,' I said in a different voice. 'Tried to kiss you, eh? Where is this big slab of meat, darling? Have you any idea at all? It seems hardly likely he would be hanging around on the street corner for me to punch his nose for him.'

Ellen lowered her long silky eyelashes at me—and when she does that I go limp as a scrubwoman's back hair.

'He didn't run away. He must have known the pearls were false and that he was safe enough to blackmail Mrs Penruddock. I called up the agency he came from and he has been back there and registered again for employment. But they said it was against their rules to give his address.'

'Why couldn't somebody else have taken the pearls? A burglar, for instance?'

'There is no one else. The servants are beyond suspicion and the house is locked up as tight as an icebox every night and there were no signs of anybody having broken in. Besides Henry Eichelberger knew where the pearls were kept, because he saw me putting them away after the last time she wore them—which was when she had two very dear friends in to dinner on the occasion of the anniversary of Mr Penruddock's death.'

'That must have been a pretty wild party,' I said. 'All right, I'll go down to the agency and make them give me his address. Where is it?'

'It is called the Ada Twomey Domestic Employment Agency, and it is in the two-hundred block on East Second, a very unpleasant neighborhood.'

'Not half as unpleasant as my neighborhood will be to Henry Eichelberger,' I said. 'So he tried to kiss you, eh?'

'The pearls, Walter,' Ellen said gently, 'are the important thing. I do hope he hasn't already found out they are false and thrown them in the ocean.'

'If he has, I'll make him dive for them.'

'He is six feet three and very big and strong, Walter,' Ellen said coyly.

'But not handsome like you, of course.'

'Just my size,' I said. 'It will be a pleasure. Good-bye, darling.'

She took hold of my sleeve. 'There is just one thing, Walter. I don't mind a little fighting because it is manly. But you mustn't cause a disturbance that would bring the police in, you know. And although you are very big and strong and played right tackle at college, you are a little weak about one thing. Will you promise me not to drink any whiskey?'

'This Eichelberger,' I said, 'is all the drink I want.'

2

The Ada Twomey Domestic Employment Agency on East Second Street proved to be all that the name and location implied. The odor of the anteroom, in which I was compelled to wait for a short time, was not at all pleasant. The agency was presided over by a hard-faced middle-aged woman who said that Henry Eichelberger was registered with them for employment as a chauffeur, and that she could arrange to have him call upon me, or could bring him there to the office for an interview. But when I placed a ten-dollar bill on her desk and indicated that it was merely an earnest of good faith, without prejudice to any commission which might become due to her agency, she relented and gave me his address, which was out west on Santa Monica Boulevard, near the part of the city which used to be called Sherman.

I drove out there without delay, for fear that Henry Eichelberger might telephone in and be informed that I was coming. The address proved to be a seedy hotel, conveniently close to the interurban car tracks and having its entrance adjoining a Chinese laundry. The hotel was upstairs, the steps being covered—in places—with strips of decayed rubber matting to which were screwed irregular fragments of unpolished brass. The smell of the Chinese laundry ceased about halfway up the stairs and was replaced by a smell of kerosene, cigar butts, slept-in air and greasy paper bags. There was a register at the head of the stairs on a wooden shelf. The last entry was in pencil, three weeks previous as to date, and had been written by someone with a very unsteady hand. I deduced from this that the management was not over-particular.

There was a bell beside the book and a sign reading: MANAGER.

I rang the bell and waited. Presently a door opened down the hall and feet shuffled towards me without haste. A man appeared wearing frayed leather slippers and trousers of a nameless color, which had the two top buttons unlatched to permit more freedom to the suburbs of his extensive stomach. He also wore red suspenders, his shirt was darkened under the arms, and elsewhere, and his face badly needed a thorough laundering and trimming.

He said, 'Full-up, bud,' and sneered.

I said: 'I am not looking for a room. I am looking for one Eichelberger, who, I am informed lives here, but who, I observe, has not registered in your book. And this, as of course you know, is contrary to the law.'

'A wise guy,' the fat man sneered again. 'Down the hall, bud. Two-eighteen.'

He waved a thumb the color and almost the size of a burnt baked potato.

'Have the kindness to show me the way,' I said.

'Geez, the lootenant-governor,' he said, and began to shake his stomach. His small eyes disappeared in folds of yellow fat. 'O.K., bud. Follow on.' We went into the gloomy depths of the back hall and came to a wooden door at the end with a closed wooden transom above it. The fat man smote the door with a fat hand. Nothing happened.

'Out,' he said.

'Have the kindness to unlock the door,' I said. 'I wish to go in and wait for Eichelberger.'

'In a pig's valise,' the fat man said nastily, 'Who the hell you think you are, bum?'

This angered me. He was a fair-sized man, about six feet tall, but too full of the memories of beer. I looked up and down the dark hall. The place seemed utterly deserted.

I hit the fat man in the stomach. He sat down on the floor and belched and his right kneecap came into sharp contact with his jaw. He coughed and tears welled up in his eyes.

'Cripes, bud,' he whined. 'You got twenty years on me. That ain't fair.'

'Open the door,' I said. 'I have no time to argue with you.'

'A buck,' he said, wiping his eyes on his shirt. 'Two bucks and no tipoff.'

I took two dollars out of my pocket and helped the man to his feet. He folded the two dollars and produced an ordinary passkey which I could have purchased for five cents.

'Brother, you sock,' he said. 'Where you learn it? Most big guys are muscle-bound.' He unlocked the door.

'If you hear any noises later on,' I said, 'ignore them. If there is any damage, it will be paid for generously.'

He nodded and I went into the room. He locked the door behind me and his steps receded. There was silence.

The room was small, mean and tawdry. It contained a brown chest of drawers with a small mirror hanging over it, a straight wooden chair, a wooden rocking chair, a single bed of chipped enamel, with a much mended cotton counterpane. The curtains at the single window had fly marks on them and the green shade was without a slat at the bottom. There was a wash bowl in the corner with two paper-thin towels hanging beside it. There was, of course, no bathroom, and there was no closet. A piece of dark figured material hanging from a shelf made a substitute for the latter. Behind this I found a gray business suit of the largest size made, which would be my size, if I wore ready-made clothes, which I do not. There was a pair of black brogues on the floor, size number twelve at least. There was also a cheap fiber suitcase, which of course I searched, as it was not locked.

I also searched the bureau and was surprised to find that everything in it was neat and clean and decent. But there was not much in it. Particularly there were no pearls in it. I searched in all other likely and unlikely places in the room but I found nothing of interest.

I sat on the side of the bed and lit a cigarette and waited. It was now apparent to me that Henry Eichelberger was either a very great fool or entirely innocent. The room and the open trail he had left behind him did not suggest a man dealing in operations like stealing pearl necklaces.

I had smoked four cigarettes, more than I usually

smoke in an entire day, when approaching steps sounded. They were light quick steps but not at all clandestine. A key was thrust into the door and turned and the door swung carelessly open. A man stepped through it and looked at me. I am six feet three inches in height and weigh over two hundred pounds. This man was tall, but he seemed lighter. He wore a blue serge suit of the kind which is called neat for lack of anything better to say about it. He had thick wiry blond hair, a neck like a Prussian corporal in a cartoon, very wide shoulders and large hard hands, and he had a face that had taken much battering in its time. His small greenish eyes glinted at me with what I then took to be evil humor. I saw at once that he was not a man to trifle with, but I was not afraid of him. I was his equal in size and strength, and, I had small doubt, his superior in intelligence.

I stood up off the bed calmly and said: 'I am looking for one Eichelberger.'

'How you get in here, bud?' It was a cheerful voice, rather heavy, but not unpleasant to the ear.

'The explanation of that can wait,' I said stiffly. 'I am looking for one Eichelberger. Are you he?'

'Haw,' the man said. 'A gut-buster. A comedian. Wait'll I loosen my belt.' He took a couple of steps farther into the room and I took the same number towards him.

'My name is Walter Gage,' I said. 'Are you Eichelberger?'

'Gimme a nickel,' he said, 'and I'll tell you.'

I ignored that. 'I am the fiancé of Miss Ellen Macintosh,' I told him coldly. 'I am informed that you tried to kiss her.'

He took another step towards me and I another towards him. 'Whaddaya mean—tried?' he sneered.

I led sharply with my right and it landed flush on his chin. It seemed to me a good solid punch, but it scarcely moved him. I then put two hard left jabs into his neck and landed a second hard right at the side of his rather wide nose. He snorted and hit me in the solar plexus.

I bent over and took hold of the room with both hands and spun it. When I had it nicely spinning I gave it a full swing and hit myself on the back of the head with the floor. This made me lose my balance temporarily and while I was thinking about how to regain it a wet towel began to slap at my face and I opened my eyes. The face of Henry Eichelberger was close to mine and bore a certain appearance of solicitude.

'Bud,' his voice said, 'your stomach is as weak as a Chinaman's tea.'

'Brandy!' I croaked. 'What happened?'

'You tripped on a little tear in the carpet, bud. You really got to have liquor?'

'Brandy,' I croaked again, and closed my eyes.

'I hope it don't get me started,' his voice said.

A door opened and closed. I lay motionless and tried to avoid being sick at my stomach. The time passed slowly, in a long gray veil. Then the door of the room opened and closed once more and a moment later something hard was being pressed against my lips. I opened my mouth and liquor poured down my throat. I coughed, but the fiery liquid coursed through my veins and strengthened me at once. I sat up.

'Thank you, Henry,' I said. 'May I call you Henry?'

'No tax on it, bud.'

I got to my feet and stood before him. He stared at me curiously. 'You look O.K.,' he said. 'Why'n't you told me you was sick?'

'Damn you, Eichelberger!' I said and hit with all my strength on the side of his jaw. He shook his head and his eyes seemed annoyed. I delivered three more punches to his face and jaw while he was still shaking his head.

'So you wanta play for keeps!' he yelled and took hold of the bed and threw it at me.

I dodged the corner of the bed, but in doing so I moved a little too quickly and lost my balance and pushed my head about four inches into the baseboard under the window.

A wet towel began to slap at my face. I opened my eyes.

'Listen, kid. You got two strikes and no balls on you. Maybe you oughta try a lighter bat.'

'Brandy,' I croaked.

'You'll take rye.' He pressed a glass against my lips and I drank thirstily. Then I climbed to my feet again.

The bed, to my astonishment, had not moved. I sat down on it and Henry Eichelberger sat down beside me and patted my shoulder.

'You and me could get along,' he said. 'I never kissed your girl, although I ain't saying I wouldn't like to. Is that all is worrying at you?'

He poured himself half a waterglassful of the whiskey out of the pint bottle which he had gone out to buy. He swallowed the liquor thoughtfully.

'No, there is another matter,' I said.

'Shoot. But no more haymakers. Promise?'

I promised him rather reluctantly. 'Why did you leave the employ of Mrs Penruddock?' I asked him.

He looked at me from under his shaggy blond eyebrows. Then he looked at the bottle he was holding in his hand. 'Would you call me a looker?' he asked.

'Well, Henry—'

'Don't pansy up on me,' he snarled.

'No, Henry, I should not call you very handsome. But unquestionably you are virile.'

He poured another half-waterglassful of whiskey and handed it to me.

'Your turn,' he said. I drank it down without fully realizing what I was doing. When I had stopped coughing Henry took the glass out of my hand and refilled it. He took his own drink moodily. The bottle was now nearly empty.

'Suppose you fell for a dame with all the looks this side of heaven. With a map like mine. A guy like me, a guy from the stockyards that played himself a lot of very tough left end at a cow college and left his looks and education on the scoreboard. A guy that has fought everything but whales and freight hogs—engines to you—and licked 'em all, but naturally had to take a sock now and then. Then I get a job where I see this lovely all the time and every day and know it's no dice. What would you do, pal? Me, I just quit the job.'

'Henry, I'd like to shake your hand,' I said.

He shook hands with me listlessly. 'So I ask for my time,' he said. 'What else would I do?' He held the bottle up and looked at it against the light.

'Bo, you made an error when you had me get this. When I start drinking it's a world cruise. You got plenty dough?'

'Certainly,' I said. 'If whiskey is what you want, Henry, whiskey is what you shall have. I have a very nice apartment on Franklin Avenue in Hollywood and while I cast no aspersions on your own humble and of course quite temporary abode, I now suggest we repair to my apartment, which is a good deal larger and gives one more room to extend one's elbow.' I waved my hand airily.

'Say, you're drunk,' Henry said, with admiration in his small green eyes.

'I am not yet drunk, Henry, although I do in fact feel the effect of that whiskey and very pleasantly. You must not mind my way of talking which is a personal matter, like your own clipped and concise method of speech. But before we depart there is one other rather insignificant detail I wish to discuss with you. I am empowered to arrange for the return of Mrs. Penruddock's pearls. I understand there is some possibility that you may have stolen them.'

'Son, you take some awful chances,' Henry said softly.

'This is a business matter, Henry, and plain talk is the best way to settle it. The pearls are only false pearls, so we should very easily be able to come to an agreement. I mean you no ill will, Henry, and I am obliged to you for procuring the whiskey, but business is business. Will you take fifty dollars and return the pearls and no questions asked?'

Henry laughed shortly and mirthlessly, but he seemed to have no animosity in his voice when he said: 'So you think I stole some marbles and am sitting around here waiting for a flock of dicks to swarm me?'

'No police have been told, Henry, and you may not have known the pearls were false. Pass the liquor, Henry.'

He poured me most of what was left in the bottle, and I drank it down with the greatest good humor. I threw the glass at the mirror, but unfortunately missed. The glass, which was of heavy and cheap construction, fell on the floor and did not break. Henry Eichelberger laughed heartily.

'What are you laughing at, Henry?'

'Nothing,' he said. 'I was just thinking what a

sucker some guy is finding out he is—about them marbles.'

'You mean you did not steal the pearls, Henry?'

He laughed again, a little gloomily. 'Yeah,' he said, 'meaning no. I oughta sock you, but what the hell? Any guy can get a bum idea. No, I didn't steal no pearls, bud. If they was ringers, I wouldn't be bothered, and if they was what they looked like the one time I saw them on the old lady's neck, I wouldn't decidedly be holed up in no cheap flat in LA. Waiting for a couple carloads of johns to put the sneeze on me.'

I reached for his hand again and shook it.

'That is all I required to know,' I said happily. 'Now I am at peace. We shall now go to my apartment and consider ways and means to recover these pearls. You and I together should make a team that can conquer any opposition, Henry.'

'You ain't kidding me, huh?'

I stood up and put my hat on—upside down. 'No, Henry. I am making you an offer of employment which I understand you need, and all the whiskey you can drink. Let us go. Can you drive a car in your condition?'

'Hell, I ain't drunk,' Henry said, looking surprised.

We left the room and walked down the dark hallway. The fat manager very suddenly appeared from some nebulous shade and stood in front of us rubbing his stomach and looking at me with small greedy expectant eyes.

'Everything okey?' he inquired, chewing on a time-darkened toothpick.

'Give him a buck,' Henry said.

'What for, Henry?'

'Oh, I dunno. Just give him a buck.'

I withdrew a dollar bill from my pocket and gave it to the fat man.

'Thanks, pal,' Henry said. He chucked the fat man under the Adam's apple, and removed the dollar bill deftly from between his fingers. 'That pays for the hooch,' he added. 'I hate to have to bum dough.'

We went down the stairs arm in arm, leaving the manager trying to cough the toothpick up from his esophagus.

3

At five o'clock that afternoon I awoke from slumber and found that I was lying on my bed in my apartment in the Chateau Moraine, on Franklin Avenue near Ivar Street, in Hollywood. I turned my head, which ached, and saw that Henry Eichelberger was lying beside me in his undershirt and trousers. I then perceived that I also was as lightly attired. On the table near by there stood an almost full bottle of Old Plantation rye whiskey, the full quart size, and on the floor lay an entirely empty bottle of the same excellent brand. There were garments lying here and there on the floor, and a cigarette had burned a hole in the brocaded arm of one of my easy chairs.

I felt myself over carefully. My stomach was stiff and sore and my jaw seemed a little swollen on one side. Otherwise I was none the worse for wear. A sharp pain darted through my temples as I stood up off the bed, but I ignored it and walked steadily to the bottle on the table and raised it to my lips. After a steady draught of the fiery liquid I suddenly felt much better. A hearty and cheerful mood came over me and I was ready for any adventure. I went back to the bed and shook Henry firmly by the shoulder.

'Wake up, Henry,' I said. 'The sunset hour is nigh. The robins are calling and the squirrels are scolding and the morning glories furl themselves in sleep.'

Like all men of action Henry Eichelberger came awake with his fist doubled. 'What was that crack?' he snarled. 'Oh, yeah. Hi, Walter. How you feel?'

'I feel splendid. Are you rested?'

'Sure.' He swung his shoeless feet to the floor and rumpled his thick blond hair with his fingers. 'We was going swell until you passed out,' he said. 'So I had me a nap. I never drink solo. You O.K.?'

'Yes, Henry, I feel very well indeed. And we have work to do.'

'Swell.' He went to the whiskey bottle and quaffed from it freely. He rubbed his stomach with the flat of his hand. His green eyes shone peacefully.

'I'm a sick man,' he said, 'and I got to take my medicine.' He put the bottle down on the table and surveyed the apartment. 'Geez,' he said, 'we thrown it into us so fast I ain't hardly looked at the dump. You got a nice little place here, Walter. Geez, a white typewriter and a white telephone. What's the matter, kid—you just been confirmed?'

'Just a foolish fancy, Henry,' I said, waving an airy hand. Henry went over and looked at the typewriter and the telephone side by side on my writing desk, and the silver-mounted desk set, each piece chased with my initials.

'Well fixed, huh?' Henry said, turning his green gaze on me.

'Tolerably so, Henry,' I said modestly;

'Well, what next pal? You got any ideas or do we just drink some?'

'Yes, Henry, I do have an idea. With a man like you to help me I think it can be put into practice. I feel that we must, as they say, tap the grapevine. When a string of pearls is stolen, all the underworld knows it at once. Pearls are hard to sell, Henry, inasmuch as they cannot be cut and can be identified by experts, I have read. The underworld will be seething with activity. It should not be too difficult for us to find someone who would send a message to the proper quarter that we are willing to pay a reasonable sum for their return.'

'You talk nice—for a drunk guy,' Henry said, reaching for the bottle. 'But ain't you forgot these marbles are phonies?'

'For sentimental reasons I am quite willing to pay

for their return, just the same.'

Henry drank some whiskey, appeared to enjoy the flavor of it and drank some more. He waved the bottle at me politely.

'That's O.K.—as far as it goes,' he said. 'But this underworld that's doing all this here seething you spoke of ain't going to seethe a hell of a lot over a string of glass beads. Or am I screwy?'

'I was thinking, Henry, that the underworld probably has a sense of humor and the laugh that would go around would be quite emphatic.'

'There's an idea in that,' Henry said. 'Here's some mug finds out lady Penruddock has a string of oyster fruit worth oodles of kale, and he does hisseif a neat little box job and trots down to the fence. And the fence gives him the belly laugh. I would say something like that could get around the poolrooms and start a little idle chatter. So far, so nutty. But this box man is going to dump them beads in a hurry, because he has a three-to-ten on him even if they are only worth a nickel plus sales tax. Breaking and entering is the rap, Walter.'

'However, Henry,' I said, 'there is another element in the situation. If this thief is very stupid, it will not, of course, have much weight. But if he is even moderately intelligent, it will. Mrs Penruddock is a very proud woman and lives in a very exclusive section of the city. If it should become known that she wore imitation pearls, and above all, if it should be even hinted in the public press that these were the very pearls her own husband had given her for her golden wedding present—well, I am sure you see the point, Henry.'

'Box guys ain't too bright,' he said and rubbed his stony chin. Then he lifted his right thumb and bit it thoughtfully. He looked at the windows, at the corner of the room, at the floor. He looked at me from the corners of his eyes.

'Blackmail, huh?' he said. 'Maybe. But crooks don't mix their rackets much. Still, the guy might pass the word along. There's a chance, Walter. I wouldn't care to hock my gold fillings to buy me a piece of it, but there's a chance. How much you figure to put out?'

'A hundred dollars should be ample, but I am willing to go as high as two hundred, which is the actual cost of the imitations.'

Henry shook his head and patronized the bottle. 'Nope. The guy wouldn't uncover hisself for that kind of money. Wouldn't be worth the chance he takes. He'd dump the marbles and keep his nose clean.'

'We can at least try, Henry.'

'Yeah, but where? And we're getting low on liquor. Maybe I better put my shoes on and run out, huh?'

At that very moment, as if in answer to my unspoken prayer, a soft dull thump sounded on the door of my apartment. I opened it and picked up the final edition of the evening paper. I closed the door again and carried the paper back across the room, opening it up as I went. I touched it with my right forefinger and smiled confidently at Henry Eichelberger.

'Here. I will wager you a full quart of Old Plantation that the answer will be on the crime page of this paper.'

'There ain't any crime page,' Henry chortled. 'This is Los Angeles. I'll fade you.'

I opened the paper to page three with some trepidation, for, although I had already seen the item I was looking for in an early edition of the paper while waiting in Ada Twomey's Domestic Employment Agency, I was not certain it would appear intact in the later editions. But my faith was rewarded. It had not been removed, but appeared midway of column three exactly as before.

The paragraph, which was quite short, was headed: LOU GANDESI QUESTIONED IN GEM THEFTS. 'Listen to this, Henry,' I said, and began to read.

Acting on an anonymous tip police late last night picked up Louis C. (Lou) Gandesi, proprietor of a well-known Spring Street tavern, and quizzed him intensively concerning the recent wave of dinner party hold-ups in an exclusive western section of this city, hold-ups during which, it is alleged, more than two hundred thousand dollars' worth of valuable jewels have been torn at gun's point from women guests in fashionable homes. Gandesi was released at a late hour and refused to make any statement to reporters.

'I never kibitz the cops,' he said modestly. Captain William Norgaard, of the General Robbery Detail, announced himself as satisfied that Gandesi had no connection with the robberies, and that the tip was merely an act of personal spite.

I folded the paper and threw it on the bed.

'You win, ho,' Henry said, and handed me the bottle. I took a long drink and returned it to him. 'Now what? Brace this Gandesi and take him through the hoops?'

'He may be a dangerous man, Henry. Do you think we are equal to it?'

Henry snorted contemptuously. 'Yah, a Spring Street punk. Some fat slob with a phony ruby on his mitt. Lead me to him. We'll turn the slob inside out and drain his liver. But we're just about fresh out of liquor. All we got is maybe a pint.' He examined the bottle against the light.

'We have had enough for the moment, Henry.'

'We ain't drunk, are we? I only had seven drinks since I got here, maybe nine.'

'Certainly we are not drunk, Henry, but you take very large drinks, and we have a difficult evening before us. I think we should now get shaved and dressed, and I further think that we should wear dinner clothes. I have an extra suit which will fit you admirably, as we are almost exactly the same size. It is certainly a remarkable omen that two such large men should be associated in the same enterprise. Evening clothes impress these low characters, Henry.'

'Swell,' Henry said. 'They'll think we're mugs workin' for some big shot. This Gandesi will be scared enough to swallow his necktie.'

We decided to do as I had suggested and I laid out clothes for Henry, and while he was bathing and shaving I telephoned to Ellen Macintosh.

'Oh, Walter, I am so glad you called up,' she cried. 'Have you found anything?'

'Not yet, darling,' I said. 'But we have an idea. Henry and I are just about to put it into execution.'

'Henry, Walter? Henry who?'

'Why, Henry Eichelberger, of course, darling. Have you forgotten him so soon? Henry and I are warm friends and we—'

She interrupted me coldly. 'Are you drinking, Walter?' she demanded in a very distant voice.

'Certainly not, darling. Henry is a teetotaler.'

She sniffed sharply. I could hear the sound distinctly over the telephone.

'But didn't Henry take the pearls?' she asked, after quite a long pause.

'Henry, angel? Of course not. Henry left because he was in love with you.'

'Oh, Walter. That ape? I'm sure you're drinking terribly. I don't ever want to speak to you again. Goodbye.' And she hung the phone up very sharply so that a painful sensation made itself felt in my ear.

I sat down in a chair with a bottle of Old Plantation in my hand wondering what I had said that could be construed as offensive or indiscreet. As I was unable to think of anything, I consoled myself with the bottle until Henry came out of the bathroom looking extremely personable in one of my pleated shirts and a wing collar and black bow tie.

It was dark when we left the apartment and I, at least, was full of hope and confidence, although a little depressed by the way Ellen Macintosh had spoken to me over the telephone.

4

Mr Gandesi's establishment was not difficult to find, inasmuch as the first taxicab driver Henry yelled at on Spring Street directed us to it. It was called the Blue Lagoon and its interior was bathed in an unpleasant blue light.

Henry and I entered it steadily, since we had consumed a partly solid meal at Mandy's Caribbean Grotto before starting out to find Mr Gandesi. Henry looked almost handsome in my second-best dinner suit, with a fringed white scarf hanging over his shoulder, a lightweight black felt hat on the back of his head (which was only a little larger than mine), and a bottle of whiskey in each of the side pockets of the summer overcoat he was wearing.

The bar of the Blue Lagoon was crowded, but Henry and I went on back to the small dim dining room behind it. A man in a dirty dinner suit came up to us and Henry asked him for Gandesi, and he pointed out a fat man who sat alone at a small table in the far corner of the room. We went that way.

The man sat with a small glass of red wine in front of him and slowly twisted a large green stone on his finger. He did not look up. There were no other chairs at the table, so Henry leaned on it with both elbows.

'You Gandesi?' he said.

The man did not look up even then. He moved his thick black eyebrows together and said in an absent voice: 'Si. Yes.'

'We got to talk to you in private,' Henry told him. Where we won't be disturbed.'

Gandesi looked up now and there was extreme boredom in his flat black almond-shaped eyes. 'So?' he asked and shrugged. 'Eet ees about what?'

'About some pearls,' Henry said. 'Forty-nine on the string, matched and pink.'

'You sell—or you buy?' Gandesi inquired and his chin began to shake up and down as if with amusement.

'Buy,' Henry said.

The man at the table crooked his finger quietly and a very large waiter appeared at his side. 'Ees dronk,' he said lifelessly. 'Put dees men out.'

The waiter took hold of Henry's shoulder. Henry reached up carelessly and took hold of the waiter's hand and twisted it. The waiter's face in that bluish light turned some color I could not describe, but which was not at all healthy. He let out a low moan. Henry dropped the hand and said to me: 'Put a C-note on the table.'

I took my wallet out and extracted from it one of

the two hundred-dollar bills I had taken the precaution to obtain from the cashier at the Chateau Moraine. Gandesi stared at the bill and made a gesture to the large waiter, who went away rubbing his hand and holding it tight against his chest.

'What for?' Gandesi asked.

'Five minutes of your time alone.'

'Ees very fonny. O.K., I bite.' Gandesi took the bill and folded it neatly and put it in his vest pocket. Then he put both hands on the table and pushed himself heavily to his feet. He started to waddle away without looking at us.

Henry and I followed him among the crowded tables to the far side of the dining room and through a door in the wainscoting and then down a narrow dim hallway. At the end of this Gandesi opened a door into a lighted room and stood holding it for us, with a grave smile on his olive face. I went in first.

As Henry passed in front of Gandesi into the room the latter, with surprising agility, took a small shiny black leather club from his clothes and hit Henry on the head with it very hard. Henry sprawled forward on his hands and knees. Gandesi shut the door of the room very quickly for a man of his build and leaned against it with the small club in his left hand. Now, very suddenly, in his right hand appeared a short but heavy black revolver.

'Ees very fonny,' he said politely, and chuckled to himself.

Exactly what happened then I did not see clearly. Henry was at one instant on his hands and knees with his back to Gandesi. In the next, or possibly even in the same instant, something swirled like a big fish in water and Gandesi grunted. I then saw that Henry's hard blond head was buried in Gandesi's stomach and that Henry's large hands held both of Gandesi's hairy wrists.

Then Henry straightened his body to its full height and Gandesi was high up in the air balanced on top of Henry's head, his mouth strained wide open and his face a dark purple color. Then Henry shook himself, as it seemed, quite lightly, and Gandesi landed on his back on the floor with a terrible thud and lay gasping. Then a key turned in the door and Henry stood with his back to it, holding both the club and the revolver in his left hand, and solicitously feeling the pockets which contained our supply of whiskey. All this happened with such rapidity that I leaned against the side wall and felt a little sick at my stomach.

'A gut-buster,' Henry drawled. 'A comedian. Wait'll I loosen my belt.'

Gandesi rolled over and got to his feet very slowly and painfully and stood swaying and passing his hand up and down his face. His clothes were covered with dust.

'This here's a sap,' Henry said, showing me the small black club. 'He hit me with it, didn't he?'

'Why, Henry, don't you know?' I inquired.

'I just wanted to be sure,' Henry said. 'You don't do

that to the Eichelbergers.'

'O.K., what you boys want?' Gandesi asked abruptly, with no trace whatever of his Italian accent.

'I told you what we wanted, dough-face.'

'I don't think I know you boys,' Gandesi said and lowered his body with care into a wooden chair beside a shabby office desk. He mopped his face and neck and felt himself in various places.

'You got the wrong idea, Gandesi. A lady living in Carondelet Park lost a forty-nine bead pearl necklace a couple of days back. A box job, but a pushover. Our outfit's carrying a little insurance on those marbles. And I'll take that C note.'

He walked over to Gandesi and Gandesi quickly reached the folded bill from his pocket and handed it to him. Henry gave me the bill and I put it back in my wallet.

'I don't think I hear about it,' Gandesi said carefully.

'You hit me with a sap,' Henry said. 'Listen kind of hard.'

Gandesi shook his head and then winced. 'I don't back no petermen,' he said, 'nor no heist guys. You got me wrong.'

'Listen hard,' Henry said in a low voice. 'You might hear something.' He swung the small black club lightly in front of his body with two fingers of his right hand. The slightly too small hat was still on the back of his head, although a little crumpled.

'Henry,' I said, 'you seem to be doing all the work

this evening. Do you think that is quite fair?'

'O.K., work him over,' Henry said. 'These fat guys bruise something lovely.'

By this time Gandesi had become a more natural color and was gazing at us steadily. 'Insurance guys, huh?' he inquired dubiously.

'You said it, dough-face.'

'You try Melachrino?' Gandesi asked.

'Haw,' Henry began raucously, 'a gut-buster. A—' but I interrupted him sharply.

'One moment, Henry,' I said. Then turning to Gandesi, 'Is this Melachrino a person?' I asked him.

Gandesi's eyes rounded in surprise. 'Sure—a guy. You don't know him, huh?' A look of dark suspicion was born in his shoeblack eyes, but vanished almost as soon as it appeared.

'Phone him,' Henry said, pointing to the instrument which stood on the shabby office desk.

'Phone is bad,' Gandesi objected thoughtfully.

'So is sap poison,' Henry said. Gandesi sighed and turned his thick body in the chair and drew the telephone towards him. He dialed a number with an inky nail and listened.

After an interval he said: 'Joe?…Lou. Couple insurance guys tryin' to deal on a Carondelet Park job…Yeah…No, marbles…You ain't heard a whisper, huh?…O.K., Joe.'

Gandesi replaced the phone and swung around in the chair again. He studied us with sleepy eyes. 'No soap. What insurance outfit you boys work for?'

'Give him a card,' Henry said to me.

I took my wallet out once more and withdrew one of my cards from it. It was an engraved calling card and contained nothing but my name. So I used my pocket pencil to write, Chateau Moraine Apartments, Franklin near Ivar, below the name. I showed the card to Henry and then gave it to Gandesi. Gandesi read the card and quietly bit his finger. His face brightened suddenly.

'You boys better see Jack Lawler,' he said.

Henry stared at him closely. Gandesi's eyes were now bright and unblinking and guileless.

'Who's he?' Henry asked.

'Runs the Penguin Club. Out on the Strip—Eighty-six Forty-four Sunset or some number like that. He can find out, if any guy can.'

'Thanks,' Henry said quietly. He glanced at me. 'You believe him?'

'Well, Henry,' I said, 'I don't really think he would be above telling us an untruth.'

'Haw!' Gandesi began suddenly. 'A gut-buster! A—'

'Can it!' Henry snarled. 'That's my line. Straight goods, is it, Gandesi? About this Jack Lawler?'

Gandesi nodded vigorously. 'Straight goods, absolute. Jack Lawler got a finger in everything high class that's touched. But he ain't easy to see.'

'Don't worry none about that. Thanks, Gandesi.'

Henry tossed the black club into the corner of the

room and broke open the breech of the revolver he had been holding all this time in his left hand. He ejected the shells and then bent down and slid the gun along the floor until it disappeared under the desk. He tossed the cartridges idly in his hand for a moment and then let them spill on the floor.

'So long, Gandesi,' he said coldly. 'And keep that schnozzle of yours clean, if you don't want to be looking for it under the bed.'

He opened the door then and we both went out quickly and left the Blue Lagoon without interference from any of the employees.

5

My car was parked a short distance away down the block. We entered it and Henry leaned his arms on the wheel and stared moodily through the windshield.

'Well, what you think, Walter?' he inquired at length.

'If you ask my opinion, Henry, I think Mr Gandesi told us a cock-and-bull story merely to get rid of us. Furthermore I do not believe he thought we were insurance agents.'

'Me too, and an extra helping,' Henry said. 'I don't figure there's any such guy as this Melachrino or this Jack Lawler and this Gandesi called up some dead number and had himself a phony chin with it. I oughta go back there and pull his arms and legs off. The hell with the fat slob.'

'We had the best idea we could think of, Henry, and we executed it to the best of our ability. I now suggest that we return to my apartment and try to think of something else.'

'And get drunk,' Henry said, starting the car and guiding it away from the curb.

'We could perhaps have a small allowance of liquor, Henry.'

'Yah!' Henry snorted. 'A stall. I oughta go back there and wreck the joint.'

He stopped at the intersection, although no traffic signal was in operation at the time; and raised a bottle of whiskey to his lips. He was in the act of drinking when a car came up behind us and collided with our car, but not very severely. Henry choked and lowered his bottle, spilling some of the liquor on his garments.

'This town's getting too crowded,' he snarled. 'A guy can't take hisself a drink without some smart monkey bumps his elbow.'

Whoever it was in the car behind us blew a horn with some insistence, inasmuch as our car had not yet moved forward. Henry wrenched the door open and got out and went back. I heard voices of considerable loudness, the louder being Henry's voice. He came back after a moment and got into the car and drove on.

'I oughta have pulled his mush off,' he said, 'but I went soft,' He drove rapidly the rest of the way to Hollywood and the Chateau Moraine and we went up to my apartment and sat down with large glasses in our hands.

'We got better than a quart and a half of hooch,' Henry said, looking at the two bottles which he had placed on the table beside others which had long since been emptied. 'That oughta be good for an idea.'

'If it isn't enough, Henry, there is an abundant further supply where it came from,' I drained my glass cheerfully.

'You seem a right guy,' Henry said. 'What makes you always talk so funny?'

'I cannot seem to change my speech, Henry. My father and mother were both severe purists in the New England tradition, and the vernacular has never come naturally to my lips, even while I was in college.'

Henry made an attempt to digest this remark, but I could see that it lay somewhat heavily on his stomach.

We talked for a time concerning Gandesi and the doubtful quality of his advice, and thus passed perhaps half an hour. Then rather suddenly the white telephone on my desk began to ring. I hurried over to it, hoping that it was Ellen Macintosh and that she had recovered from her ill humor. But it proved to be a male voice and a strange one to me. It spoke crisply, with an

unpleasant metallic quality of tone.

'You Walter Gage?'

'This is Mister Gage speaking.'

'Well, *Mister* Gage, I understand you're in the market for some jewelry.'

I held the phone very tightly and turned my body and made grimaces to Henry over the top of the instrument. But he was moodily pouring himself another large portion of Old Plantation.

'That is so,' I said into the telephone, trying to keep my voice steady, although my excitement was almost too much for me. 'If by jewelry you mean pearls.'

'Forty-nine in a rope, brother, And five grand is the price.'

'Why that is entirely absurd,' I gasped. 'Five thousand dollars for those—'

The voice broke in on me rudely. 'You heard me, brother. Five grand. Just hold up the hand and count the fingers. No more, no less. Think it over. I'll call you later.'

The phone clicked dryly and I replaced the instrument shakily in its cradle.

I was trembling. I walked back to my chair and sat down and wiped my face with my handkerchief.

'Henry,' I said in a low tense voice, 'it worked. But how strangely.'

Henry put his empty glass down on the floor. It was the first time that I had ever seen him put an empty glass down and leave it empty. He stared at me closely with his tight unblinking green eyes.

'Yeah?' he said gently. 'What worked, kid?' He licked his lips slowly with the tip of his tongue.

'What we accomplished down at Gandesi's place, Henry. A man just called me on the telephone and asked me if I was in the market for pearls.'

'Geez.' Henry pursed his lips and whistled gently. 'That damn dago had something after all.'

'But the price is five thousand dollars, Henry. That seems beyond reasonable explanation.'

'Huh?' Henry's eyes seemed to bulge as if they were about to depart from their orbits. 'Five grand for them ringers? The guy's nuts. They cost two C's, you said. Bugs completely is what the guy is. Five grand? Why, for five grand I could buy me enough phony pearls to cover an elephant's caboose.'

I could see that Henry seemed puzzled. He refilled our glasses silently and we stared at each other over them. 'Well, what the heck can you do with that, Walter?' he asked after a long silence.

'Henry,' I said firmly, 'there is only one thing to do. It is true that Ellen Macintosh spoke to me in confidence, and as she did not have Mrs Penruddock's express permission to tell me about the pearls, I suppose I should respect that confidence. But Ellen is now angry with me and does not wish to speak to me, for the reason that I am drinking whiskey in considerable quantities, although my speech and brain are still reasonably clear. This last is a very strange development and I think, in spite of everything, some close friend of the family should be consulted. Preferably of course, a man, someone of large business experience, and in addition to that a man who understands about jewels. There is such a man, Henry, and tomorrow morning I shall call upon him.'

'Geez,' Henry said. 'You coulda said all that in nine words, bo. Who is this guy?'

'His name is Mr Lansing Gallemore, and he is president of the Gallemore Jewelry Company on Seventh Street. He is a very old friend of Mrs Penruddock—Ellen has often mentioned him—and is, in fact, the very man who procured for her the imitation pearls.'

'But this guy will tip the bulls,' Henry objected.

'I do not think so, Henry. I do not think he will do anything to embarrass Mrs Penruddock in any way.'

Henry shrugged. 'Phonies are phonies,' he said. 'You can't make nothing else outa them. Not even no president of no jewlery store can't.'

'Nevertheless, there must be a reason why so large a sum is demanded, Henry. The only reason that occurs to me is blackmail and, frankly, that is a little too much for me to handle alone, because I do not know enough about the background of the Penruddock family.'

'Okey,' Henry said, sighing. 'If that's your hunch, you better follow it, Walter. And I better breeze on home and flop so as to be in good shape for the rough work, if any.'

'You would not care to pass the night here, Henry?'

'Thanks, pal, but I'm O.K. Back at the hotel. I'll just take this spare bottle of the tiger sweat to put me to sleep. I might happen to get a call from the agency in the A.M. And would have to brush my teeth and go after it. And I guess I better change my duds back to where I can mix with the common people.'

So saying he went into the bathroom and in a short time emerged wearing his own blue serge suite. I urged him to take my car, but he said it would not be safe in his neighborhood. He did, however, consent to use the topcoat he had been wearing and, placing in it carefully the unopened quart of whiskey, he shook me warmly by the hand.

'One moment, Henry,' I said and took out my wallet. I extended a twentydollar bill to him.

'What's that in favor of?' he growled.

'You are temporarily out of employment, Henry, and you have done a noble piece of work this evening, puzzling as are the results. You should be rewarded and I can well afford this small token.'

'Well, thanks, pal,' Henry said. 'But it's just a loan.' His voice was gruff with emotion. 'Should I give you a buzz in the A.M.?'

'By all means. And there is one thing more that has occurred to me. Would it not be advisable for you to change your hotel? Suppose, through no fault of mine, the police learn of this theft. Would they not at least suspect you?'

'Hell, they'd bounce me up and down for hours,' Henry said. 'But what'll it get them? I ain't no ripe peach.'

'It is for you to decide, of course, Henry.'

'Yeah. Good night, pal, and don't have no nightmares.'

He left me then and I felt suddenly very depressed and lonely. Henry's company had been very stimulating to me, in spite of his rough way of talking. He was very much of a man. I poured myself a rather large drink of whiskey from the remaining bottle and drank it quickly but gloomily. The effect was such that I had an overmastering desire to speak to Ellen Macintosh at all costs. I went to the telephone and called her number.

After a long wait a sleepy maid answered. But Ellen, upon hearing my name, refused to come to the telephone. That depressed me still further and I finished the rest of the whiskey almost without noticing what I was doing. I then lay down on the bed and fell into fitful slumber.

6

The busy ringing of the telephone awoke me and I saw that the morning sunlight was streaming into the room. It was nine o'clock and all the lamps were still burning. I arose feeling a little stiff and dissipated, for I was still wearing my dinner suit. But I am a healthy man with very steady nerves and I did not feel as badly as I expected. I went to the telephone and answered it.

Henry's voice said: 'How you feel, pal? I got a hangover like twelve Swedes.'

'Not too badly, Henry.'

'I got a call from the agency about a job. I better go down and take a gander at it. Should I drop around later?'

'Yes, Henry, by all means do that. By eleven o'clock I should be back from the errand about which I spoke to you last night.'

'Any more calls from you know?'

'Not yet, Henry.'

'Check. Abyssinia.' He hung up and I took a cold shower and shaved and dressed. I donned a quiet brown business suit and had some coffee sent up from the coffee shop downstairs. I also had the waiter remove the empty bottles from my apartment and gave him a dollar for his trouble.

After drinking two cups of black coffee I felt my own man once more and drove downtown to the Gallemore Jewelry Company's large and brilliant store on West Seventh Street. It was another bright, golden morning and it seemed that somehow things should adjust themselves on so pleasant a day.

Mr Lansing Gallemore proved to be a little difficult to see, so that I was compelled to tell his secretary that it was a matter concerning Mrs Penruddock and of a confidential nature. Upon this message being carried in to him I was at once ushered into a long paneled office, at the far end of which Mr Gallemore stood behind a massive desk. He extended a thin pink hand to me.

'Mr Gage? I don't believe we have met, have we?'

'No, Mr Gallemore, I do not believe we have. I am the fiancé—or was until last night—of Miss Ellen Macintosh, who, as you probably know, is Mrs Penruddock's nurse. I am come to you upon a very delicate matter and it is necessary that I ask for your confidence before I speak.'

He was a man of perhaps seventy-five years of age, and very thin and tall and correct and well preserved. He had cold blue eyes but a warming smile. He was attired youthfully enough in a gray flannel suit with a red carnation at his lapel.

'That is something I make it a rule never to promise, Mr Gage,' he said.

'I think it is almost always a very unfair request. But if you assure me the matter concerns Mrs Penruddock and is really of a delicate and confidential nature, I will make an exception.'

'It is indeed, Mr Gallemore,' I said, and thereupon told him the entire story, concealing nothing, not even the fact that I had consumed far too much whiskey the day before.

He stared at me curiously at the end of my story. His finely shaped hand picked up an old-fashioned white quill pen and he slowly tickled his right ear with the feather of it.

'Mr Gage,' he said, 'can't you guess why they ask five thousand dollars for that string of pearls?'

'If you permit me to guess, in a matter of so personal a nature, I could perhaps hazard an explanation, Mr Gallemore.'

He moved the white feather around to his left ear and nodded. 'Go ahead, son.'

'The pearls are in fact real, Mr Gallemore. You are

a very old friend of Mrs Penruddock—perhaps even a childhood sweetheart. When she gave you her pearls, her golden wedding present, to sell because she was in sore need of money for a generous purpose, you did not sell them, Mr Gallemore. You only pretended to sell them. You gave her twenty thousand dollars of your own money, and you returned the real pearls to her, pretending that they were an imitation made in Czechoslovakia.'

'Son, you think a lot smarter than you talk,' Mr Gallemore said. He arose and walked to a window, pulled aside a fine net curtain and looked down on the bustle of Seventh Street. He came back to his desk and seated himself and smiled a little wistfully.

'You are almost embarrassingly correct, Mr Gage,' he said, and sighed.

'Mrs Penruddock is a very proud woman, or I should simply have offered her the twenty thousand dollars as an unsecured loan. I happened to be the co-administrator of Mr Penruddock's estate and I knew that in the condition of the financial market at that time it would be out of the question to raise enough cash, without damaging the corpus of the estate beyond reason, to care for all those relatives and pensioners. So Mrs Penruddock sold her pearls—as she thought—but she insisted that no one should know about it. And I did what you have guessed. It was unimportant. I could afford the gesture. I have never married, Gage, and I am rated a wealthy man. As a matter of fact, at that time, the pearls would not have fetched more than half of what I gave her, or of what they should bring today.'

I lowered my eyes for fear this kindly old gentleman might be troubled by my direct gaze.

'So I think we had better raise that five thousand, son,' Mr Gallemore at once added in a brisk voice. 'The price is pretty low, although stolen pearls are a great deal more difficult to deal in than cut stones. If I should care to trust you that far on your face, do you think you could handle the assignment?'

'Mr Gallemore,' I said firmly but quietly, 'I am a total stranger to you and I am only flesh and blood. But I promise you by the memories of my dead and revered parents that there will be no cowardice.'

'Well, there is a good deal of the flesh and blood, son,' Mr Gallemore said kindly. 'And I am not afraid of your stealing the money, because possibly I know a little more about Miss Ellen Macintosh and her boy friend than you might suspect. Furthermore, the pearls are insured, in my name, of course, and the insurance company should really handle this affair. But you and your funny friend seem to have got along very nicely so far, and I believe in playing out a hand. This Henry must be quite a man.'

'I have grown very attached to him, in spite of his uncouth ways,' I said. Mr Gallemore played with his white quill pen a little longer and then he brought out a large checkbook and wrote a check, which he carefully blotted and passed across the desk.

'If you get the pearls, I'll see that the insurance people refund this to me,' he said. 'If they like my business, there will be no difficulty about that. The bank is down at the corner and I will be waiting for their call. They won't cash the check without telephoning me, probably. Be careful, son, and don't get hurt.'

He shook hands with me once more and I hesitated. 'Mr Gallemore, you are placing a greater trust in me than any man ever has,' I said. 'With the exception, of course, of my own father.'

'I am acting like a damn fool,' he said with a peculiar smile. 'It is so long since I heard anyone talk the way Jane Austen writes that it is making a sucker out of me.'

'Thank you, sir. I know my language is a bit stilted. Dare I ask you to do me a small favor, sir?'

'What is it, Gage?'

'To telephone Miss Ellen Macintosh, from whom I am now a little estranged, and tell her that I am not drinking today, and that you have entrusted me with a very delicate mission.'

He laughed aloud. 'I'll be glad to, Walter. And as I know she can be trusted, I'll give her an idea of what's going on.'

I left him then and went down to the bank with the check, and the teller, after looking at me suspiciously, then absenting himself from his cage for a long time, finally counted out the money in hundred-dollar bills with the reluctance one might have expected, if it had been his own money.

I placed the flat packet of bills in my pocket and said: 'Now give me a roll of quarters, please.'

'A roll of quarters, sir?' His eyebrows lifted.

'Exactly. I use them for tips. And naturally I should prefer to carry them home in the wrappings.'

'Oh, I see. Ten dollars, please.'

I took the fat hard roll of coins and dropped it into my pocket and drove back to Hollywood.

Henry was waiting for me in the lobby of the Chateau Moraine, twirling his hat between his rough hard hands. His face looked a little more deeply lined than it had the day before and I noticed that his breath smelled of whiskey. We went up to my apartment and he turned to me eagerly.

'Any luck, pal?'

'Henry,' I said, 'before we proceed further into this day I wish it clearly understood that I am not drinking. I see that already you have been at the bottle.'

'Just a pick-up, Walter,' he said a little contritely. 'That job I went out for was gone before I got there. What's the good word?'

I sat down and lit a cigarette and stared at him evenly. 'Well, Henry, I don't really know whether I should tell you or not. But it seems a little petty not to do so after all you did last night to Gandesi.' I hesitated a moment longer while Henry stared at me and pinched the muscles of his left arm.

'The pearls are real, Henry. And I have instructions

to proceed with the business and I have five thousand dollars in cash in my pocket at this moment.'

I told him briefly what had happened.

He was more amazed than words could tell. 'Cripes!' he exclaimed, his mouth hanging wide open. 'You mean you got the five grand from this Gallemore—just like that?'

'Precisely that, Henry.'

'Kid,' he said earnestly, 'You got something with that daisy pan and that fluff talk that a lot of guys would give important dough to cop. Five grand—out of a business guy—just like that. Why, I'll be a monkey's uncle. I'll be a snake's daddy. I'll be a mickey finn at a woman's-club lunch.'

At that exact moment, as if my entrance to the building had been observed, the telephone rang again and I sprang to answer it.

It was one of the voices I was awaiting, but not the one I wanted to hear with the greater longing. 'How's it looking to you this morning, Gage?'

'It is looking better,' I said. 'If I can have any assurance of honorable treatment, I am prepared to go through with it.'

'You mean you got the dough?'

'In my pocket at this exact moment.'

The voice seemed to exhale a slow breath. 'You'll get your marbles O.K.—if we get the price, Gage. We're in this business for a long time and we don't welsh. If we did, it would soon get around and nobody would play with us any more.'

'Yes, I can readily understand that,' I said. 'Proceed with your instructions,' I added coldly.

'Listen close, Gage. Tonight at eight sharp you be in Pacific Palisades. Know where that is?'

'Certainly. It is a small residential section west of the polo fields on Sunset Boulevard.'

'Right. Sunset goes slap through it. There's one drugstore there—open till nine. Be there waiting a call at eight sharp tonight. Alone. And I mean alone, Gage. No cops and no strongarm guys. It's rough country down there and we got a way to get you to where we want you and know if you're alone. Get all this?'

'I am not entirely an idiot,' I retorted.

'No dummy packages, Gage. The dough will be checked. No guns. You'll be searched and there's enough of us to cover you from all angles. We know your car. No funny business, no smart work, no slip-up and nobody hurt. That's the way we do business. How's the dough fixed?'

'One-hundred-dollar bills,' I said. 'And only a few of them are new.'

'Attaboy. Eight o'clock then. Be smart, Gage.'

The phone clicked in my ear and I hung up. It rang again almost instantly.

This time it was the one voice.

'Oh, Walter,' Ellen cried, 'I was so mean to you! Please forgive me, Walter. Mr Gallemore has told me everything and I'm so frightened.'

'There is nothing of which to be frightened,' I told her warmly. 'Does Mrs Penruddock know, darling?'

'No, darling. Mr Gallemore told me not to tell her. I am phoning from a store down on Sixth Street. Oh, Walter, I really am frightened. Will Henry go with you?'

'I am afraid not, darling. The arrangements are all made and they will not permit it. I must go alone.'

'Oh, Walter! I'm terrified. I can't bear the suspense.'

'There is nothing to fear,' I assured her. 'It is a simple business transaction. And I am not exactly a midget.'

'But, Walter—oh, I *will* try to be brave, Walter. Will you promise me just one teensy-weensy little thing?'

'Not a drop, darling,' I said firmly. 'Not a single solitary drop.'

'Oh, Walter!'

There was a little more of that sort of thing, very pleasant to me in the circumstances, although possibly not of great interest to others. We finally parted with my promise to telephone as soon as the meeting between the crooks and myself had been consummated.

I turned from the telephone to find Henry drinking deeply from a bottle he had taken from his hip pocket.

'Henry!' I cried sharply.

He looked at me over the bottle with a shaggy determined look. 'Listen, pal,' he said in a low hard voice. 'I got enough of your end of the talk to figure the set-up. Some place out in the tall weeds and you go alone and they feed you the old sap poison and take your dough and leave you lying—with the marbles still in their kitty. Nothing doing, pal. I said—nothing doing!' He almost shouted the last words.

'Henry, it is my duty and I must do it,' I said quietly.

'Haw!' Henry snorted. 'I say no. You're a nut, but you're a sweet guy on the side. I say no. Henry Eichelberger of the Wisconsin Eichelbergers—in fact, I might just as leave say of the Milwaukee Eichelbergers—says no. And he says it with both hands working.' He drank again from his bottle.

'You certainly will not help matters by becoming intoxicated,' I told him rather bitterly.

He lowered the bottle and looked at me with amazement written all over his rugged features. 'Drunk, Walter?' he boomed. 'Did I hear you say drunk? An Eichelberger drunk? Listen, son. We ain't got a lot of time now. It would take maybe three months. Some day when you got three months and maybe five thousand gallons of whiskey and a funnel, I would be glad to take my own time and show you what an Eichelberger looks like when drunk. You wouldn't believe it. Son, there wouldn't be nothing left of this town but a few sprung girders and a lot of busted bricks, in the middle of which—Geez, I'll get talking English myself if I hang around you much longer—in the middle of which, peaceful, with no human life nearer than maybe fifty miles, Henry Eichelberger will be on his back smiling at the sun. Drunk, Walter. Not stinking drunk, not even country-club drunk. But you could use the word drunk and I wouldn't take no offense.'

He sat down and drank again. I stared moodily at the floor. There was nothing for me to say.

'But that,' Henry said, 'is some other time. Right now I am just taking my medicine. I ain't myself without a slight touch of delirium tremens, as the guy says. I was brought up on it. And I'm going with you, Walter. Where is this place at?'

'It's down near the beach, Henry, and you are not going with me. If you must get drunk—get drunk, but you are not going with me.'

'You got a big car, Walter. I'll hide in back on the floor under a rug. It's a cinch.'

'No, Henry.'

'Walter, you are a sweet guy,' Henry said, 'and I am going with you into this frame. Have a smell from the barrel, Walter. You look to me kind of frail.'

We argued for an hour and my head ached and I began to feel very nervous and tired. It was then that I made what might have been a fatal mistake. I succumbed to Henry's blandishments and took a small portion of whiskey, purely for medicinal purposes. This made me feel so much more relaxed that I took another and larger portion. I had had no food except coffee that morning and only a very light dinner the evening before. At the end of another hour Henry had been out for two more bottles of whiskey and I was as bright as a bird. All difficulties had now disappeared and I had agreed heartily that Henry should lie in the back of my car hidden by a rug and accompany me to the rendezvous. We had passed the time very pleasantly until two o'clock, at which hour I began to feel sleepy and lay down on the bed, and fell into a deep slumber.

7

When I awoke again it was almost dark. I rose from the bed with panic in my heart, and also a sharp shoot of pain through my temples. It was only six-thirty, however. I was alone in the apartment and lengthening shadows were stealing across the floor. The display of empty whiskey bottles on the table was very disgusting. Henry Eichelberger was nowhere to be seen. With an instinctive pang, of which I was almost immediately ashamed, I hurried to my jacket hanging on the back of a chair and plunged my hand into the inner breast pocket. The packet of bills was there intact. After a brief hesitation, and with a feeling of secret guilt, I drew them out and slowly counted them over. Not a bill was missing. I replaced the money and tried to smile at myself for this lack of trust, and then switched on a light and went into the bathroom to take alternate hot and cold showers until my brain was once more comparatively clear.

I had done this and was dressing in fresh linen when a key turned in the lock and Henry Eichelberger entered with two wrapped bottles under his arm. He looked at me with what I thought was genuine affection.

'A guy that can sleep it off like you is a real champ, Walter,' he said admiringly. 'I snuck your keys so as not to wake you. I had to get some eats and some more hooch. I done a little solo drinking, which as I told you is against my principles, but this is a big day. However, we take it easy from now on as to the hooch. We can't afford no jitters till it's all over.'

He had unwrapped a bottle while he was speaking and poured me a small drink. I drank it gratefully and immediately felt a warm glow in my veins.

'I bet you looked in your poke for that deck of mazuma,' Henry said, grinning at me.

I felt myself reddening, but I said nothing. 'Okay, pal, you done right. What the heck do you know about Henry Eichelberger anyways? I done something else.' He reached behind him and drew a short automatic from his hip pocket. 'If these boys wanta play rough,' he said, 'I got me five bucks worth of iron that don't mind playin' rough a little itself. And the Eichelbergers ain't missed a whole lot of the guys they shot at.'

'I don't like that, Henry,' I said severely. 'That is contrary to the agreement.'

'Nuts to the agreement,' Henry said. 'The boys get their dough and no cops. I'm out to see that they hand over them marbles and don't pull any fast footwork.'

I saw there was no use arguing with him, so I completed my dressing and prepared to leave the apartment. We each took one more drink and then Henry put a full bottle in his pocket and we left.

On the way down the hall to the elevator he explained in a low voice: 'I got a hack out front to tail you, just in case these boys got the same idea. You might circle a few quiet blocks so as I can find out. More like they don't pick you up till down close to the beach.'

'All this must be costing you a great deal of money, Henry,' I told him, and while we were waiting for the elevator to come up I took another twenty-dollar bill from my wallet and offered it to him. He took the money reluctantly, but finally folded it and placed it in his pocket.

I did as Henry had suggested, driving up and down a number of the hilly streets north of Hollywood Boulevard, and presently I heard the unmistakable hoot of a taxicab horn behind me. I pulled over to the side of the road. Henry got out of the cab and paid off the driver and got into my car beside me.

'All clear,' he said. 'No tail. I'll just keep kind of slumped down and you better stop somewhere for some groceries on account of if we have to get rough with these mugs, a full head of steam will help.'

So I drove westward and dropped down to Sunset Boulevard and presently stopped at a crowded drive-in restaurant where we sat at the counter and ate a light meal of omelette and black coffee. We then proceeded on our way. When we reached Beverly Hills, Henry again made me wind in and out through a number of residential streets where he observed very carefully through the rear window of the car.

Fully satisfied at last we drove back to Sunset, and without incident onwards through Bel-Air and the fringes of Westwood, almost as far as the Riviera Polo field. At this point, down in the hollow, there is a canyon called Mandeville Canyon, a very quiet place. Henry had me drive up this for a short distance. We then stopped and had a little whiskey from his bottle and he climbed into the back of the car and curled his big body up on the floor, with the rug over him and his automatic pistol and his bottle down on the floor conveniently to his hand. That done I once more resumed my journey.

Pacific Palisades is a district whose inhabitants seem to retire rather early. When I reached what might be called the business center nothing was open but the drugstore beside the bank. I parked the car, with Henry remaining silent under the rug in the back, except for a slight gurgling noise I noticed as I stood on the dark pavement. Then I went into the drugstore and saw by its clock that it was now fifteen minutes to eight. I bought a package of cigarettes and lit one and took up my position near the open telephone booth.

The druggist, a heavy-set red-faced man of uncertain age, had a small radio up very loud and was listening to some foolish serial. I asked him to turn it down, as I was expecting an important telephone call. This he did, but not with any good grace, and immediately retired to the back part of his store whence I saw him looking out at me malignantly through a small glass window.

At precisely one minute to eight by the drugstore clock the phone rang sharply in the booth. I hastened into it and pulled the door tight shut. I lifted the receiver, trembling a little in spite of myself.

It was the same cool metallic voice. 'Gage?'

'This is Mr Gage.'

'You done just what I told you?'

'Yes,' I said. 'I have the money in my pocket and I am entirely alone.' I did not like the feeling of lying so brazenly, even to a thief, but I steeled myself to it.

'Listen, then. Go back about three hundred feet the way you come. Beside the firehouse there's a service station, closed up, painted green and red and white. Beside that, going south, is a dirt road. Follow it three quarters of a mile and you come to a white fence of four-by-four built almost across the road. You can just squeeze your car by at the left side. Dim your lights and get through there and keep going down the little hill into a hollow with sage all around. Park there, cut your lights, and wait. Get it?'

'Perfectly,' I said coldly, 'and it shall be done exactly that way.'

'And listen, pal. There ain't a house in half a mile, and there ain't any folks around at all. You got ten minutes to get there. You're watched right this minute. You get there fast and you get there alone—or you got a trip for biscuits. And don't light no matches or pills nor use no flashlights. On your way.'

The phone went dead and I left the booth. I was scarcely outside the drugstore before the druggist rushed at his radio and turned it up to a booming blare. I got into my car and turned it and drove back along Sunset Boulevard, as directed. Henry was as still as the grave on the floor behind me.

I was now very nervous and Henry had all the liquor which we had brought with us. I reached the firehouse in no time at all and through its front window I could see four firemen playing cards. I turned to the right down the dirt road past the red-and-green-and-white service station and almost at once the night was so still, in spite of the quiet sound of my car, that I could hear the crickets and tree-frogs chirping and trilling in all directions, and from some nearby watery spot came the hoarse croak of a solitary bullfrog.

The road dipped and rose again and far off there was a yellow window. Then ahead of me, ghostly in the blackness of the moonless night, appeared the dim white barrier across the road. I noted the gap at the side and then dimmed my headlamps and steered carefully through it and so on down a rough short hill into an oval-shaped hollow space surrounded by low brush and plentifully littered with empty bottles and cans and pieces of paper. It was entirely deserted, however, at this dark hour.

I stopped my car and shut off the ignition, and the

lights, and sat there motionless, hands on the wheel. Behind me I heard no murmur of sound from Henry. I waited possibly five minutes, although it seemed much longer, but nothing happened. It was very still, very lonely, and I did not feel happy.

Finally there was a faint sound of movement behind me and I looked back to see the pale blur of Henry's face peering at me from under the rug.

His voice whispered huskily. 'Anything stirring, Walter?'

I shook my head at him vigorously and he once more pulled the rug over his face. I heard a faint sound of gurgling. Fully fifteen minutes passed before I dared to move again. By this time the tensity of waiting had made me stiff. I therefore boldly unlatched the door of the car and stepped out upon the rough ground. Nothing happened. I walked slowly back and forth with my hands in my pockets. More and more time dragged by. More than half an hour had now elapsed and I became impatient.

I went to the rear window of the car and spoke softly into the interior.

'Henry, I fear we have been victimized in a very cheap way. I fear very much that this is nothing but a low practical joke on the part of Mr Gandesi in retaliation for the way you handled him last night. There is no one here and only one possible way of arriving. It looks to me like a very unlikely place for the sort of meeting we have been expecting.'

'The son of a bitch!' Henry whispered back, and the gurgling sound was repeated in the darkness of the car. Then there was movement and he appeared free of the rug. The door opened against my body. Henry's head emerged. He looked in all directions his eyes could command. 'Sit down on the running board,' he whispered. 'I'm getting out, If they got a bead on us from them bushes, they'll only see one head.'

I did what Henry suggested and turned my collar up high and pulled my hat down over my eyes. As noiselessly as a shadow Henry stepped out of the car and shut the door without sound and stood before me ranging the limited horizon with his eyes. I could see the dim reflection of light on the gun in his hand. We remained thus for ten more minutes.

Henry then got angry and threw discretion to the winds. 'Suckered!' he snarled. 'You know what happened, Walter?'

'No, Henry. I do not.'

'It was just a tryout, that's what it was. Somewhere along the line these dirty-so-and-so's checked on you to see did you play ball, and then again they checked on you at that drugstore back there. I bet you a pair of solid platinum bicycle wheels that was a long-distance call you caught back there.'

'Yes, Henry, now that you mention it, I am sure it was,' I said sadly.

'There you are, kid. The bums ain't even left town. They are sitting back there beside their plush-lined spittoons giving you the big razzoo. And tomorrow this guy calls you again on the phone and says O.K. So far, but they had to be careful and they will try again tonight maybe out in San Fernando Valley and the price will be upped to ten grand, on account of their extra trouble. I oughta go back there and twist that Gandesi so he would be lookin' up his left pants leg.'

'Well, Henry,' I said, 'after all, I did not do exactly what they told me to, because you insisted on coming with me. And perhaps they are more clever than you think. So I think the best thing now is to go back to town and hope there will be a chance tomorrow to try again. And you must promise me faithfully not to interfere.'

'Nuts!' Henry said angrily. 'Without me along they would take you the way the cat took the canary. You are a sweet guy, Walter, but you don't know as many answers as Baby Leroy. These guys are thieves and they have a string of marbles that might probably bring them twenty grand with careful handling. They are out for a quick touch, but they will squeeze all they can just the same. I oughta go back to that fat wop Gandesi right now. I could do things to that slob that ain't been invented yet.'

'Now, Henry, don't get violent,' I said.

'Haw,' Henry snarled. 'Them guys give me an ache in the back of my lap.' He raised his bottle to his lips with his left hand and drank thirstily. His voice came down a few tones and sounded more peaceful. 'Better dip the bill, Walter. The party's a flop.'

'Perhaps you are right, Henry,' I sighed. 'I will admit that my stomach has been trembling like an autumn leaf for all of half an hour.'

So I stood up boldly beside him and poured a liberal portion of the fiery liquid down my throat. At once my courage revived. I handed the bottle back to Henry and he placed it carefully down on the running board. He stood beside me dancing the short automatic pistol up and down on the broad palm of his hand.

'I don't need no tools to handle that bunch. The hell with it.' And with a sweep of his arm he hurled the pistol off among the bushes, where it fell to the ground with a muffled thud. He walked away from the car and stood with his arms akimbo, looking up at the sky.

I moved over beside him and watched his averted face, insofar as I was able to see it in that dim light. A strange melancholy came over me. In the brief time I had known Henry I had grown very fond of him.

'Well, Henry,' I said at last, 'what is the next move?'

'Beat it on home, I guess,' he said slowly and mournfully. 'And get good and drunk.' He doubled his hands into fists and shook them slowly. Then he turned to face me. 'Yeah,' he said. 'Nothing else to do. Beat it on home, kid, is all that is left to us.'

'Not quite yet, Henry,' I said softly.

I took my right hand out of my pocket. I have large hands. In my right hand nestled the roll of wrapped quarters which I had obtained at the bank that morning.

My hand made a large fist around them.

'Good night, Henry,' I said quietly, and swung my fist with all the weight of my arm and body. 'You had two strikes on me, Henry,' I said. 'The big one is still left.'

But Henry was not listening to me. My fist with the wrapped weight of metal inside it had caught him fairly and squarely on the point of his jaw. His legs became boneless and he pitched straight forward, brushing my sleeve as he fell. I stepped quickly out of his way.

Henry Eichelberger lay motionless on the ground, as limp as a rubber glove. I looked down at him a little sadly, waiting for him to stir, but he did not move a muscle. He lay inert, completely unconscious. I dropped the roll of quarters back into my pocket, bent over him, searched him thoroughly, moving him around like a sack of meal, but it was a long time before I found the pearls. They were twined around his ankle inside his left sock.

'Well, Henry,' I said, speaking to him for the last time, although he could not hear me, 'you are a gentleman, even if you are a thief. You could have taken the money a dozen times this afternoon and given me nothing. You could have taken it a little while ago when you had the gun in your hand, but even that repelled you. You threw the gun away and we were man to man, far from help, far from interference. And even then you hesitated, Henry. In fact, Henry, I think for a successful thief you hesitated just a little too long. But as a man of sporting feelings I can only think the more highly of you. Goodbye, Henry, and good luck.'

I took my wallet out and withdrew a one-hundred-dollar bill and placed it carefully in the pocket where I had seen Henry put his money. Then I went back to the car and took a drink out of the whiskey bottle and corked it firmly and laid it beside him, convenient to his right hand. I felt sure that when he awakened he would need it.

8

It was past ten o'clock when I returned home to my apartment, but I at once went to the telephone and called Ellen Macintosh. 'Darling!' I cried. 'I have the pearls.'

I caught the sound of her indrawn breath over the wire. 'Oh darling,' she said tensely and excitedly, 'and you are not hurt? They did not hurt you, darling? They just took the money and let you go?'

'There were no 'they,' darling,' I said proudly. 'I still have Mr Gallemore's money intact. There was only Henry.'

'Henry!' she cried in a very strange voice. 'But I thought—Come over here at once, Walter Gage, and tell me—' 'I have whiskey on my breath, Ellen.'

'Darling! I'm sure you needed it. Come at once.'

So once more I went down to the street and hurried to Carondelet Park and in no time at all was at the

Penruddock residence. Ellen came out on the porch to meet me and we talked there quietly in the dark, holding hands, for the household had gone to bed. As simple as I could I told her my story.

'But darling,' she said at last, 'how did you know it was Henry? I thought Henry was your friend. And this other voice on the telephone—' 'Henry *was* my friend,' I said a little sadly, 'and that is what destroyed him. As to the voice on the telephone, that was a small matter and easily arranged. Henry was away from me a number of times to arrange it. There was just one small point that gave me thought. After I gave Gandesi my private card with the name of my apartment house scribbled upon it, it was necessary for Henry to communicate to his confederate that we had seen Gandesi and given him my name and address. For of course when I had this foolish, or perhaps not so very foolish idea of visiting some well-known underworld character in order to send a message that we would buy back the pearls, this was Henry's opportunity to make me think the telephone message came as a result of our talking to Gandesi, and telling him our difficulty. But since the first call came to me at my apartment before Henry had had a chance to inform his confederate of our meeting with Gandesi, it was obvious that a trick had been employed.

'Then I recalled that a car had bumped into us from behind and Henry had gone back to abuse the driver. And of course the bumping was deliberate, and

Henry had made the opportunity for it on purpose, and his confederate was in the car. So Henry, while pretending to shout at him, was able to convey the necessary information.'

'But, Walter,' Ellen said, having listened to this explanation a little impatiently, 'that is a very small matter. What I really want to know is how you decided that Henry had the pearls at all.'

'But you told me he had them,' I said. 'You were quite sure of it. Henry is a very durable character. It would be just like him to hide the pearls somewhere, having no fear of what the police might do to him, and get another position and then after perhaps quite a long time, retrieve the pearls and quietly leave this part of the country.'

Ellen shook her head impatiently in the darkness of the porch. 'Walter,' she said sharply, 'you are hiding something. You could not have been sure and you would not have hit Henry in that brutal way, unless you had been sure. I know you well enough to know that.'

'Well, darling,' I said modestly, 'there was indeed another small indication, one of those foolish trifles which the cleverest men overlook. As you know, I do not use the regular apartment house telephone, not wishing to be annoyed by solicitors and such people. The phone which I use is a private line and its number is unlisted. But the calls I received from Henry's confederate came over that phone, and Henry had been in my apartment a great deal, and I had been careful not to give Mr Gandesi that number, because of course I did not expect anything from Mr Gandesi, as I was perfectly sure from the beginning that Henry had the pearls, if only I could get him to bring them out of hiding.'

'Oh, darling,' Ellen cried, and threw her arms around me. 'How brave you are, and I really think that you are actually clever in your own peculiar way. Do you believe that Henry was in love with me?'

But that was a subject in which I had no interest whatever. I left the pearls in Ellen's keeping and late as the hour now was I drove at once to the residence of Mr Lansing Gallemore and told him my story and gave him back his money.

A few months later I was happy to receive a letter postmarked in Honolulu and written on a very inferior brand of paper.

Well, pal, that Sunday punch of yours was the money and I did not think you had it in you, altho of course I was not set for it. But it was a pip and made me think of you for a week every time I brushed my teeth. It was too bad I had to scram because you are a sweet guy altho a little on the goofy side and I'd like to be getting plastered with you right now instead of wiping oil valves where I am at which is not where this letter is mailed by several thousand miles. There is just two things I would like you to know and they are both kosher. I did fall hard for that tall blonde and this was the main reason I took my time from the old lady. Glomming the pearls was just one of those screwy ideas a guy can get when he is dizzy with a dame. It was a crime the way they left them marbles lying around in that bread box and I worked for a Frenchy once in Djibouty and got to know pearls enough to tell them from snowballs. But when it came to the clinch down there in that brush with us two alone and no holds barred I just was too soft to go through with the deal. Tell that blonde you got a loop on I was asking for her.

YRS. As ever,
HENRY EICHELBERGER (Alias)
P. S. What do you know, that punk that did the phone work on you tried to take me for a fifty cut on that C note you tucked in my vest. I had to twist the sucker plenty.
Yrs. H. E. (Alias)